Praise for Sh

"Angels are intriguing indeed, and with engaging folks driving the story, Nancy Panko has penned a thought-provoking work. Maybe we are all blessed with guardian angels."
—Scott Mason, WRAL-TV's *Tar Heel Traveler* and author of the *Tar Heel Traveler* book series

"I love the way Nancy weaves love and trust into her stories, like a gentle wind blowing across your face—touched by a loving hand. Yes, I believe!"
—Willa Brigham, *Smart Start* host WRAL-TV

"It inspired me to read the Bible from an new perspective—a fresh awareness of God working behind the scenes through His Angel Armies."
—Juni Felix, Host of *Moving Forward, Tiny Habits for Successful Soul Care*

"Characters from this world and the one beyond will generate smiles, an occasional tear and a great deal of interest."
—Rev. Richard E. Zajac, Staff Chaplain at Sisters of Charity Hospital in Buffalo, NY, *Life Injections 1,2,3,*and *4*

"A beautiful depiction of what takes place around us every day as our angelic guardians work with us and for us at God's direction to help us through this journey of earthly life."
—Deacon Charles Zlamal, *A Single Rock Foundation*

"The Bible speaks about angels who watch over us and interact with us. *Sheltering Angels* will encourage you and cause you to think about how angels interact in our lives."
—Nathan Redinger, Pastor, LifePoint Community Church

"A 20th Century *Little House on the Prairie*—with angels! Highly recommended."
—E. E. Kennedy, author of the *Miss Prentice* mystery series.

"Nancy Panko has a real gift for creating loveable characters, whose personalities are revealed through wonderful dialogue and ways they interact with each other. Understanding creative ways God protects us makes this a faith-builder as well as a moving, perfectly-paced story."
—Laurie Winslow Sargent, Author of *Delight in Your Child's Design* and other titles

"Nancy Panko has artfully sifted together a little fiction with a little personal experience to create a story that keeps the reader turning the pages. The tone and pace of *Sheltering Angels* lends a comforting, 'settle down and put your feet up' quality while depicting undeniable angelic interventions; a treasured addition to any library."
—Debbie Dillon, former magazine publisher/editor

"An unforgettable story of triumphant faith spanning generations of a close-knit family and the angels who care for them."
—Barbara Parentini, *Feasting with Angels, Divine Interventions: Heartwarming Stories of Answered Prayer, Soaring Hearts* Cards, *and Living Letters*®Seminars

Sheltering Angels

*To Sandy,
Be Inspired!*

Sheltering
Angels

a novel

Believe!

NANCY PANKO

Nancy Panko

Torchflame Books

Durham, NC

To
Fred and Cora who gave us roots
and
Butch and Mary who gave us wings

"May God grant you always:
A sunbeam to warm you,
A moonbeam to charm you,
A sheltering angel so nothing can harm you.
Laughter to cheer you. Faithful friends near you.
And whenever you pray, heaven to hear you."
—Irish blessing

One

Spring 1946

Mary Emig negotiated the awkward turn onto the one-lane dirt road. The well-worn tire tracks made it difficult to control the old truck as it chugged its way up the winding path to the neighboring Meek farm. Her knuckles whitened as she grappled with the vibrating steering wheel. Mary struggled to downshift as beads of sweat formed on her upper lip. The last thing she wanted to do was drive off this road with its eight-foot drop-offs.

At that moment, the pickup hit an unexpected bump. Mary's nearly three-year-old daughter Betsy, standing on the seat next to her mother, lost her balance. She pitched forward. Mary reflexively reached out with one hand attempting to stop her daughter's fall, and as she did so, jerked the steering wheel to the right. The child hit her head on the flat dashboard with a sound that made her mother sick to her stomach.

Mary needed to get the tires back in the tracks. She wrenched the steering wheel to the left but overcorrected.

The old green truck careened off the narrow, rutted road on two wheels, became airborne, and tumbled into the swampy brambles, landing on the driver's side. As the chilly marsh water hit the warm radiator, steam poured out from under the hood. The passenger-side tires spun in futility as the left side wheels sank deep into the mud. Brown water began to seep into the cab.

Birds chirped in the meadow. A train whistle pierced the air as a locomotive crossed onto the Lyon Brook Bridge.

Guardian angels hovering nearby were the only ones to hear a cry for help from inside the truck.

Two

One Hour Earlier

I t began as an ordinary day. Mary and her daughter Betsy emerged onto a covered porch from their apartment. Setting the picnic basket and thermos down, Mary reached back to close the door behind her. A brisk breeze swooped under her faded print dress and ballooned the skirt over the toddler's head.

"Mommy! Can't see!"

"Hold still, honey. It's like a tent, isn't it?

"Uh-huh."

Mary laughed as she worked to untangle stray threads from the seam of her house dress caught on the butterfly barrettes securing her child's blonde pigtails. She leaned over her daughter to release the mess. "Is that better, sweetie?"

Betsy giggled and bobbed her head up and down. "Yes."

Mary picked up the basket and thermos in one arm and held her daughter's hand with the other while walking down the wide porch steps.

"Going for a ride?"

"Yes, we are, honey. We're having a picnic lunch with

Daddy. He's plowing fields at Archie Meek's farm next door. We'll meet Daddy in the back yard."

"Can Sandy come?"

Mary's freckled brow furrowed while she tried to hide her concern about her precocious daughter's imaginary friend. Betsy had been babbling and gesturing to an empty room even as an infant in her crib. Mary spoke to their family doctor, who didn't seem to think it was anything to be concerned about. He reassured the young mother, saying, "She's likely to be a chatterbox when she starts talking."

Somehow that was of little comfort now that Betsy had daily conversations with her friend. Mary would have to see if Butch noticed it too. Maybe it was time for Betsy to have an occasional playmate her own age.

"Sure, Sandy can come." Changing the subject, Mary said, "Daddy's been working since early this morning and has to be hungry."

"How 'bout Terry?" Betsy asked.

"Grandma is watching your baby brother, so this is a good time to go. After we have our picnic and Daddy goes back to the field, we can see if Miss Trudy is home. I know she'd love to show you her new puppy."

"A puppy?" The little girl squealed. "Can I hold him?"

"I'm sure Miss Trudy will let you hold the puppy. But first, would you like to be my helper?" She shifted the basket of food to her other arm and held a thermos out to her daughter.

"I carry Daddy's water. I be careful. Be a helper jus' like Sandy."

"Is she a good helper like you are?"

"Yup! But he's a boy, Mommy."

This information was new. "Oh, Sandy's a boy?" Mary held her breath, not knowing what else was coming.

"Yup, he told me."

Mary breathed. "He talks to you?"

"Yup, lots of times."

"How does he help you, honey?"

"Plays with me. Sings. Holds my hand if I'm scared."

"I'd say that you have a good friend if he does that."

"Yup. Him and the others."

"The others? What others?" Mary swallowed.

"Angels, Mommy. Angels."

"Real angels?"

"Yup! Real angels. They help you and Daddy and Terry and me."

"Do the other angels have names?"

"Yup. And wings!" Betsy took a breath.

Mary said, "Wings? Wings like birds?" Her child certainly had an active imagination.

"No, bigger."

"Big wings," Mary repeated mechanically. "How big, honey?"

"So-o-o-o-o big." The little girl raised her arms as high as she could.

"Wow!" Mary was stunned. "And he's a real angel?"

"Uh-huh, and he's my friend."

"I'm sure he is, honey."

"See him, Mommy?"

"No honey, I don't see him, but I believe you when you say you do. Let's hope our angels can help me start the truck."

Mary paused in the driveway to gaze at the farmhouse owned by her in-laws, Fred and Cora Emig. Betsy picked up a stick and drew in the dust. The wide porch on the larger part of the homestead spanned the width of the house. It was great on rainy days when Betsy wanted to ride her tricycle back and forth with plenty of room to turn around. Mary's in-laws had added a two-story apartment on the backside of the house for Butch and Mary. It had an enclosed sun porch and a small front entrance porch at right angles to the main house. A bird's-eye view showed an L-shaped structure with lovely porches everywhere. Fred and Cora's yellow barns and outbuildings stood out from the traditional red barns of the neighboring farms, making Lyon Brook Farm unforgettable.

Mary loved her life here, and she loved her home. She sighed as she opened the creaky vehicle door with the Lyon Brook Farm logo. She fumbled for the keys in her dress pocket and found a hole instead. Another dress would be going in the sewing pile. The key ring had gotten hung up on torn fabric, keeping it from tumbling out. At least she hadn't lost the keys. After loading the basket and thermos into the back compartment, she lifted Betsy onto the worn leather seat. Mary stood on the rusted running board, grasped the steering wheel, and swung herself into the driver's position.

She studied the flat, featureless dashboard, thinking how much she disliked that shade of green. "Almost as much as I hate driving this truck," she muttered. Mary reviewed Butch's instructions aloud. "There's the choke, the speedometer, and the map compartment." Her hand rested on the spindly gear shift extending from the floorboard, which reminded her of an oversized jointed limb of a daddy longlegs spider.

"Betsy, you stand here on the seat next to me, sweetie, so you can see everything." Mary shifted into neutral, pulled the choke, pumped the gas pedal, depressed the clutch with one foot and the brake with the other, and prayed as she turned the key.

The engine coughed and started on the first try. Mary maneuvered the spider-leg shifter into low gear as

Butch taught her, and with a sigh of relief, slowly pulled out of the driveway. She gained more confidence as the vehicle picked up speed on the main dirt road.

Betsy hung tight to her mother's shoulder as they passed fields dotted with cows and horses grazing on lush green grasses.

"Horsies!" Betsy squealed, clapping her hands. "Sandy, look!"

"They like this warm sunny day. Here's our turn, sweetie. Hang on to Mommy's shoulder. Look up the hill, behind the house. See the red barn? Daddy's plowing the field next to the barn."

That was the last thing Mary said to her daughter before losing control of the old vehicle.

Muddy water seeped into the cab to cover Mary's arm and shoulder. The chill awakened her. She remembered the truck rolling down the bank into the marsh. Her eyes flew open. "Betsy! Bets?" Mary wailed when she saw her daughter's crumpled form on top of her legs. "Help! Someone, help us."

The toddler had a nasty bump on her head but stirred when she heard her mother's cries.

"Mommy?"

"Yes, baby girl, I'm here. We're gonna be okay. I've gotta get us out of here. Can you move, honey?"

Betsy stirred and struggled to move but couldn't do anything but squirm in place.

Mary was on her side against the driver's door, looking up at the partly open passenger window. Using the steering wheel for leverage, she managed to push herself up to a sitting position. She pulled Betsy into her lap. Bracing her feet on the edge of the truck seat and part of the submerged door, Mary stood. With Betsy over one shoulder, she reached up, grasping the passenger window frame with the other hand. Thank God, the windows had been slightly opened. "Betsy, honey. Can you roll the window down all the way?"

The child managed to reach the handle and struggled to turn it. The window started moving upward. "No, honey, the other way. Roll it the other way."

Betsy pushed the handle, and the window went down smoothly. "Sandy's helping," she announced.

"Atta, girl!" her mother encouraged. "You got it!"

With the window down, Mary thought of a plan to get Betsy and herself out of the sinking truck. If she boosted Betsy out of the passenger window, Betsy could lie flat on the passenger door until Mary pulled herself out. The plan had to work before the truck sank any deeper into the watery mud.

Wading through all that muck would be another obstacle. "Lord, please help us," Mary prayed.

Guardian angels heard the young mother's plea.

Three

Driving the John Deere tractor back and forth in the field, Butch watched behind him as the plow blades sliced through the rich, brown earth. His stomach growled. He hoped for good weather with enough rain to make this an abundant crop. It sure would help the family's bottom line. The Emigs were struggling financially after several lousy growing seasons.

Suddenly, a big rock rolled up out of the earth in front of one of the plow blades. Butch heard the dreaded sound of metal hitting something hard.

"Dang, this is the last thing I need!" He knew that a broken plow blade would necessitate going back to the barn to fetch another, as well as the tools to change it.

The young man's guardian angel nodded with satisfaction. *That's exactly what I want him to do: go back to the barn. I do feel some remorse about breaking his plow blade, but an angel must do what an angel has to do.*

Butch's brow furrowed as he brought the tractor to a stop. An unusual feeling of dread gripped his gut. "I wonder where Mary is," he said aloud as he glanced at his watch. They were supposed to meet at noon for a picnic, and it was well past the hour. She usually parked the truck where Butch could see it. He hoped everything was okay.

He dismounted and walked back toward the plow. There it was—a broken blade. Moving with a new sense of urgency, Butch unhooked the tractor from the plow, jumped back in the seat, and drove toward the barn. Coming to a stop in front of the barn, he hopped down and jogged toward the house, hoping that Trudy was there so he could use the telephone to check on Mary's whereabouts. He caught a glimpse of someone walking in the driveway around the corner of the Meeks' house. It was a woman. His wife.

Mary was limping; her legs were streaked with blood. She was carrying a feedbag draped over her arms. With a second look, Butch could see it wasn't a feedbag. Mary was carrying the limp form of his daughter, dressed in a romper his wife had made from floral feedbag material.

He screamed, "No! Oh, dear God!"

The family's guardian angels heard his urgent invoking of God. They unfurled their wings and prepared for action.

Seeing Trudy's car parked in front of the house, Butch bellowed, "Help, Trudy! Help!"

"Oh, Butch!" Mary gasped. "I went off the road, the truck rolled, we were in the marsh and I had to get out of the truck." She dropped to her knees in the driveway, laying Betsy at his feet. The child's eyes fluttered open and closed. She had a sizable purplish bruise in the center of her forehead. Thorns protruded from both of Betsy's legs.

Butch picked up his daughter. Gently laying her on the grass, he returned to get Mary. She slumped down next to Betsy, crooning softly, "It's gonna be okay, baby. Mommy's right here."

Trudy came out of the house with a basin of warm water, washcloths, and antiseptic. She was at the kitchen sink when she heard Butch's cries and saw the spectacle in the driveway. Butch leaned over his child to reassure himself that she was still breathing.

"Here, Butch, you work on pulling thorns out of Betsy's legs while she's groggy. I'll work on Mary." Trudy handed him a pair of tweezers.

Trudy talked to Mary while gently cleaning dirt and blood from her legs and pulling out nasty thorns at the same time.

Butch turned to Mary, tweezers in midair, and asked, "What happened? How'd you manage to get through the marsh and up the bank?"

"The only way I could. I began tramping through the brambles and mud, trying to find solid footing. I prayed for help. But...but then I felt as if I was being lifted up. Strange, I know. Maybe it was my imagination." She rambled on, "I didn't know there were so many thorny bushes down there. Just look at us, we're a mess. Right before I lost control of the truck, we hit a bump, and Betsy flew off the seat, hitting her forehead on the map compartment."

"Yeah, I saw the knot, it's a beaut!"

Trudy had already seen the swollen black and blue area above Betsy's nose and had gone back into the house to get a cold compress, which now covered the area. Butch ran both his hands over her entire head, feeling for other bumps. Looking under the compress, Butch said, "Mary. It's the only bump I found, and it's quite a goose egg." Betsy's eyes fluttered open, and she looked up at her father.

"Daddy. We bringed you a pic-a-nick." The little girl yawned.

"Yes, baby girl, I know you did. You just rest while we get your legs all cleaned up."

Mary lifted herself on one elbow. "I'm sorry, honey.

Lunch is still in the truck. By the way, how is it you're here and not out in the field?"

"I hit a big rock with the plow. I guess it's a darn good thing, or I wouldn't have been here when you came around the corner."

"I guess so," Mary murmured as she reached over to stroke some strands of her daughter's blonde hair that had escaped from one of the pigtails.

When Trudy and Butch had finished tweezing thorns, Butch gently lifted the washcloth from his daughter's forehead to check the bump. It was gone! The skin was flawless as if nothing had happened. He ran his hand over the spot in disbelief. Butch exchanged glances with Trudy. Mary's eyes were closed.

"Mary, there's no goose egg on Betsy's forehead. It's gone! How could that be from just a cold compress? You both saw how bad it was." He shook his head in amazement.

Mary sat up. Both she and Trudy looked at Betsy's face.

Betsy had stopped crying and was more alert. "Daddy, Sandy kissed my booboo, and it's all better."

Butch and Mary exchanged concerned glances. Trudy looked puzzled.

"Sandy?" Mary questioned.

"See, Mommy? Sandy helps!"

Butch's high school first-aid training kicked in. "Bets, you can tell Mommy and me more about Sandy later." Turning to his wife, he whispered, "Mary, she did have quite a blow to her head. It would make me feel better if we kept her quiet for a while." Mary nodded.

"Hey, Betsy, I have an idea! Do you think you and Mommy can lie back down on the grass and tell us what animals you see in the clouds?"

"Uh-huh." Betsy settled back on the grass and rested her arms behind her head.

Trudy went back into the house to rinse out the basin and fill it with fresh water. Both girls needed a final cleaning before salve could be applied.

Butch's attention shifted to Mary. He wiped her dirt-streaked face with his handkerchief.

"I see a ducky, Daddy."

"I do, too," said Mary.

Butch smiled as his girls shared what critters they were seeing in the sky.

Mary turned to her husband. "I think it might be a couple of days before we can dance again." She gestured to her blood-streaked legs and thought of their special time together after they tucked the children into bed. That's when they'd turn the radio on to listen to big band music. Butch would lead her in a slow dance across the hardwood floors to the strains of Glenn Miller's "Sentimental Journey." Mary lapsed into a daydream about melting into her husband's muscular body, inhaling the scent of his Old Spice, grateful that he was her man.

Butch interrupted her reverie. "Right now all that matters is that you and Betsy get better. I signed your dance card for life, remember? We'll be under the spell of Glenn Miller in no time." Butch leaned down and gently embraced his wife.

She grinned. He must have been reading her mind. "Butch," Mary whispered, "I need to talk to you about a conversation Bets and I had before driving over here. You won't believe what she told me."

"About what?"

"About her friend, Sandy... and others."

"Others?"

"Betsy says they're angels."

"Angels."

"Yeah, it's kind of imaginative and, at the same time, very believable."

"Later, then."

Mary and Betsy had blankets loosely wrapped around their shoulders as they moved onto Trudy's front porch. Their legs had been cleaned and bandaged after all the thorns were removed. Trudy went back into the house and returned with a tray of lemonade and chocolate chip cookies. She set the refreshments on a table between the girls. Trudy's puppy sniffed around their bandaged legs. Betsy giggled as she attempted to pet the wiggling ball of fur.

Helping to tidy up, Butch said, "Trudy, I can't thank you enough for all your help today. I don't know where we'd be without you."

As they walked into the house, Trudy said, "You're welcome. I'm glad I was here to help." She paused and lowered her voice, "Butch, I'm confused. Who's Sandy?"

Butch hesitated. "Oh, Betsy has this imaginary friend. You know how kids are. Trudy, I gotta go look at my truck in the marsh." Butch bolted out the door.

Trudy's eyebrows rose. She had more questions, but Butch didn't seem in the mood to answer.

Returning to the porch, he announced to his wife and daughter, "It looks like you two are in good hands, so I'm going to walk down the driveway to check on the truck. I gotta figure out how the heck we're gonna get it out of that muck."

Butch rounded the corner of the house and walked down the rutted road. With his hands shoved deep in his denim overalls, he surveyed the scene. He could see his trusted work truck lying on its side in the marsh. He wondered how many tractors it would take to get it back onto the road and concluded it would definitely need a miracle. Butch raised his arms and eyes to the blue sky. "God, what am I going to do?"

Covering his eyes with the heels of his hands, he allowed tears to flow. He was shaken to the core to think of what could have happened to his wife and child.

Butch's angel gave him a gentle caress of support and went to work on his vehicle.

Feeling a soft warm breeze swirling around his shoulders, Butch turned around and began to trudge up the winding driveway.

Behind him, the wind increased in intensity. Swirling around the inert form of green metal, the wind gently lifted the truck up and out of the marsh. With the agility of a performing Lipizzaner stallion, the muddy vehicle righted itself in a four-point stance. Its tires were perfectly placed in the tracks of the narrow road as if nothing had happened.

Hearing a noise of metal creaking, Butch glanced over his shoulder toward the scene of the accident.

His mouth dropped open in shock as he turned. "What in tarnation?" He couldn't believe his eyes. If he hadn't seen the truck in the marsh, he never would have believed what he was looking at now. "How...?"

Butch ran toward his vehicle. Circling it to survey the damage, he spun around, looking for evidence of the miracle that just happened. The only thing he saw were the deep ruts that sent his wife and daughter careening into the marsh. Finally, he approached the truck. When he opened the driver's door, he wasn't surprised to find the interior wet and muddy. But he was surprised to see the keys still in the ignition. He climbed onto the driver's seat, pulled the choke, depressed the clutch, and gave it some gas. The old truck started on the first try.

"Thank God!" Butch exclaimed with a big smile. He drove the muddy vehicle up the rutted path toward the house. The unexpected sight created quite a reaction from Trudy and Mary as Butch drove around the corner. He parked in the driveway and got out of the truck.

"Butch! How? What happened? How did you...? Mary stammered.

"I don't know, Mary. I just don't know. I think we experienced a miracle. I don't have any idea how, but I sure am grateful."

Mary wondered if it could have anything to do with Sandy and the other angels.

Sandy hovered around Betsy. The guardian angel acknowledged other angels perched on Miss Trudy's roof, watching and listening to everything below. Sandy chuckled and told the heavenly beings, "In Chenango County, New York, not many hard-working farm families ever think about guardian angels in their midst. But one small person knows and is assured that we are here."

Betsy was the only human to hear the declaration. The toddler smiled at Sandy and waved to the others.

Four

Three Years Earlier, June 1943

Butch nudged the rust-colored stallion with his heels as they approached the railroad tracks that cut through the upper pastures. Once or twice a week, he checked the gates to the grazing fields to make sure they were closed and locked. Although their land was posted against trespassers, some dared to break the locks, breach the gate, and hunt illegally on Emig property. Once in a while, the dirty devils even left the gate open, creating a risk for his cows. His prize-winning herd could get onto the tracks and into the path of a train.

The very thought of the carnage made Butch shiver. He adjusted his 30/30 rifle across his lap and wondered if he would have the nerve to hold someone at gunpoint if he caught them in the act. For that matter, he wondered what kind of soldier he would have made. Like most of the men in the farming community, he had tried to enlist when the war broke out. But since his older brother Chet was in the Army, he had been refused. Somebody had to keep the dairy farm going. It was essential for the country.

As Butch turned Duke toward the trail back to the barn, he heard a shout. He pulled up on the reins and pivoted in his saddle. Butch saw his friend and neighbor, Jim Fisher, emerge from the guard shack. He was waving. Like Butch, Jim had been exempted from military service. He and his two brothers were the only family left to run their adjacent farm. In addition to that, they'd been called upon to guard the Lyon Brook railroad bridge in case of sabotage.

Butch returned the salutation. "Hey, Jim! How the heck are you?"

"Great, Butch. I pulled the four-to-twelve shift this week. Randy has something going on with his daughter at school. You know the end-of-year stuff they do, even in kindergarten. Paul, well, Paulie's running around with some of his friends from Norwich." Jim grimaced then shrugged.

"Hey, we were all eighteen once. Don't worry; with you and Randy as good examples, Paul isn't likely to get into trouble. Just keep on talking to him. As far as end-of-year school activities, I remember those with my little sis Beverly—which wasn't so long ago. Now Mary and I are gonna have a baby of our own in a couple of months. It'll be a while before we have to worry about kindergarten activities."

"How's Mary doing?"

"She's getting anxious to meet the baby. You know, it's getting a little harder to dance, with her belly in the way. She's due in September, so we've got a few months to finish getting ready."

Jim chuckled, "You two sure can cut a rug. I always loved watching your smooth moves on the dance floor... almost as much as I enjoyed your smooth moves on the football field. You gonna have Doc Mayhew come out for the birthing?"

"Aw, thanks. Yeah, Doc Mayhew and his nurse are supposed to come. That's what we're thinking. And both our mothers want to be in on the action. We'll see who gives

in first and leaves the room. Who knows, it could be me."
Butch chuckled.

"Nah, you'll be fine, with all the calves you've helped
come into this world. Sounds like a great way to welcome a
new baby, a real family get-together. I hope for your sake the
baby don't come at milking time!"

They shared a laugh, knowing that not much stops
milking time.

"Say, Jim, have you seen anything suspicious up here
since you boys started?"

"No, all's quiet. Except the rumors, that is. You know
how it goes."

"Yup, I sure do. Well, still and all, we Emigs appreciate
you guys pulling duty up here. Stay safe." Butch waved as he
flicked the reins.

Jim sauntered down the tracks to check all eight
hundred twenty feet of the bridge.

Five

In the early morning hours of Labor Day 1943, eighteen-year-old Mary reclined on the bed, propped up with multiple pillows. Moaning softly with each contraction, Mary was exhausted from being in labor for twenty hours.

The day before, she mentioned her "gas pains" to her mother-in-law as they hung the wash on the clothesline. Having experienced childbirth four times, Cora started asking her daughter-in-law questions.

"Any nausea?"

"Maybe, a little."

"How about backache?"

"Now that you mention it, it kinda feels like the backache I used to get when I had my period."

"Well now, dear, I think you might be starting labor. That's fitting, with tomorrow being Labor Day and all." Cora's smile couldn't have been wider. She loved Mary as much as each of her daughters. "We should probably call Doc Mayhew to let him know it's started."

As reality set in, Mary's face turned pale, her freckles more apparent. "I'll give my mom a call too. This is her first grandchild, and she'll want to be here. My dad's been sick off and on, but I know Mom's sister, Aunt Gertrude, will stay with him so Mom can come... I think I'm a little nervous, but excited to meet my baby," she rambled on. "I can't wait to find out what I'm having. It doesn't matter to me, but I think Butch would like a boy."

Cora put her arm around Mary's shoulders. "I'm also anxious to meet my grandchild. This is number three for us and just as exciting as the first. It's going to be fine, and you and your baby are going to be fine. I'll make some soup, so you have some nourishment. It may be hours before things really start to happen."

Now, in the early hours of the morning, the petite young woman lay on the bed, her red curls pushed off her forehead by a cool washcloth placed there by Bivi, Doc Mayhew's nurse. Mary was dwarfed by her substantial pregnant belly as she dozed off and on from the Twilight Sleep medication Doc had given her to help her rest.

When he wasn't holding Mary's limp hand, twenty-one-year-old Butch paced around the compact dining room, into the kitchen, then back through the dining room into the living room. Butch and his father had pushed the dining table and chairs flush against the bay window to make room for the single bed on which Mary would give birth.

"Birthing a calf is nothing like this," Butch muttered.

Cora busied herself in Mary's small kitchen, making coffee and refilling glasses of water. Fifteen-year-old Beverly poked her head into the living room. "Can I come in yet?"

A chorus of "No" echoed throughout the small apartment.

Cora told her daughter to whip up a coffee cake because everyone was working up an appetite. Everyone but Mary.

"While the coffee cake is baking, dear, would you make some egg salad sandwiches? Oh, and Bev, honey, don't forget to put the icing on the coffee cake. You know, the drizzle we've made before."

"Okay, Mom, but promise me you'll call me when the baby is here."

"I will." Cora winked at Bivi. "That food fixin' will keep her busy for a while."

Mary's mother had gone to bed hours ago. Her nerves had gotten the best of her when she saw her daughter in labor. "Cora, please wake me when my daughter has the baby in her arms," Helen had instructed.

Nurse Bivi was strategically preparing a table of supplies needed for the delivery. A white-skirted bassinet was set up, ready for an occupant. A metal scale draped with a soft pale-yellow baby blanket sat on the dining room table.

At a quarter of three in the morning, Doc Mayhew checked his patient's progress. "Places everyone; it's time to have a baby." Doc proceeded to put on a surgical apron and a pair of rubber gloves. "Butch, you sit next to Mary's head. I need you to keep her awake so she can push."

"How do I wake her up?" Butch asked innocently.

"You slap her face."

"I can't slap her, Doc."

"Yes, you can. Now do it."

Butch gently tapped Mary's cheeks. "Come on, honey. Wake up, it's time. We're having a baby."

Doc stood behind Butch. "Son, harder than that. You're being too gentle."

"I... I just can't hit her."

Doc reached over Butch's shoulder, slapping Mary's face soundly. "Mary, it's Doc Mayhew. Time to get this baby out. Come on, wake up. That's what I need you to do, Butch."

With the slap of Doc's hand, Mary's eyes fluttered

open. "What? Time to have a baby?" she said, slurring her words.

Doc repeated, "Time to push, Mary. We gotta get this baby out. Take a deep breath and hold it while you bear down, like you're trying to poop. Can you do that? I'll tell you when." With one hand on Mary's belly, Doc said, "Here comes another contraction. Big deep breath, Mary. Bear down and push, push, push. That's it, you're doing great!"

Mary nodded. Her body took over with the urge to expel the little human inside her, and Mary was now wide awake from the exertion. Resting between contractions, she glanced up at her handsome husband's pale face and grimaced.

Butch and Mary's guardian angels perched at the head of the bed. They watched as the couple exchanged glances. It was evident to them that Butch realized new respect for his beautiful wife and what she was capable of doing to produce this child. This was good for him. The angels prayed for a speedy and uneventful delivery.

After several hard pushes, a head full of dark hair appeared, quickly followed by a scrunched-up little face. With one more effort, the rest of the baby entered the world.

Doc proclaimed, "It's a girl!" He gently smacked her bottom to get her to take a deep breath. The baby loudly expressed her displeasure. Doc placed the infant on a blanket on her mother's chest.

Mary closed her eyes in exhaustion. "Is she all there and all right, Doc?" Mary placed her hand on the baby's back.

Butch swiped at a tear that had escaped from one of his eyes. "She's beautiful, Mary."

Doc answered Mary, "I counted ten toes, ten fingers; I'll check the rest in a minute when I'm finished with you, young lady." With that, he delivered the placenta. Satisfied that Mary was stable, Doc picked up the baby and took her to the scale. Butch followed.

Everyone smiled and chuckled at the delightful sounds of a newborn baby.

Cora pulled a lace handkerchief from underneath the shoulder strap of her bra. Wiping the tears streaming down her face, she said, "I better go wake Helen."

Bivi towel-dried the baby girl and placed her on the scale, noting the child's weight in her notebook. "Doc, I have an eight-pound twelve-ounce bundle here." Doc had his stethoscope out and was listening to the baby's heart and lungs. He checked her muscle tone, reflexes, and skin color, then handed her back to his nurse. Bivi swaddled the child and handed the little bundle to Butch, who walked to Mary's side. The nurse gathered all the medical supplies and wrapped all the used equipment in a towel, to be washed and sterilized back at the office.

The room quieted down as everyone started to feel the fatigue.

Butch placed the baby across Mary's chest. She drew the little one to her lips and kissed her forehead, her nose, and each cheek. "So pretty," she said. "She's got your hair, Butch."

Helen came around the corner and began fussing over her daughter and the baby. "Oh my, oh my, oh my." She couldn't seem to get any other words out.

"Mother, we're fine. Would you like to hold her?"

Helen reached out and drew her granddaughter to her bosom. The ordinarily stoic woman didn't even notice when a tear escaped her left eye. She stared into the angelic face, kissed the baby's cheek, and handed the newborn to her mother.

"Mom, why don't you join Fred and Cora for

something to eat? You might want to ask Doc and Bivi some questions."

"That sounds like a good idea." Helen turned to go and paused. "We have a beautiful baby, you know. What a great job you did, Mary. I'm proud of you."

The touching scene was interrupted by a high-pitched voice. "Can I come in now?" Beverly squealed from the doorway into Fred and Cora's part of the house.

"Yes, come meet your niece," Butch called to his little sister.

Beverly stared at the sleeping child. "Wow! She looks like a perfect baby doll. I can't believe I'm an aunt for the third time, and I'm only fifteen," she whispered as she gazed at her niece.

As Doc Mayhew scrubbed his hands in the kitchen sink, he turned to Cora and said, "I'm famished! Sure could use a sandwich and a piece of Bev's famous coffee cake."

Cora invited everyone into her kitchen next door for refreshments. She had to pull Beverly away from Mary's bedside. "Let's give them a little time together, dear."

While Doc and Bivi were eating their sandwiches and coffee cake, he wrote up his invoice for twenty-five dollars: for services rendered. Fred paid him in fives and single dollar bills before Doc left the house.

It was four o'clock in the morning.

Butch had never been happier as he gazed at his two girls. He began to softly sing Glenn Miller's "Don't Sit Under the Apple Tree." Mary smiled as her husband bent forward to kiss her. "Nice job, honey. She's a keeper."

The baby slept under the watchful eyes of her parents as the angels maintained a protective vigil.

"In my capacity as Archangel," Michael said to the gathered host, "I sent Sandalphon to be a guardian for Butch and Mary's first-born child. The baby and Sandalphon are a package deal. In Psalm Ninety-One, scripture assures His people that God surrounds them with heavenly angels to guide and protect them. Today, Sandalphon joined a flock of angels already protecting others in this family. His assignment has an unusual stipulation, though. Sandalphon is to reveal himself to the child and—when she gets a little older—tell her about a unique and special gift. I know the Lord has a reason for this, and I serve the Lord. I have counseled Sandalphon to do what he has to do without revealing himself to anyone but the child.

"The Emigs are not aware of the presence of the guardians. In due time, their new baby will know and be able to see them all. It's a special gift with which she's been endowed—one that will be hard for her parents and others to understand. Sandalphon, can you share with us how you and the Emig baby entered into this world?"

"It was a long and arduous journey," Sandalphon said, "but she could see the light. I had been consoling her for the previous twenty hours. As she finally entered the room, I stood alongside her and couldn't help but smile. She's a beautiful baby.

"She was greeted with oohs and ahs. Someone sniffled; another emitted a deep-throated laugh. Her eyebrows lifted. Unexpectedly, someone smacked her on the bottom, causing a furrowed brow and cry of alarm. Her head turned toward me as if asking for help. I reached out to hold her hand."

The assembled angels nodded in approval.

"The lights were brighter than the darkened environment we had been used to," Sandalphon continued.

"She was carried to another corner of the room. I hovered at her side as two pairs of hands turned her this way and that. Soon, the scrutiny was over. She was wrapped in a soft blanket and placed into the arms of someone whose voice was familiar. Overcome with emotion from the exhausting journey, the baby's eyes filled with tears, and at the same time, she stifled a yawn. A fleeting smile crossed her face, but she was much too tired to be social. My presence calmed her, and she knew it was safe to accept the sleep coming to claim her.

"I watched as her eyelids closed and heard a voice say, 'Butch and Mary, meet your daughter. Do you have a name for the birth certificate?' Mary said, 'Yes, her name is Elizabeth Lee—Betsy for short. She's our little angel.' I floated around them, smiled, and thought: two angels for the price of one.

Six

F all came late to Central New York that year. It was mid-October and the leaves were just beginning to turn. Indian Summer was in full swing. Herb Brunner sat at the dimly lit hole-in-the-wall bar on a side street in Norwich, New York, brooding over his beer. The neon sign in the window proclaimed the establishment name as The Cabooze, but the first two letters had burned out some time ago, enabling the local patrons to call it The Booze. Fired from the New York, Ontario, and Western Railway for insubordination, Herb had been a regular at the dingy bar every day for the last week. It was one of the favorite watering holes for railroad workers to gather between or after runs. Today the place was buzzing with excitement. Herb couldn't help overhearing a conversation among four men at a nearby table.

One of the denim-clad men leaned forward. "You got some scuttlebutt, Joe?"

The man called Joe leaned back in his chair. "Yeah, the bosses say the Lyon Brook Bridge is a war-time target, and they're taking it serious."

"Where'd you hear this? Who told you?"

Joe took off his cap and held it in one hand while he smoothed back his shiny black hair. "From my supervisor.

He's a straight shooter. If anyone would know, he would." Joe put his hat back on.

Another man piped up, "Well, you know the railroad figures the bridge is important enough to build a guard shack on the eastern side of the tracks, and it's manned around the clock."

Herb turned on his perch at the bar to look at the men engaged in conversation. "Say, couldn't help but overhear. Has the Lyon Brook Bridge been threatened?"

"Yessiree," one of the other men answered.

"Do they know where the threat came from?" Herb probed.

Joe replied, "The boss is thinking a Nazi or Jap sympathizer."

Herb turned around, sipping his beer, and thought of getting even for his firing. He'd show them some insubordination, all right. Maybe, just maybe, this would be the perfect time for him to get even. He drained his beer glass in several gulps, slammed it on the bar, and headed out to the feed store for supplies.

The startled men at the adjacent table watched as Herb rushed out the door.

꽃

The bell over the door jingled as Herb entered the Norwich Feed and Grain store. Phil Rogers looked up from the ledger on the counter to ask, "What can I do you for?"

"Yeah, I'm looking to get rid of some stumps. Whaddya got that'll do the trick?" Herb knew that dynamite was the way to go. He'd watched his dad and uncles clear land and blow out the stumps on their farms.

"I'll be right with you as soon as I finish helping Mr. Emig load his pickup with feed. Won't be but a minute or two." Phil disappeared around the corner but reappeared before Herb could think about being impatient.

Butch Emig walked up to the counter and stepped ahead of the man seeking to buy dynamite. "Time to settle up, Phil."

Butch's guardian sensed an evil force nearby and unfurled his wings, assuming a protective stance.

"Do you want it on the Lyon Brook Farm account, Butch?"

"I reckon that's the best way to keep track. Hey, while I'm thinking of it, don't forget to tune in to NBC on the radio tonight for the Glenn Miller broadcast. Mary and I will have our dancing shoes on." Butch looked over his shoulder at the man behind him, now tapping his foot impatiently. "I'll get outta here now so you can tend to your next customer, Phil. See you next week. Give my best to Sadie, will ya?"

"You bet. She's at home churning butter today. I'm salivating just thinking about homemade bread and butter for supper. And thanks for the tip. We'll be sure to tune in."

Butch turned and walked out of the feed store. His angel followed, feeling the evil dissipate as they moved farther away from the building. The angel maintained a defensive posture until Butch's vehicle left the parking lot and then relaxed, thinking, *Bingo! The evil I sensed was standing behind Butch inside the feed store. I'll need to let Sandalphon and the others know about this guy. He sure was giving Butch the evil eye.*

Phil turned to the waiting customer. "Now about your stumps; everybody's still using dynamite. Got some in the back. How much do you need? Usually, one stick per stump."

"I got six real beauts to take out. I'm gonna need caps and fuses, too." And then it dawned on Herb that he didn't know where to place the explosives to actually take the bridge down. He might need more than six. "Uh, I may be back for more, depending on how successful I am. How much fuse material do you think I need to get myself clear?"

"I can sell you a short spool leftover from other purchasers. I'd recommend timing a length of fuse, so you know how many inches per minute it burns. No sense in taking your life in your hands unnecessarily. I'll be here if you have any questions or if you need more supplies. Do you want to put this on your account?"

Herb maintained his casual demeanor. "Nah, I'll just give you cash."

They settled up, and Herb took his purchases home. He knew how and where to get the information he needed. Things were going well. "I'm gonna tune in to wrastling tonight. None of that sissified Glenn Miller stuff for me," he muttered to himself, thinking again of the Lyon Brook farmer.

Seven

Fred Emig gently rocked in the white wicker chair on the front porch of the farmhouse, enjoying the sunny fall day. It was his after-lunch-quiet-time. Cora had prepared his favorite open-face roast beef sandwiches on homemade bread smothered with lump-free gravy, after his morning of hard work in and around the barn. The wooden screen door creaked as she came onto the porch to join her husband. He smiled at her. She maneuvered herself into the adjacent matching rocker while balancing her Bible and two glasses of ice water, one for him and one for her. Cora leaned back in the rocker and sighed.

"Sure feels good to sit, don't it, Mother?" Fred briefly lowered the Bible he was reading to gaze at his wife of many years.

"Yes, it does. We don't have much time in between chores on this farm. It makes me grateful for these settin' spells." She opened her Bible to the crocheted marker in the center of the well-worn book. The couple sat quietly engrossed in their respective reading under the shade of the towering maple trees lining their property. A thick canopy of leaves shaded the front porch, making it the coolest spot on any summer day. In a few short months, they'd be tapping those same trees for the sweet sap they produced to make a year's supply of maple syrup for the entire family.

"You've got a lot of markers in your Bible, Dad."

"Yes, I do. I'm searching out passages about angels."

"Angels? What brought about this sudden interest in angels?"

"Well, this war has me wondering about our children and grandchildren having guardian angels to watch over them. We've been fighting the Germans and Japanese for two years now with no end in sight, and we don't even know for sure where Chet is. Makes me wonder what is in store for our family."

Fred and Cora were blessed to have four children and three grandchildren. The couple prayed for their family's safety every day, especially for their older son Chet, a bombardier gunner in the Army.

Fred paused as if he wanted to say more, reconsidered, and went back to reading his Bible.

Cora studied her husband. He was a scholar and had been ever since she'd known him. Cora remembered Fred's excitement as they traveled with their three children, Chet, Louise, and Butch, to this New York State farm after he'd finally completed his studies at Normal School. She smiled, recalling the day in 1928 when Beverly, their youngest daughter, was born—right here on this farm. Now she and Fred had in-law children and grandchildren.

The couple didn't get to see their grandchildren as often as they'd like. Wartime gas rationing coupons had to be used for the farm machinery. So they'd been thrilled that Butch and Mary lived in the attached apartment and wanted a home-delivery for their first child.

Cora glanced at her husband, with his glasses perched

at the end of his nose. He rocked gently in his cushioned wicker chair.

Fred was a voracious reader. He was curious, always wanting to know the "who, what, when, where, and why" of everything. The Bible, historical books, various farming periodicals—and anything that came across his desk—often were tucked in his barn jacket or coverall pocket. He read whenever there was a lull in farm chores or while suffering the monotonous driving of the tractor and manure spreader back and forth across the fields.

Cora tilted her head. "Well, what did you learn about angels so far?"

"Interestingly, guardian angels are real. According to several books in the Bible, God surrounds us with heavenly angels to guide and protect us from evil forces. That's why I was wondering if every baby comes with a guardian angel to watch over them."

"I wonder too." Cora sighed. "I know firsthand that babies don't come with instructions, but with an angel? Wouldn't that be nice?"

The green Lyon Brook Farm pickup truck driving toward the farm stirred up a dust trail behind it, and they both watched as it slowed when approaching their driveway. The discussion about guardian angels had made their quiet time pass quickly.

"I'll bet Butch made a run to the feed store right after the milking," Fred said. "I better help him unload the truck. You know, Cora, one of these days we're gonna have to get us a hired farm hand. There's more work with the increased size of our herd; we can hardly keep up."

Fred bolted from his chair, leaving in such a hurry that the empty chair continued to rock.

Cora got up, gathering books and empty glasses.

With her arms full, she started for the screen door. But a slight movement caught her eye. She paused, turning to look over her shoulder. As Fred's chair rocked slower and slower, her chair began to rock as if it were occupied. Cora felt a shiver travel down her back. She could swear she felt someone caress her cheek. "Maybe I have a guardian angel, too," she said to no one in particular.

Indeed, you do, Cora's angel thought. *And so does Fred. You both are believers in God's love and grace. We are here to guide and watch over you.*

Eight

The next day, Herb sat in his usual spot at the bar. He waited patiently. Within twenty minutes, his hunch paid off. Joe and the others burst through the door and settled at the same worn round table as the day before. Joe nodded to Herb. Herb nodded back.

Herb inquired, "Any more news on the people who threatened to blow up the Lyon Brook Bridge?"

"Nah, nothing that I heard." Joe signaled to the bartender for beers all around.

"I couldn't sleep last night thinking about the sabotage," Herb said truthfully. "That's quite a structure to try to take down. Someone would have to be pretty sure his efforts would work to risk getting caught."

"Got that right, with the guard there and all." Joe helped the bartender pass the beers to the rest of the guys.

A pale freckle-faced man in a denim jacket piped up, "Besides, that bridge was built in sections when it was rebuilt in 1894. I know about this because my pa was a supervisor on the job."

Herb's eyes widened, and his pulse quickened. Here was a guy who could tell him what he needed to know. "I bet that was some complicated project," he said, hoping to get more details.

Red took a deep breath and said, "The masonry for the new piers began in May. A month later, the steelwork started going up."

"Wow, that was fast," Herb remarked.

Red seemed to be chomping at the bit. "You bet! There's eight spans of thirty feet each, three spans of eighty feet, four spans of sixty feet, and two spans of fifty feet. All told it's eight hundred twenty feet long. It stands one hundred fifty-five feet above the ravine and was finished in mid-August."

The three other men at the table applauded Red's ability to rattle off his memorized railroad bridge construction facts.

Apparently, Red wasn't done. He waved his hand, took a drink of his beer, and continued. "That sucker cost more than thirty-five thousand dollars. Here's something amazing; all the work was done without interruption of rail service. Daddy said they all got bonuses of twenty-five bucks each!"

"That's interesting, Red. I'm surprised you remembered it all!" Joe poked the guy with his elbow.

Red blushed.

Herb listened intently. Nodding with each bit of information, he smiled, mentally taking notes.

"If someone don't know what he's doing planting a charge up there, the bridge may not be outta commission very long." Red snorted. "Besides, a bad guy would have to take care of the Fisher boys, and they're armed. Maybe. Uh, well, I'm not exactly sure. But I do know for sure that they carry radios."

Herb signaled the bartender to bring the guys another round to further loosen their tongues. The men thanked him.

"The Fisher boys?" Herb scratched his two-day-old beard with a puzzled look on his face. "Who are the Fisher boys?"

"Randy, Jim, and Paul," Joe responded. "They're farmers, but they also guard the bridge, get paid by the county for doing it. Randy and Jim are real dependable, being older and all, but young Paul can be a fat-head. They work eight-hour shifts and even got themselves an outhouse. The railroad property is wide enough for the guard shack and the privy. It's right where the easternmost line butts right up against the Emig's fenced-off pasture land."

"The Emigs?" Herb cocked his head, wondering where he'd heard that name.

"The Lyon Brook Farm Emigs," Leon chimed in. "You've heard of them?"

"Of course!" Herb acted like it was something he'd known about all along. Emig was the name of the kid he saw in the feed store. And the truck he'd been driving had the farm logo on the door.

"I can't figure out how in the world one guy would be able to take that bridge down without being an engineering genius." Red swallowed a mouthful of beer. "Think of it, you'd have to know where the spans connect to blow one or two of the eighty-foot lengths. I guess the weight of a fully-loaded train would do the rest of the job for ya! That's how I see it."

Joe looked at Red with newfound respect. "You may have something there, Red."

Herb finished the beer in his glass and made some notes on a napkin before tucking it in his shirt pocket. "Well, guys, the wife's waiting for me. I better get along before I get the rolling pin," he lied with ease.

They all laughed as they waved goodbye to the guy who'd bought them a round of drinks.

"See ya around, Herb," Joe called after him.

On his way home, Herb fumed about never finding a convenient parking spot on Broad Street. These days he was angry about everything. He got out of his beat-up car and stomped down the block toward the entrance to his second-floor apartment. Spotting a five-foot section of rusted downspout dangling precariously from the roof of the stationery store, Herb reached up for the mangled metal and gave it a yank. The broken spout separated easily from the gutter above.

"Well, I guess that's that," he said as he tucked the newly acquired treasure under his arm, thinking it might come in handy.

Walking into his shabby one-room flat over the J. C. Penney store, Herb leaned the piece of broken downspout against the wall and scrounged around for paper and pencil. Clearing one side of his cluttered gray Formica table, he pulled out a chair and sat. Pulling the crumpled napkin out of his pocket, Herb transposed the information to his tablet. Next, he started a shopping list of all the materials needed to carry out his plan. Herb paused to think while he chewed on the end of the pencil. How would he get onto the bridge to plant the dynamite? He jotted down two possible routes, making a mental note to drive through the ravine to look closely at the iron structure and the stone abutments. He was reasonably sure he would have to scale the bridge to see if he could do it. That was one route. The timing would be crucial, so it was essential to see how long it took to climb to the top but more importantly to climb back down to the ground. His life would depend on being accurate. The other route meant trespassing on Emig land without getting caught. He'd prefer to climb if all the numbers worked out.

Herb got up and crossed the room to a dilapidated desk butted up against a sagging green sofa. He coaxed open the handle-less top drawer of the desk with a rusty screwdriver and dug out the last train schedule he had from work. Returning to the table, he looked at his calendar showing the phases of the moon. Herb compared it to the railroad schedule and decided on the perfect date to take down a big payload for the New York, Ontario, and Western Railroad. Things were coming together.

Herb grabbed a towel from the hook on the back of the bathroom door. After spreading it across the cleared Formica tabletop, he reached for the broken downspout. Using his tin snips, Herb cut the metal open until he had a piece about three feet long. With the spool of fuse material set up on a chair, he cut off exactly two feet of it and laid it inside the cut metal piece, reaching for his stopwatch. Herb torched the end of the fuse. When the fuse was extinguished, he scribbled his notes on a piece of paper and put his stopwatch away.

"Just a few more things to do," he said smugly. "I'll show that railroad that they messed with the wrong guy when they fired me."

Nine

Shortly after dusk the following Wednesday, Randy Fisher lay unconscious in the guard shack after being hit on the head with a baseball bat. Herb had tried not to hit him too hard, but the kid fought back and now was bleeding profusely. If Herb was going to be successful in blowing the bridge, he had to work quickly and put the Fisher kid out of his thoughts.

Remembering Red's description of the bridge spans, Herb strapped four sticks of dynamite in two strategic places. The fully loaded train was due to come along in thirty minutes. As inexperienced as he was with dynamite, he had tested carefully. Herb planned for an extra-long fuse to give him enough time to get away and watch the fireworks from a safe distance.

He worked feverishly to tie the deadly packages to the bridge with bailing twine. He looked down into the gorge at his car parked on the side of the road. It was gassed up and ready to go as soon as he reached the bottom of the iron superstructure and abutment. The climb up wasn't as bad as he'd thought it would be, as long as he didn't look down. With a twelve-foot ladder on the backside of the flagstone foundation, Herb figured that he'd not be noticed going up or down. Once he finished, he planned to watch the explosions and the train go down with the bridge while he was having a drink at the bar across the river

Sitting high in the saddle on his rust-colored horse, Butch breached the crest of the hill. It was later than his usual rounds to check the gate, but he'd been waylaid by chores and a new calf who decided to enter the world early. With a lantern hooked over the saddle horn and cradling his rifle in his right arm, Butch called out, "Fisher-man, you up here?"

Hearing Butch's call-out to the guard, Herb finished tying the last knot and lit each fuse as he low-crawled across the bridge to the spot where he planned to descend. He certainly hadn't counted on someone coming upon him up here. Having to climb down the steel latticework in a hurry on this leg of the bridge was not something he wanted to do. He was supposed to have time to do it safely. His heart pounded, and his throat was dry. Despite his moist palms, Herb began his quick descent as the fuses burned. Sweat dripped into his eyes.

In the distance, the train whistle sounded, and the rails started to vibrate.

Butch strained to hear a reply from the guard. But with the sound of the train whistle and the stiff breeze ruffling through his hair, none came. Duke snorted and tossed his head.

"Easy boy, what's got you spooked?" Butch approached the gate, dismounted, and tied the reins around the metal bars. He called out again and placed his lantern onto the ground before climbing through the bars. Retrieving the lantern, he approached the guard shack.

A flicker caught his eye in the increasing darkness.

He muttered, "What the heck? Looks like a sparkler." Butch picked up the pace to see what the flickering was.

"No! It can't be!" he blurted as he drew near. His brain was slow in registering the danger his eyes were seeing. Holding the lantern high in the air, Butch shouted, "Good God! It's a dynamite fuse! Fisher-man, get out here!"

Butch ran toward the flickering, and as he did, he spotted another farther down the track. Both were on the center section of the trestle spanning the gorge. Without a thought to his safety, Butch acted instinctively.

His guardian angel unfurled his mighty wings and sprang into action.

Reaching the first device, Butch saw something metallic winking in the lantern light. A knife. With the lantern resting on a railroad tie, he knelt and picked it up before seeing that the crudely-made explosive was tied to the side of the trestle with bailing twine. The fuse was getting shorter, so he had to detach the explosive quickly, opting for the knife in his hand rather than the knife he always carried in his pocket. His steady hands worked as if guided by an unseen force.

Having cut the twine attachments, Butch watched as the deadly package dropped one hundred fifty-five feet. The dynamite exploded as it entered the dark water below, sending up a geyser of spray. At the same time, he saw headlights near the bridge abutment by the creek below. A car pulled away and sped down the dirt road toward the river.

The train whistle blew again. Vibrations shook the rails. It was getting closer by the second, and Butch had to hurry. He felt a calm come over him and the wind at his back as he ran toward the second explosive.

Again, his deft fingers worked with a speed Butch

didn't know he was capable of as he dispatched the second device into the water below. It must have had a slightly longer fuse because it was extinguished when it hit the water.

"Thank God!" Butch uttered in prayer. Neither the bridge nor the abutments were damaged. Despite the urgency of the situation, he had a fleeting thought of the family's swimming hole, wondering if the first blast had made it bigger.

As the train whistle sounded again, Butch sprinted from the tracks. The huge locomotive was already on the first span of the bridge. The engineer saw movement on the eastern edge of the structure near the guard shack. Assuming it was the guard, the engineer gave him two short blasts on the horn. Butch waved.

With lantern in hand, Butch ran to the small building. The door wouldn't open all the way. Holding the lamp inside the narrow opening, Butch could see why. A crumpled body lay on the floor, blocking the entrance. He lifted the light higher and stuck his head around the corner of the door. Butch saw the bloodied head of his friend, Randy Fisher.

As Butch pushed on the door to the guard shack, Randy's legs moved enough to allow an opening for Butch to squeeze through.

"Randy! Randy! Can you hear me?" Butch placed the lantern on the floor and knelt next to his friend, working to straighten out Randy's contorted body. He was sickened at the pasty color of his buddy's skin in the lamplight. Leaning his head toward Randy's face, Butch could feel his breath. "Thank God! I know you can hear me, Randy. You stay with me buddy; I'm gonna get some help."

Butch looked around for the walkie-talkie each guard carried, wondering which brother was on the other end. Butch gently lifted each of Randy's limbs to look for the radio and found it tucked inside a jacket pocket.

Pushing the talk button, Butch called out, "Mayday, Mayday, Mayday!"

The radio squawked. Butch heard static and then, "This better not be a joke, Randy. I'm in the middle of a great poker hand, and I'm about to win some money."

Butch replied, "This is Butch Emig. Randy's hurt. Who's this? Over."

"What? Did you say Randy's hurt? How'd he get hurt? Over."

"Who is this? Over," Butch repeated.

"It's Paul Fisher. Over."

"Paul, someone tried to blow up the railroad bridge, and he got away. What are your instructions in case of an emergency? Over."

"Well, lemme see, there's a list of stuff..."

Butch heard the sound of shuffling papers. "Paul! Listen to me. Randy's hurt bad and he's bleeding. We need to get him to the hospital quick. Can you call the switchboard operator? Tell her to get my dad at the farm. He needs to hitch up the team and bring the buckboard to the upper pasture near the guard shack. We gotta get Randy down to the main road right quick. Oh, and tell Dad to have Mom gather up a bunch of pillows and some bandages so we can stop the bleeding and cushion Randy's head. Then call Doc Mayhew. Tell him to get out to the Emig farm right away. After that, report the incident to your superiors in charge of bridge security. Paul, do you read? Over."

"I read you, Butch. Call Fred, pillows and bandages, Doc Mayhew, and report the incident. I'll make the calls right away. Over."

"Roger, Paul."

Butch took a red bandana out of his back pocket and wrapped it around Randy's head. He hoped his twenty-four-year-old friend would live to see twenty-five. Butch sat back against the wall of the guard shack with Randy's head in his lap. Waiting for help to arrive, Butch prayed.

It occurred to him that he and his injured friend were not alone.

Ten

Herb drove his old car down the rutted dirt road as fast as he dared in the dark. The steering wheel was slick from his sweaty palms. Still shaking from nearly being caught, Herb fumed.

"My plot was fool-proof. It was brilliant! No one could have planned better." Spittle flew from his lips as he spoke aloud. "It was all spoiled by that damn Emig kid. I was supposed to be sitting at the Halfway Bar having a beer right now, but, no-o-o-o-o, that snot-nosed kid had to show up and screw up my plan. I was damn lucky not to get caught." He sucked in a deep breath and let it out slowly. "I gotta think. I gotta get myself together. I gotta give myself an alibi if anyone wants to know where I was and what I was doing."

He pulled into the bowling alley parking lot. Stopping his car in the shadow of a maple tree at the edge of the lot closest to the side entrance, Herb slipped out of his vehicle and entered the building through the conveniently unlocked door. He found himself in a back hallway adjacent to the men's room—just what he needed. Herb examined himself in the mirror as he soaped up his hands. Next, he washed the sweat-streaked dirt from his face.

"I feel better already," Herb said to his reflection as he ran wet fingers through his hair several times to cool his head. Straightening his shirt, Herb walked casually out of the men's room, darting around the corner into the empty billiards room. He picked up a cue stick and racked up the balls. Holding his bridge steady, he controlled his erratic breathing and took careful aim. The whole process helped to calm his nerves. Herb played all shots before a waitress noticed he was there.

"Oh, I'm so sorry; I didn't see you come in or I would have been here sooner. Would you care for a drink?"

"A beer'll do," he answered curtly.

As the barmaid turned to leave the room, they heard a siren approaching. Herb and the waitress walked to the window and parted the blinds.

"It's one of Seymour's hearses with the lights flashing," she said. "It's turning onto Lyon Brook Road. Wonder if someone's hurt on the Emig farm."

"Yeah, I wonder," Herb said as he rolled his eyes and walked back to the billiards table.

"They only use the flashing red lights and siren if they're acting as a hospital transport." The waitress chuckled. "Not many people get to ride in a hearse while they're still alive!" Still giggling, she left the room to get Herb's beer.

Fred's massive draft horses never sounded as good to Butch as they did that night, clomping up over the ridge of the pasture. By the light of several lanterns, Fred and Butch loaded Randy onto the buckboard as gently as possible and cushioned his head and neck with the pillows from the house. Fred signaled the team. The brute strength of the animals controlled the buckboard on the rough descent. Randy's only responses were groans.

"Hopefully, Doc will be waiting for us," said Fred, as

he patted Butch's shoulder. "Paul said Doc was his next call after me."

"Dad, I feel so helpless. There wasn't much I could do for him."

"Butch, you kept your wits about you and gave young Paul specific instructions. I just hope he was able to remember everything you said and made all the calls."

"Paul's not so bad, Dad. He's just still sowing his wild oats. I know Randy and Jim don't like those guys he runs with, but I believe that his brothers will help keep him in line."

The journey seemed to take forever. When the buckboard rounded the corner of the barn, Fred was the first to spot Doc Mayhew. He was standing beside the big black hearse from the Seymour Funeral Home, parked in the driveway.

"He's not dead, Doc!" Butch hollered.

"I know. The hospital ambulance is busy right now, and Bub Seymour volunteered their hearse for transport."

"All's I can say is Randy better not wake up in a hearse. It'll scare him out of his wits."

Despite the gravity of the situation, Butch chuckled as he and Fred assisted the funeral home driver in getting Randy onto the stretcher and into the big black vehicle.

Eleven

Herb tossed and turned in his bed. The bedsheets were torn free from the bottom of his mattress and wrapped tightly around his legs. He was trying to run away, but he couldn't get his footing. Crashing into an embankment, he'd had to jump out of his disabled vehicle to escape the giant fireball and collapsing bridge. Breathing hard and soaked with sweat, Herb's frustration grew as he couldn't move his legs. He gasped for air and woke up shaking. Sunlight streamed through the cracks and splits in the dark green window shades. Herb sat up and ran his hand through his matted hair.

"Crap!" He realized that it was all a dream and struggled to untangle the sheets from his lower limbs. Finally, he was able to swing his legs around to sit on the edge of the bed. His plot to blow up the bridge was a failure.

"That damn Emig kid," he muttered. "That's a score I've gotta settle." Herb got up to start the coffee percolating on the tiny hot plate set next to the sink. "I need money. Gotta get a job. Who's gonna hire me, knowing I got fired from the railroad?"

Coffee would help clear his head.

Reality hit him when he thought about the cops looking for the person who tried to blow the bridge. What could they trace back to him? He knew the Emig kid didn't see his face, and he was sure the Fisher boy never saw him coming. He hoped he hadn't killed the kid...

Herb was a little surprised about his unexpected concern. That kernel of caring was something he wasn't used to. He wondered where it came from. Then speaking aloud to no one but himself, he announced, "First order of business today is to get outta town and start looking for a job."

After breakfast and a shower, Herb shaved his beard and dressed in overalls and a t-shirt topped by an open flannel shirt, the standard uniform for this farming community. He packed his cardboard suitcase, secured it with a belt, and set out for his cousin's place in Ithaca.

"That's far enough away," he grumbled as he slammed the door behind him. "But I'll come back to settle the score after things die down!"

Twelve

A week later, Butch entered the kitchen of his parent's house from the adjoining apartment door. He saw his father sitting at the hand-hewn oak breakfast table, carefully working with different lengths of finished wood.

"Morning, Dad. What are you working on?"

"I'm piecing together a picture frame. It's a special project."

"Any news about Randy?"

"Jim stopped by a little bit ago. He already told the railroad they'll need to get the Army or someone else to do guard duty at the bridge, now that the threat is credible. Randy's conscious and resting. He doesn't remember anything about the attack, which is a doggone shame. I hoped he'd be able to tell us who hit him. The doctors think he'll be okay, but they're going to keep him awhile. Every time I look up at that majestic railroad trestle overlooking this beautiful Lyon Brook valley, I realize what could have happened if that scoundrel had succeeded in blowing up the bridge. It sure does show the danger we're living in these days. I praise God for His protection that night and the fact that Randy didn't die."

"Amen to that. So, what's your special project?"

"I visited the Farm Bureau office yesterday," said Fred.

"They were getting ready to paint and were throwing away some stuff. I spotted this architectural drawing of the Lyon Brook Bridge and asked if I could have it. They said sure, so I fished it off the junk pile. It was drawn in the late 1800s, and at the time it was an engineering marvel. I think I got a real find. As I look at this drawing, there's something intriguing about it. Can't quite put my finger on it..." Fred angled his head to look at the drawing from a different perspective. "On another subject, Butch, I have to talk to you about our workload. You've seen yourself how much we have to do with our expanding role as an experimental site for Cornell. We're already using the latest in animal husbandry techniques. Now they want us to start using some new crop-planting and soil-enrichment tactics. Of course, everything has to be documented, so it's hours of extra work for me when I should be helping you."

"I know, Dad." Butch picked up the dented aluminum coffee pot from the stove and poured some of the hot brew into his mug. "I've been thinking a lot about our situation." He walked over to the table and sat on the corner next to his father.

Fred looked at his son. "I'm being asked to speak on our experiences with Cornell just about every week. And the Farm Bureau approached me the other day about doing a weekly broadcast on the Norwich radio station." He tapped a tiny nail into the corner of the picture frame. "There, it's finished." He held up the black and white drawing to admire his handiwork.

Butch's brown eyes widened. "Yeah, it looks nice, Dad. It's different, kinda. About this broadcast offer, are you gonna do it?"

"Well, I suppose I could if we had enough help on the farm. Then I could also say yes to the farming magazine that wants me to write a column each month."

"Well, I'll be, Dad! You're getting to be famous."

"I don't know about that. I'm still a simple Chenango County farmer."

"Well, it looks like I'll be the farmer, and you'll be the famous farming expert everyone wants to talk to, listen to, and read about."

Fred's belly bounced up and down as he chuckled and picked up the morning newspaper.

"I think we ought to put an ad in the paper for an experienced farmhand." Fred looked over at Butch. "What do you think?"

"Good idea. But why don't I go to the high school in Oxford first to ask the Agriculture Department if they would recommend any junior or senior young men as part-time help? Then I can put ads up on the bulletin boards at the feed store and the post office for a full-time hand. If we get some interest, we won't have to pay for an ad."

"You know, Butch, it may take a while to find a permanent fella. Lots of men have been drafted, and others are working on the railroad or in plants supporting the war effort. It may be slim pickings."

Butch took a sip of coffee, "Let's see what happens, and keep our fingers crossed. With the baby here and all, I'm not sure I'll be able to handle all the chores without some extra help."

"I know that, son." Fred put the paper down and lifted his coffee cup to his lips. He paused. "There's something else I need to tell you. Your mother and I have been doing some talking about turning the whole operation over to you. Eventually, we'd move into town. That is, when Chet gets out of the Army, and if he'll consider partnering with you on the farm. Right now, moving is just talk, but it's gonna happen in the next few years. I'm sure of that. In the meantime, I hope we can find dependable help."

"Say, Dad, have you thought about talking to the Fisher boys? Maybe they know someone who's looking for work."

"By cracky! That's a good idea. Do you think you could pay them a visit? Since you'll be running the show someday, it'll be a good experience for you. In the meantime, I'm gonna hang this picture. Say, it kind of resembles a pair of angel wings. Well, I'll be jiggered."

The next week, Butch swung by the Fisher place. Randy was back, working in the barn with his brothers. After asking Randy details of his recovery, Butch told the three boys about his needs at Lyon Brook Farm. Randy and Jim figured they could run the farm on their own if Butch wanted to hire Paul. Butch made an offer to Paul Fisher to come on board as a full-time hand. It happened that the young man was looking to make some extra money so he could buy a red sports car. It was all he talked about. They shook hands and agreed that Paul would start the next day.

Butch returned to his home, feeling a measure of relief. He was hopeful that Paul would work out because help was sorely needed.

Thirteen

Baby Betsy was almost four months old, alert, and happy. Mary was feeling and looking great. Christmas was just weeks away. It would be Betsy's first. Butch should have been on top of the world, but he was more than a little uneasy with the way things were working out with his hired hand Paul.

While setting up the milking machines one day, Butch called Paul over to discuss the day's plans. "Paul, I smell beer on your breath, and it looks like you slept in those clothes."

Paul burped noisily, not attempting to hide it.

Butch continued, "This isn't the first time it's happened. What's going on with you?"

Butch's guardian angel cringed. *Ugh! The stench of booze accompanies every belch Paul emits. Even an angel is repulsed by it.*

Paul crossed his arms over his chest and took two steps back. He couldn't look Butch in the eye. "It's not me, Butch. I dunno what you smell."

"Are you telling me you haven't had anything to drink? Or that you don't have a hangover?"

Paul licked his lips then blew out a loud breath. "You don't believe me?"

"Paul, I don't want you here like this. You need to go home and sober up. Don't come to work tomorrow smelling like the inside of a barrel. You understand?"

"I didn't do nuthin'. You gotta believe me, Butch; I really need this job," Paul slurred as he staggered off toward his truck to drive home two miles up the road.

"Hold up, Paul. I'm gonna drive you. Toss me your keys."

Paul rolled his eyes but did as he was told. Sullenly, he got into the passenger side and slammed the door. He didn't say a word all the way home.

Cora gladly watched the baby as Mary donned one of her husband's old brown barn coats. She followed Butch in the Lyon Brook truck to drive him home. They'd have some talking to do on the way back.

Butch knew he'd have to talk to Jim and Randy. He just didn't want Paul around his family.

Morning barn chores took longer than usual the next day without Paul to help. Fred arrived in the barn around seven o'clock. Butch waved him over to the piglet pen to see some new arrivals nursing while their exhausted mama slept.

"Look what happened before dawn. They seem to be doing fine. Cute, aren't they?"

"Yeah, they sure are. Morning, son. Where's Paul?"

"I had to send him home yesterday."

"Yeah, your mother told me it happened while I was in town."

"He was drunk as a skunk. I told him not to come back until he sobered up. He insisted that he hadn't been drinking up until I drove him home."

"What in tarnation has gotten into that young man? Is he running with those hoods from Norwich again? When

I was in town for my radio broadcast the other day, I heard that the police have their hands full with vandalism. I sure hope Paul's not involved with any of that stuff."

"I wonder too, Dad. I'm thinking about paying a visit to his brothers and having a chat. We have to do something. Can you help me finish up? I'd like to drive to the Fisher farm before three o'clock this afternoon."

჻

Butch walked into the milking parlor of the Fisher Farm. Randy and Jim were finishing up cleaning out the gutters and filling up the manure spreader. Butch called out, "Hey, neighbors, do you have ten minutes to talk?"

"Sure, pull up a bale and have a seat." Jim began spreading hay for the cattle. "I'm getting ready to sprinkle some blackstrap molasses on this stuff. The cows think they're getting dessert first when they come in for milking."

"Molasses is great for increasing milk production. My cows love it," Butch said. "I appreciate you guys taking the time to talk to me today. And I'm glad to see you're doing so well, Randy. You sure did give us all a fright. I hope someday the son of a gun who hit you is caught and punished."

"We're with you on that, Butch. Thanks for your help that night. I might not have been so lucky if you hadn't found me right away." Randy's eyes were downcast at the thought.

Butch shifted on his bale of hay. "I'll get right to it. I got serious concerns about your little brother."

Jim pulled up a wooden stool and sat.

"Paul?" Randy asked as his eyes widened. "I thought he was doing a good job for you. Isn't he back at your farm finishing chores so you can visit?"

"No, I sent him home yesterday because I smelled beer on him. I told him not to come back unless he was sober. He was doing a good job until he started showing up late, or not at all."

"What?" Jim bellowed. He stood up from the stool so fast that it tipped over and rolled. He began to pace. "Paul's drinking? I can't believe it! I can't believe he'd touch the stuff since he saw what it did to our dad. Now, I wonder where the heck he is."

Butch nodded. "I can tell you he was slurring his words and couldn't walk straight to save his soul. I had to drive him home. I'm worried about him."

"Well, to be honest, he hasn't been himself for a while." Randy rubbed the palms of his hands across the rough fabric of his barn pants. "He always says he's going to Norwich to see his friends. Then he leaves, and I don't usually see him till morning."

"What else, Randy?" Jim asked.

"Well, before I got whacked on the head, I noticed a couple of things about our little brother but didn't say anything. I thought I'd keep an eye on him. But, well, you know what happened, and then I got laid up. What I did notice is that Paul was never on time. He always had some lame excuse for being late or not showing up at all. He didn't want to accept any responsibility when he messed up or forgot to do something. His temper got the best of him—a lot." Randy hung his head as he jammed his hands in his pockets, murmuring, "I feel kinda responsible because I didn't say anything."

Jim lifted his cap with one hand and smoothed his thick brown hair back with the other. His brow furrowed as he processed the information. "We appreciate your concern, Butch. You're a good neighbor and friend."

It was Butch's cue to leave so the brothers could talk. Butch's angel lingered behind, thinking, *As an angel,*

I should be able to see other angels, and lately I haven't seen one around Paul.

Rubbing the back of his neck, Randy turned to face his brother. "Jim, I'm really worried. If Paul's running with those bozos that are causing all the trouble in Norwich, they'll get him landed in jail sooner or later. What are we gonna do?"

Jim brushed his face with both hands and sighed. "The only thing we can do is talk to our little brother and lay down the law. It's what Mom would do after she chased him around with the broom and hit him a couple of times."

He's going to need more than talking to, boys, Butch's guardian thought. *Paul's soul is in danger.*

After dinner, Randy and Jim sat at the kitchen table with their younger brother Paul.

Paul nervously rubbed his hands together. "What's up, guys?"

"Butch paid us a visit today and told us he had to drive you home yesterday." Randy's eyes bore into Paul's, trying to read him. "What do you have to say for yourself?"

Paul lifted his chin in defiance but didn't say a word.

"What do you have to say for yourself?" Randy insisted.

"Okay, okay. I was with friends, and yeah, we were at the inn shootin' pool. Those guys made me join a drinking game. It was all their fault."

Randy frowned at his younger brother. "You could've said no, you know."

Jim stood up and started to pace as he spoke. "We've heard the reports of vandalism and fights in town and don't want you getting caught up in something that would spell J-A-I-L. The bottom line is that we are having this talk because we don't like what we're seeing and hearing. And since we are all part of this family, we're stepping in, little brother."

"I just wanna know where does Butch Emig get off sticking his nose in my business?" Paul demanded.

"First off, he's your boss. Second, he actually cares about you, Paul. Third, we're neighbors and went to school together. And fourth, you're the one that wanted extra money so's you could save up for a car." Jim stood next to his brother to put a hand on his shoulder. Paul pushed it away.

"I don't need his caring. I'm fine."

"Paul, we all know what living with Dad was like." Randy paused. "We're not saying you can't have a beer with your friends, we're telling you to watch how much you drink."

"And to choose your friends wisely," interjected Jim.

"But they like me. And I'm not Dad," Paul whined.

"You do realize that this drinking has messed up your job," Randy pointed out.

"So I drank some beer and missed some work. Big deal!"

"It's a big enough deal for Butch to talk to us. He depends on you to show up and work." Jim stood up to face his defiant younger brother.

"That Butch Emig should'a minded his own business. He needs to be taught a thing or two." Paul clenched and unclenched his fists. It did not go unnoticed by his brothers.

"He's concerned about you, Paul," Randy reiterated.

"Yeah, right." Paul stood as if ready to throw a punch. "Well, what the hell are you gonna do, since you think I have a problem?"

Randy got up and approached his younger brother. Poking his index finger in the center of Paul's chest, he emphasized every word when he said, "I'm gonna be watching you like a hawk, little brother. No more hanging out with those hoodlums from Norwich. You want to act like an immature idiot, that's how we're going to treat you. And we'll make sure you get to work. Sober."

Paul reached in his back pocket and pulled out a blue and white handkerchief to blow his nose. "If it's all the same to you, I need to go to bed now. I'm wiped out." Paul headed toward the stairs.

"Okay, see you tomorrow," Jim said as he and Randy walked into the living room.

"Yup," Randy called over his shoulder, "one of us will take you to work."

Paul sullenly trudged upstairs. In his bedroom, he lay on his back, looking at the ceiling, fuming. "Somebody's gotta pay for this," he muttered before closing his eyes. "I will get even..."

Fourteen

Randy Fisher's wife Ginny pulled into the Emig driveway in an old black Plymouth. She drove directly to the barn and parked in front of the double sliding doors. She threw the car door open and struggled to maneuver her cumbersome pregnant belly out from behind the steering wheel. Waddling to a small door, she entered the room where stainless steel cans of fresh cow's milk were immersed in ice-cold water until they were picked up and taken for pasteurization. Shivering, she pulled her coat around her belly. As far as she was concerned, spring couldn't come soon enough.

Ginny opened the next door, which led into the milking parlor. Each cow, secured in stanchions, patiently chewed on her hay while awaiting a turn to be hooked up to a milking machine. Ginny saw Butch moving from one animal to the next, keeping an eye on the process. She waved to get his attention.

"Hey, Ginny, how are you doing?" The new dad eyed her belly.

"I'm at that uncomfortable stage now, Butch. You know how it goes."

"I can vaguely remember what Mary went through. What can I do for you?"

"Jim wanted me to come speak to Paul. Is he here?"

"No, he's not, Ginny. Paul has only showed up for work off and on for weeks. Told me that he's needed at home to help you and that you'd been told by Doc Mayhew that you needed to stay in bed."

"Well, you can see that he wasn't telling the truth. But I don't understand; he's been leaving the house in the morning like he's coming here to work. He promised he'd..."

"Ginny, are you okay?"

"No, I guess I'm not. Jim and Randy trusted Paul to do the right thing. I think Paul is pulling the wool over his brothers' eyes. It makes me so mad. I think he's running with that Norwich gang and drinking again. The police even came to the house, asking questions about a stolen car."

"Yikes, that doesn't sound good." Butch wiped his hands on a towel dangling from his overalls.

"Paul seems angry all the time, and he hasn't been going to church. I'm so worried."

"I'm sorry to hear this, Ginny. Paul's irresponsible behavior has caused a problem for both you and me. I've given him three months, but he doesn't seem to care. In a couple weeks it'll be March and we'll have even more work. I've got to think about how to handle it on my end. I need help on the farm, and Paul isn't giving it to me."

Ginny pondered that last statement. While Butch walked her out to the car, she wondered what would happen to Paul's job. She was reasonably sure that Butch's patience was at an end.

"Well, Dad, what do you think about all this stuff

Ginny had to say?" Butch poured himself a mug of hot coffee. The two men sat at the rectangular farm table in front of a large picture window in the kitchen.

"Frankly, Butch, we'll help the Fisher family when and where we can. But we're gonna have to hire someone else, because our workload isn't getting lighter or easier. We've got a bigger herd than ever, and Cornell wants us to try a new wheat seed, which means a lot more paperwork in addition to the manpower hours." He picked up a pencil and made a note on one of the papers to his right.

"I know." Butch got up and took his empty mug to the sink. He paced around the kitchen table. "I put out the word that we're hiring. Got ads on the bulletin board at both the feed store and the post office."

"That's as good a place as any, I suppose," Fred said. "It may take a little while to find someone, which means more work for us."

Butch stood at the window overlooking the back yard, both hands shoved deep into his pants pockets. He looked out over the fields toward the barn and the three-story chicken house, wondering where he could find someone who would care as much about the land as he did.

Fifteen

Herb Brunner walked into the Norwich post office to arrange for a mailbox. He made it a point to scan the bulletin boards for notes of interest, and he needed to find a job. Exacting revenge was Herb's focus and he felt a sense of satisfaction being back in Chenango County after living in Ithaca for half a year. He'd found work within a week at the Ithaca Gun Company—an interesting job with unexpected perks: Ithaca Gun allowed employees to purchase their product at less than wholesale prices. Herb had taken advantage of that, buying an engraved special edition shotgun, complete with case and gun-cleaning kit. After staying with his cousin for a few weeks, he'd found a furnished room with an efficiency kitchen above a corner drugstore. It was more than comfortable, better than what he was used to, and had access to a shared bathroom across the hall.

However, all he could think of was getting back to Chenango County to settle a score. Hatred burned inside his gut, and the time had come for him to carry out his mission. His eyes widened as he saw what seemed too good to be true. Lyon Brook Farm was looking for a hand and provided room and board if needed. He reached for the card and pulled it down. It said to call 22F5 and ask for Butch. It seemed fate was finally working in Herb's favor.

Herb was driving an old Ford truck when he pulled into the dirt driveway of the Emig farm, glad he had gotten rid of the old green Plymouth he was driving when he tried to blow up the railroad bridge. He'd arranged to meet with Butch at the barn at three o'clock, well before evening milking time.

Butch greeted Herb in the driveway. "Hello, I'm Butch Emig. Welcome to Lyon Brook Farm. And thanks for coming out on such short notice."

"You're welcome. Nice to meet you. I'm glad it worked out for both of us." Herb sized up the muscular man in front of him, realizing there was no way he'd want to take Butch on, man to man.

"As we discussed on the telephone, the job is full-time, starting as soon as possible. I'd like to show you around the barn and outbuildings while we talk." Butch slid open the massive barn door. "You'll be working with a 'sometime' hand, Paul. I say that because sometimes he shows up and sometimes he doesn't. I don't condone it, but I'm giving the kid a second chance. I'll see how it works out, but I gotta admit I'm about outta patience."

Herb tucked that information away as Butch showed him the expansive milking parlor for forty head of dairy cows. "We have a full hayloft up overhead. That hay keeps the herd fed all winter. Any surplus, I sell off to neighbors if they're running short."

Herb asked a few questions about the machinery he'd be using. Butch answered each of them in detail. They toured the pig pens, horse stables, brood houses for the chicks, and the three-story chicken house.

Butch sized up the man who seemed interested and

not much older than Butch. He was asking all the right questions about the animals and equipment. And he said he had farming experience. They stopped in the driveway once the tour was over. Butch extended his hand.

"Herb, it's been a pleasure meeting you. I'd like to offer you the job. If you accept, you can live in a spare room in the main house with my mom and dad, Fred and Cora. I live in the attached apartment. You'll eat meals with us if you choose, and the women will do your laundry."

Herb took a minute before answering. "That's a mighty generous deal, Butch. I accept all you're offering. Right now, I'm in a rooming house, but this would save me some money and allow me to build up a savings account for my own place someday. I have a change of clothes in my truck, and I'd be glad to help with the evening milking chores tonight if you need a hand."

Butch looked surprised. "Well, that would be great. Yes, I can use the help. 'Sometime' Paul didn't show up today. The women will have dinner ready for us after the chores are done if you'd like to stay."

Now it was Herb's turn to look surprised. "Thanks. Home cooking would be a real treat for me." He figured he'd done an excellent job of making a positive first impression because he got the job. The mission had begun.

Later that night, Herb moved his belongings from the boarding house to Lyon Brook Farm. He sat on the bed and carefully unwrapped his shotgun. Placing the weapon across his lap, he rubbed the stock with a soft cloth. As he plotted his revenge, he smiled. "Things couldn't have gone any better today," he told himself. "I'll do my job, Butch will find out how much he needs my help, I'll be his trusted indispensable right-hand man, and he'll never see what's coming!"

Sixteen

"Son, what are you going to do about this Paul problem?" Fred leaned on a barn broom as he watched Butch scoop cow feed into a pail.

"Well, Dad, he's finished here on this farm. I'm done messing around with his erratic work habits. I sent him a letter telling him his services were no longer needed. I included a check for the times he worked. Nothing he says or does is gonna make me hire him again. Paul Fisher used up all his chances with Lyon Brook Farm and me. I'm grateful that we could hire Herb; I like the guy. He seems responsible."

"From the short time your mother and I have spent with him at the dinner table, he seems likable enough. I sure hope he does a good job for you."

"Working alongside the man, I'm impressed with him already, Dad."

"That's good, Butch because we just got a letter from Chet and he doesn't want to have anything to do with farming. He says that being in the war has clarified his thinking and life is too short to do something he doesn't love. I think a full-time hand and a part-timer is your best option for help, going forward." Fred's head drooped, his lips pressed together, showing disappointment in his older son's decision.

"But what will Chet do when the war ends, Dad?"

Fred shrugged his shoulders. "He said something about trying to get a job at Christman Motors. Hope it works out."

"So do I, Dad." Butch hung the feed pail on its peg and watched his dad shuffle back to his sweeping.

Later Sandalphon and the Emig guardians made their reports to Archangel Michael.

"Herb seems like a decent man," Sandalphon said, "but I sense he has secrets. I have not yet seen his guardian, and it makes me wonder about his soul. Herb's extra help allows Fred to do the mountains of paperwork associated with Cornell as an experimental farm. And Butch has more time to spend with his family. I wish I could see into the future, but that ability is strictly in God's hands. Anyway, I'm glad for the opportunity to stretch my wings as a guardian angel."

"Do you sense any other threats to the family, besides the fact that Chet is fighting in the war?" Michael asked.

"Well, I have serious misgivings about Paul. He has a dark side, and I can see he's in trouble and has resumed bad habits. I finally caught a glimpse of his guardian. I was taken aback. The angel had his wings bound with ties of hostility, envy, and greed. At one point, I thought his older brothers had convinced Paul to turn over a new leaf, but I fear he is in the clutches of the Evil One. Paul's mistakes and negligence were affecting the farm's bottom line. Butch saw the troubling signs and reminded Paul not to squander the second chance he'd been given. But it's too late. Butch is finished with him. With Paul becoming more resentful and angry... I sense dark forces gathering on the horizon."

"It will take a bevy of angels to keep this farm and its family safe," Michael said.

"With all that's going on, it warms our hearts to see Betsy's parents dancing to Big Band music in the evening. Watching them glide across the floor around the dining room table brings us joy. Sometimes we angels take a spin around the floor too. I'm happy to see them have these respites because living and working on a dairy farm has many challenges and dangers."

The angels agreed and knelt to pray at the conclusion of the report. "Lord, bless this family and keep them safe from the evil forces that seek to do them harm. Amen."

Each night at bedtime, Mary rocked her baby girl while saying, "Now I lay me down to sleep, I pray the Lord my soul to keep. Angels watch me through the night, and wake me with the morning light." Mary then kissed her sleeping child and placed her in the crib.

The guardian angels basked in pleasure from her faithfulness.

At the tender age of six months, Betsy acknowledged Sandalphon's presence. Her face lit up and her blue eyes followed Sandy as he moved around her. Betsy pursed her rosebud lips, making baby sounds in an attempt to imitate the words she heard over and over from her parents and grandparents. She studied her guardian angel, staring intently. Her plump arms and legs moved as if she were pedaling an invisible baby bike.

Sandy whispered into her ear, "Betsy, one day, you and I have to talk. I will tell you who I am, about our journey together, and why you have an incredibly special gift."

Seventeen

Paul Fisher sat at the bar at The River Inn with a group of scruffy-looking guys huddled up and talking about having a "big payday." Bradley Sawyer, more commonly known as Buzz, one of the rougher looking guys, was making notes on a bar napkin.

"Yup, we're gonna be rich this time," Buzz said, slamming his fist on the bar.

One of the other rabble-rousers asked, "Is your brother Huck in on this?"

"Listen, you jerk, I've told you a dozen times, don't call him Huck. He likes to be called 'The Saw,' and if he was here now, he'd give you a knuckle sandwich. Let me give you a hint, I'm Buzz, and he's The Saw. Get it? You don't wanna mess with us because it would be like walking into a buzz saw."

"I didn't mean nuthin' by it," the hood said as he cringed against the bar.

"The Saw's not going to be helping this time on account of he's outta town. That's why I roped in that knucklehead over there." He gestured at the Fisher kid who seemed to be in his own world.

Paul wasn't paying attention to what the boys were so fired up about. He fumed about an entirely different subject as he stared into his beer, talking to himself. "I can't believe Butch fired me. He had no reason to do that. So what if I have a drink now and then? It's my business, not his." In his drunken state, Paul was not making much sense. He wanted what the Emig family had--plus a red sports car--but he didn't want to work for it. The only trouble with coveting what the Emigs had was that it chiseled away at his mind and soul and led to desperate acts.

The next day, news reached the Lyon Brook Farm that the First National Bank in Norwich had been robbed. The police had several men in custody, including young Paul Fisher.

Paul was sobering up the hard way—in jail. Being arrested only fueled his anger at Butch Emig. Paul perceived his predicament as being Butch's fault. Butch had fired him and now the cops thought he was mixed up in a robbery. Aloud he whined, "I didn't do nuthin'."

The police weren't buying it. They had an eyewitness. The assistant bank manager had returned from lunch via the back door and heard the commotion of the attempted holdup. The robbers never knew he was there or noticed when he slipped back out the door to call the police from a nearby business.

No matter how hard Paul tried to convince the police that he didn't help plan or carry out the robbery, they didn't believe him.

"So when did you come up with the scheme to rob the bank?" The detective sat across from Paul with a pen poised to take notes.

"I don't know nuthin' about robbing the bank. Buzz told me they were going to the bank to get a loan. "

"You believed him?"

"Yeah."

"Was his brother Huck in on the heist?"

"Don't call him Huck; Buzz told us to call him 'The Saw.' And no, he wasn't with us on account of he's out of town."

"What did Buzz tell you to do?"

"He told me to wait outside."

"Wait outside? And do what?"

"Well, I was supposed to watch for 'John Law,' and if I saw cops coming, I was supposed to ask directions to the hospital."

"Didn't you think that was strange, asking directions to the hospital?"

Paul shrugged his shoulders. "No, I thought that was our next stop on account of Buzz saying that he was hoping he didn't have a case of lead poisoning after being in the bank."

"Is that so?"

"Right hand to God." Paul raised his hand above his head.

"Lead poisoning?"

"I hear it can be real serious."

The wide-eyed detective stared at Paul. His face reddened, and he held back a laugh that threatened his composure. The seasoned cop held his notebook in front of his face, quickly excusing himself. He burst into the squad room, laughing uncontrollably, causing the other investigators to look his way as he staggered toward the chief's office.

"Chief, this Paul Fisher kid we've got in the box is just plain naïve... or about as dumb as a stump." The detective shared the conversation that took place in the box with the chief and said, "Let's talk to the other suspects again."

After all the suspects had been grilled repeatedly, Buzz and his gang admitted that they had given Paul a cock-and-bull story to get him to act as their lookout.

Two days later, the police released Paul into the custody of his brothers. Paul was still sullen and angry when they picked him up from jail.

"You seem like you got a burr under your saddle, little brother. Did you actually think they weren't going to give you a hard time? We warned you time and again that the gang was going to drag you down with them," Jim scolded from the front seat.

"No, I had time to think about stuff." His nostrils flared, and he lifted his chin in defiance. "You know whose fault this is, don't you?" Paul took a breath through his bared teeth.

Randy looked at Paul in the rearview mirror. "Yours? After all, they were your friends—friends who planned a bank robbery, for crying out loud!"

"No, it was Butch's fault," fumed Paul.

"What?" Jim and Randy said in unison.

"Yeah, he's the one who fired me and left me without a job."

Randy couldn't hold his temper. "See here, you blockhead. Butch fired you because you weren't showing up. You were running with those hoodlums. He didn't make you do that. Get a grip, Paul!"

Pulling into their driveway, Jim stopped the car. Paul jumped out and scurried into the house before his brothers could open their doors.

Randy and Jim sat in the car, speaking in low tones.

Jim rubbed his stubbled face. "I'm worried about him. He's acting like he's ready for the loony bin."

Randy leaned toward Jim. "Paul never could let go of a grudge. Do you suppose... could our brother be capable of... could he hurt Butch or Mary or damage their property?"

Each of the brothers had a terrible gut-wrenching feeling that Paul was still in deep trouble. And they had no idea what to do about their brother's crazy-headed anger directed at Butch.

Eighteen

A shadowy figure dressed in black walked boldly onto the snowy Emig property from the southern field. Having parked a vehicle alongside the river road, the intruder held a flashlight at his side to guide his steps. Approaching the row of six chick houses, he lifted a two-gallon can of liquid and sprinkled it from one building to the next.

It was two o'clock in the morning. The stranger was confident that everyone in the distant house was sleeping.

The intruder set the can down and fished a metal cigarette lighter from his front pocket. He walked to the first chick house, thumbing the flint, taking time to stare at the flame. The shadowy figure bent down and touched the orange tongue to the dried grass doused with gasoline. With a whoosh, the fire spread across the vegetation protruding from the light snow cover. The flames sizzled, but there wasn't enough moisture to stop the fire from approaching stacks of wooden crates piled against each coop. Walking behind the remaining five small houses, he repeated his incendiary act.

Satisfied with his work, the bold intruder retraced his steps out of the field. He seemed in no hurry. His right thumb flipped the lid of the metal lighter open and closed, open and closed. His feet crunched on the frozen remnants of hay. At the sounds of the click-crunch, click-crunch, a maniacal laugh echoed across the field and didn't stop until the figure got into a waiting truck. The intruder drove away, watching the orange and yellow flames glow in the rearview mirror. His crazy cackle echoed throughout the cab as he headed back to the bar in Norwich.

Betsy's cry woke Mary. She got out of bed and crossed the hall to her child's bedroom. Opening the door, Mary gasped at the flickering flames visible from Betsy's window. They seemed to be consuming the chick houses. Mary scooped her baby out of the crib and turning quickly, ran back across the hall to get Butch.

"Butch, we have a fire at the chick houses. Wake up, hurry."

Butch sprang out of bed and pulled on a pair of pants. Running across the hall to the window, he saw the flames. He turned and dashed down the narrow stairs, then slipped his feet into a pair of work boots sitting on a mat by the front door. He threw on his barn coat.

With his hand on the doorknob, Butch was startled to hear a loud clap of thunder. As he pulled open the front door, the sky opened up with a deluge of water so intense that he stepped back inside. He could see the row of chick houses from where he stood. Astounded, Butch watched a wall of water sweep across the lawn to the curtain of fire that looked like it would consume his brood houses and the hundreds of chicks inside. He watched in utter surprise as the flames were instantly extinguished.

The storm subsided as suddenly as it started. Butch could see steam rising from the burned grasses and wooden travel crates piled outside each coop.

Mary appeared on the porch next to him. "What happened?"

"I think I just saw a miracle," Butch answered, stunned by what he'd witnessed.

He told her everything. Mary put her hand to her mouth and said, "Oh!"

Butch turned to his wife. "Can you get me a flashlight? I've gotta check the chicks to make sure they're all right."

She disappeared into the apartment.

Deep furrows formed in Butch's brow as he stroked his chin, wondering what could have caused the fire.

With a light in hand, Butch hurried to his chick houses. Walking from one to the other, he found each coop intact and chicks unharmed.

Lifting his cap, he scratched his head. "How in the world?"

Despite the deluge of water he witnessed, Butch smelled the unmistakable odor of gasoline.

"This fire was deliberately started," he muttered. "Who would do such a thing?"

Butch and Mary's guardian angels joined Sandalphon in Betsy's bedroom, singing praises to the Lord who delivered the sheets of water. "Praise be His Holy Name!" they sang.

"Nice work getting Mary awake by waking Betsy, Sandalphon," said Butch's guardian.

"But Butch certainly has a mystery to solve," Mary's guardian said. "Maybe we can help in some way.

❦

The next morning, Butch strode into his parents' kitchen. Fred and Herb were just finishing their coffee after a breakfast of Cora's buttermilk pancakes. The two men seated at the table looked up. Both noticed that Butch had dark circles under his eyes.

"Rough night, Butch?" Fred held his mug in mid-air. "Is Betsy sick?"

"Dad, Betsy's fine, but someone tried to burn down all the chick houses in the middle of the night."

Herb's face blanched.

Fred pushed his chair back to stand. "What? How?"

"Looks like whoever did it used gasoline to start the fire. But, Dad, it was the strangest thing." Butch proceeded to relate the facts of the incident while Fred's eyes widened. Herb studied the inside of his mug. "I didn't wake you or Herb because it seemed like it was over as fast as it started. But I think we need to secure the property better. I'm not sure it'll discourage someone determined to make mischief, but it sure will take them more time to get to us."

"Before we do that, I'm gonna call the sheriff to report this," Fred said. "We can't be too careful, especially after the vicious attack on Randy Fisher and the attempt to blow up the Lyon Brook Bridge a while back."

Herb struggled to get his work gloves on. His palms were sweating profusely, even though he kept wiping them down the front of his overalls. "I'll meet you at the barn," he said as he opened the kitchen door then tore down the porch steps, still tugging at his gloves.

After the call was made to the sheriff's office, Fred and Butch followed.

"Dad, when the sheriff gets here, will you show him the chick houses and where the fire started? Herb and I will be busy putting up more barriers."

"Be glad to, son. If he needs to talk to you, I'll come looking for you."

At the machine shed, Butch and Herb gathered post-hole diggers, wood for the posts, and barbed wire. For the remainder of the day, they surrounded the property with additional razor-sharp fencing.

Herb was unusually quiet.

Nineteen

Spring 1945

While sitting on the rhythmically creaking porch swing, Mary pulled Betsy into her lap and smothered Betsy's soft cheeks with kisses. She whispered into her daughter's ear, "In six months, right about the time you have your second birthday, you'll have a baby brother or sister to play with. Won't that be nice?"

Betsy placed both her hands on her mother's cheeks as if she knew what she was being told. Leaning into her mother's freckled face, Betsy planted an open-mouthed kiss on Mary's lips. Mary giggled and hugged her precious daughter as Betsy nestled into her mother's soft bosom. Betsy's eyes closed as her thumb automatically found its way into her mouth.

"I love you so much. I can't wait to share my heart with a new baby," Mary said.

Betsy half-opened her eyes and looked over her mother's shoulder at Sandy. They locked eyes, and the child raised her hand to wave. Sandy was taken aback by the definitive recognition and realized that it was time to tell Betsy precisely who he was and why he was with her. At eighteen months, she was beginning to talk.

After Mary carried Betsy upstairs to her bedroom,

she gently placed her daughter in the pale-pink handmade crib. She pulled the window shade to block the bright afternoon sun, and tiptoed out of the room, quietly closing the bedroom door.

Sandy took that cue to reduce his height, normally twelve feet, and compact himself to curl up beside the dozing toddler. Her eyes popped open, and she looked at him intently.

"Betsy, it's time I tell you who I am. My name is Sandalphon."

Betsy whispered, "Sanny?"

"'Sanny' works for now. God is giving you the grace to hear and understand everything I'm going to say. You will subconsciously retain all this information."

As he told his precious charge the story, she bobbed her head while her big brown eyes gazed steadily into his.

"I am your protector, Betsy, and only you can see me. But I'm not alone. Each of your family members has a guardian angel that you will be able to see. We all work together to keep you safe. I promise I'll tell you more when you get older."

"'Kay," Betsy murmured as her heavy lids closed and she drifted off to sleep.

Six months later, Betsy's baby brother Terry was born. The new baby's guardian angel hovered nearby. He tilted his head in acknowledgment of the presence of the other angels. He had been briefed about this family before leaving his heavenly realm. He knew their daily challenges and was given a hint of problems to come.

The ten-pound newborn, looking more like a three-month-old, won his guardian's heart immediately—and likewise, the hearts of all the angels whose presence filled the room that sunny morning.

Sandalphon thought about his unique assignment. *In Chenango County, New York, not many hard-working farm families ever thought about guardian angels in their midst. Nor did they realize there was a little girl who could see and hear these celestial beings.*

Twenty

Late Summer 1947

Butch maneuvered the tractor as close to the empty hay wagon as he could. He and Herb were stretched thin today. Herb was working another field by himself while Butch was left to bale hay without a helper. The war had ended two years ago, but men were still coming back from Europe and Japan. Many of them took advantage of the GI bill and were going to college. Others flocked to the cities and higher paying jobs in the factories. Chet had come home safely, but still had no interest in the farm. And the hay crop had to be brought in if they were to make it through the winter.

Butch shut the tractor off, dismounted, and walked back to the trailer. Lifting up the tongue of the wagon, he jiggled it closer to the John Deere and let it fall onto the tractor hitch, securing it. He squatted down to connect the wires for the brake lights. Straightening up, Butch tugged at his ear and frowned, wondering how he could make up for missing hands to help bring in the hay crop. It was a desperate situation requiring improvisation. He had an idea and left the barn to visit Mary in the house.

Mary was concentrating on making new curtains. The sewing machine whirred as she pumped the treadle up and down. Betsy contentedly played with scraps of fabric on the floor. Next to her, Terry slept peacefully in his corner crib.

Mary looked up from her sewing machine to see her husband standing in the doorway, chewing on a piece of straw that hung from the corner of his mouth. He entered the room, scooped up his daughter, and hoisted her onto his shoulders. Betsy squealed in delight. Turning to Mary, he said, "I'm taking Betsy out to the field with me to drive the tractor."

Mary sat there, speechless at first. "Wait!" she called after him. "She's too young to drive a tractor!"

"Mary, she's almost four. She's only going to steer. Don't worry; I've got this under control." Looking at Betsy, he said, "You can do that, can't ya?"

Betsy wrapped her arms around her daddy's neck. "Yes, I can. Can Sandy come?"

Butch and Mary looked at each other. The angel-friend was a constant in Betsy's conversations and interactions, especially since the truck incident at the Meeks the year before. Even though they were used to Sandy in the abstract, the child's parents had still not gotten used to Sandy being mentioned daily. But they didn't try to discourage their daughter, either.

Butch shrugged. "Sure, fine by me. Bring Sandy." After he'd seen Betsy's head heal the way it did when she was injured in the truck accident, Butch figured Sandy was more than welcome to ride along.

Mary had to trust that her husband would see that no harm came to their firstborn. With Terry asleep, Mary returned to the task at hand as worry lines creased her face. She, too, remembered Betsy's miraculous healing after the accident, but couldn't help wonder if they should be concerned about Betsy's insistence that she could see angels.

Mary rose from the sewing machine and walked over to the end table next to the couch to pick up the family Bible. Turning to Psalm 91, she read verses nine to twelve aloud. "Because you have made the Lord your refuge, the Most High your dwelling place, no evil shall befall you, no scourge come near your tent. For he will command his angels concerning you to guard you in all your ways. On their hands, they will bear you up, so that you will not dash your foot against a stone."

She sighed and put the Bible back on the table while looking up at the architectural drawing of the Lyon Brook Bridge that Fred had given to the couple. "There's something about that picture," she mused as she returned to her sewing project.

Mary resigned herself not to think about all the "what ifs." She thought about her daughter and decided that if Sandy could heal Betsy's head, then Sandy would keep Betsy safe on the tractor. Mary felt a sense of calm come over her, and the tension in her shoulders released.

"Everything will be just fine," she said aloud.

With Betsy on his shoulders, Butch strode to the large green tractor and empty hay wagon parked in front of the barn. He lifted his daughter up over his head and placed her on the deck of the tractor. Then he hopped into the seat, perched Betsy on his knee, and started the big John Deere. Upon reaching the lower fields, Butch braked and put the vehicle in neutral. He rose and placed Betsy in the driver's seat. Her feet dangled above the deck, but her hands gripped the steering wheel.

Standing on the running board next to his daughter, Butch pointed to the brake pedal.

"When I holler 'Stop,' just jump down with both feet on this pedal and hold tight to the steering wheel. Stay there until I get to you." Simply put, he expected his daughter to comprehend and obey. "Point the nose of the tractor right down that row and keep it straight."

"I can do that, Daddy." Betsy grinned.

Sandy saw Betsy's face beam with pride. Remarkably, she didn't look a bit scared.

Butch hopped off the running board to walk alongside the trailer. He began picking up bales, loading them in neat rows on the bed of the wagon. He called out encouragement to his daughter, who was steering the slow-moving tractor.

Sandy perched on the left fender of the tractor, enjoying the ride and wishing he could bottle Betsy's bravado. Betsy smiled at Sandy and gave him a thumbs-up. Then she waved.

"Who are you waving at, honey?" Butch asked.

"Sandy."

"Is Sandy riding with you?"

"Yup, Daddy, he's on the side."

"He is?"

"Uh-huh."

"Oh." He wondered what she meant by "the side." An off-the-subject, anxious thought passed through his mind. He thought about the future talk he'd have with his daughter about boys when she approached her teens. "Why am I so worried about this now?" he mumbled. "After all, we have Sandy!" He chuckled at the visual of a boy arriving at his home to pick up his daughter. What a comfort it would be to have unexpected heavenly scrutiny. A grin spread across his face.

The work progressed with Betsy at the wheel of the tractor while her daddy picked up bales and loaded them on the wagon. She steered the tractor straight and true down the rows, one after the other. It was a day of proud accomplishment for Betsy. Sandy hovered over her the entire time, poised to take charge if necessary.

When the wagon was fully loaded, Butch said to his daughter, "I have a surprise for you."

"What, Daddy?"

He lifted her up to the top of the neatly tied bales and handed her half a peanut butter and jelly sandwich, wrapped in waxed paper. "You get to be a hay wagon queen!"

Betsy giggled and bit into her favorite sandwich. "Can Sandy ride up here, too?" Jelly squeezed out the sides of the bread. Betsy licked her sticky fingers.

"You're the queen; you can have anyone you want to ride up there with you. But there is one rule that even a queen must obey: you have to sit in the middle of the load and stay away from the sides. We're gonna take a slow ride back to the barn." Butch was once again in the driver's seat.

Sandy lay next to Betsy on the prickly hay bales. As she was finishing the last bites of her sandwich, he could see her eyelids getting heavy. Soon the child rolled on her side, sound asleep. Pieces of hay stuck to her blonde hair and her clothing. Sandy wrapped one wing around her.

The wagon pulled up perpendicular to a two-story conveyer belt and Betsy awoke.

Butch beckoned. "Come on, honey girl. Jump!" Without hesitation, Betsy dove into her father's waiting arms six feet below.

Butch looked at his girl and grinned. "You were a big help today. Now go wash up for dinner and tell Mommy you were the hay wagon queen."

"Come on, Sandy." Betsy motioned the angel to follow her. Butch scratched his head.

Sandy followed along as the grimy sweaty child ran toward the house.

Fred walked around the corner and saw the loaded hay wagon. "Hey, Butch, are you by yourself?"

"Herb's working another field, Dad. Do you think you could give me a hand if you're up to it?"

"Ayuh, son, I still have what it takes to be a farmer. And don't you forget it."

Father and son laughed as they threw bales of hay onto the conveyer belt spitting each bundle into the loft. When the wagon was empty, Butch scrambled up the conveyor, with large hooks in his hands to start stacking the bales. The loft was full almost to the ceiling. It had been a good season for making hay.

The workday was done, and Butch looked forward to dancing with his princess.

⌣✤⌣

Herb sat on the big green John Deere tractor running back and forth in the field on an adjacent farm. He was doing the work by rote because his mind was somewhere else.

"There are a hundred ways to get back at Butch," he muttered. "Where do I begin? And 'when' is another question." He continued to talk to himself. "It's been three years already, so it's a good thing I'm a patient planner."

Suddenly, Herb heard a voice saying, "Why, after all this time, do you want to get even with a man who has been nothing but good to you? Why?"

Herb gasped. A chill traveled down his spine as he listened for the familiar voice again. He stepped on the brake and stopped the tractor.

"Who's there?" Puzzled, he looked around.

Herb's angel stood nearby, his wings bound by Herb's feelings of hate and retribution. But he was not totally helpless. He had the power of the Lord at his disposal. The angel was able to mimic a voice from Herb's past, attempting to help change the man's troubled mind.

Herb demanded again, "Who's there?" He was afraid. The voice sounded so much like his mother... but she had been gone for decades. His last and fondest memory of her was when he was eight years old. They had gone on a day trip to the Finger Lakes region for a picnic and a boat ride. He felt a lump form in his throat, remembering that the following week she was gone.

Herb stopped the tractor, got off, and paced around the machine scratching his head. He looked up at the cloudless blue sky and asked, "Mom, is that you? Why are you here?" Tears began to run down Herb's face.

"I'm asking you, Herbie, why do you want to harm a man who has given you a job and welcomed you into his home—a home where you break bread with his family every day?"

"You don't understand, Mom. I hate him. He stopped me from getting back at the railroad when they fired me."

"Hate is a strong word, Herbie. Maybe he did you a favor."

Herb stopped pacing to open his thermos and take a long drink of water. He muttered, "Maybe I'm hearing things. Mom, are you there?"

All he heard was the sound of his own breathing and the wind in the trees.

"Mom?"

Herb swiped at the tears on his face. Whatever or whoever he'd heard was now silent. He got back on the tractor, started it up, and resumed his work, replaying the short conversation in his mind. His heart hurt from the re-opening of a childhood wound. How could she have left him all those years ago? He had needed her. Instead, he'd grown up living with his abusive father and escaped as soon as he could—just as he supposed his mother must have. Herb felt a lump in his throat as he thought about his mother abandoning him as a young boy.

Twenty-One

B etsy and her cousin played with a large pile of Tinker Toys on the threadbare carpet of the living room floor. Ronnie had built an impressive, complex structure for a boy five years old. He loved visiting his uncle's farm because he had more freedom to roam than he did at home.

Betsy was getting bored, trying to copy his efforts. She impatiently fumbled with the pieces and angrily threw them across the room. "They don't fit." Getting to her feet, she walked around her cousin to get his attention.

"Wanna go outside? Wanna pet the cows? Wanna look at the fishes?"

Ronnie was too engrossed in putting wheels on a wagon he had constructed to pay any attention to his cousin. Betsy walked through the kitchen and quietly passed her mother, who was concentrating on rolling out pie dough on the counter. She slipped out of the screen door to the side yard.

Spying the goldfish pond her father and grandfather built, she ran across the dirt driveway to look at the fish.

Butch was in the barn, Mary was in the kitchen, and Ronnie was still building on the living room floor. Reaching the side of the pond, Betsy knelt on the decorative raised edge. A brilliantly colored fish rose to the top of the water after seeing the child's bright yellow romper. Betsy reached out to touch it. Stretching over the water, she could almost grab the fish. Suddenly, she lost her balance. Falling with a splash, Betsy gasped from the shock of the chilly water. Panic-stricken, she flailed wildly as she sought to stay afloat. She tried her best to grab onto the concrete sides, but her fingers were too small and her grasp too weak. In seconds, she was under the water.

Sandy hovered above the surface of the water. He was the last thing Betsy saw before she lost consciousness.

Instantly, Sandy appeared outside the living room window. His wings stirred the air, fanning a breeze strong enough to knock over Ronnie's building project. The boy cried out in frustration but got up to stretch his legs. He looked around for Betsy. Then he ran out to the kitchen, but she wasn't there, either.

"Going outside," he called out to his Aunt Mary. The boy burst through the screen door to the side yard. Ronnie spotted a green frog in the grass, which Sandy kept touching with his foot, causing the little guy to hop beyond the boy's reach. Ronnie chased it until the amphibian plopped into the pond. Ronnie was kneeling on the cement edge, looking for the escapee when he spotted what looked like his cousin's romper. Then he saw Betsy's blonde hair. He shouted, "Betsy's in the water! Gotta get her out!"

Ronnie lay on his stomach and reached into the cold water. Grabbing a handful of clothing, he pulled. Betsy was heavy. He pulled until his cousin rose to the surface, face down in the water. Without letting go of the fabric, the boy sat up and braced his feet on the cement lip, pulling his cousin up and over the edge.

Ronnie neither saw nor felt Sandy's arms around his waist.

The boy was only five, but he knew that the bluish tinge of Betsy's skin wasn't a good thing. He pulled her onto the grass then ran as fast as his legs could carry him toward the barn. "Unca Butch, Unca Butch! Help!"

As Ronnie burst through the double barn doors, Butch looked up from the milk stool. He was preparing to hook up the milking machine to the cow in the end stall, but his attention quickly turned to his nephew. "Take a breath, boy. What's wrong?"

"Betsy fell in the water. I got her out, but she won't talk to me."

Butch sprang up from the milking stool, nearly tripping over it as he made a mad dash toward the goldfish pond. His heart dropped into his stomach when he saw the lifeless form of his daughter, lying on the grass.

Neither he nor Ronnie was aware of Betsy's guardian angel hovering nearby.

Butch began artificial respiration, which he'd learned years ago in high school. As he labored over his daughter's body, water poured out of her mouth and soon she coughed.

Sandy prayed over the three forms on the ground until he heard Betsy cry.

"Daaa-dddeee!"

Relieved beyond words, Butch scooped up the soggy child and carried her toward the house.

"Mary, open the door! Call Doc Mayhew," he hollered.

"What on earth happened?" Mary gasped, wiping her flour-covered hands on the floral apron around her waist.

"Looks like she fell in the pond. Ronnie got her out in the nick of time." He looked back at his nephew trailing behind him and gave him a wink. "Looks like you saved the day, buddy. And your cousin too! You're a hero!"

Wide-eyed, Ronnie grinned as his Aunt Mary took

her sopping wet daughter from her husband's arms. Betsy snuggled into her mother's shoulder and hugged her tightly. Butch ruffled his nephew's hair and walked to the phone on the wall to call their family doctor.

Sandy maintained his position nearby. Betsy looked in his direction.

"Sandy." Betsy's arms reached out to him.

Mary looked around. She wished that she could see Sandy.

The angel knelt to sing a song of praise and thanksgiving, though none but Betsy could hear the heavenly strains. "Thank you, Lord. This child has my heart, which, right now, is filled with love and thankfulness. I pray that you will keep her well."

Betsy was exhausted after her drowning ordeal. At bedtime, Mary sat in the rocking chair, holding her four-year-old daughter to her bosom. She fought back hot tears as the two of them recited the "Now I lay me down to sleep" prayer. Tenderly kissing Betsy's forehead, Mary said, "I love you, honey. Sweet dreams."

"I love you too, Mommy."

Mary turned off the pink carousel lamp and left the room.

Betsy slipped out from underneath the bed covers to kneel on the rug with her folded hands resting on the mattress. In her most grown-up voice, she recited, "Angel of God, my guardian dear, to whom His love commits me here, ever this day be at my side, to light and guard, to rule and guide."

As Betsy climbed back into bed, Sandy hovered above his small charge, astounded that she remembered what he'd taught her. He smiled and spread his massive wings, deepening Betsy's restorative, restful slumber.

Twenty-Two

T erry grew as quickly as Betsy did but was twice as adventurous. On a cold day, typical of autumn in Central New York, Betsy was making cookies with Grandma. Terry, clad in a puffy warm wool snowsuit, played outside with Buster, the family's German shepherd. Mary was sweeping snow off the steps to the front porch when she heard Butch calling to her from the open barn door.

"Mary, can you give me a hand? Herb's in town running errands for me. One of the cows is calving, and it's breech."

Mary scooped Terry into her arms and trotted to the barn. Buster followed. They saw Butch beckoning from a single pen at the rear of the barn. The laboring cow was mooing and repeatedly moaning. Mary could sympathize.

"Mary, I have to tie a rope around the calf's legs to pull it out. I need to time my pulls with her contractions. Can you put your hands on her belly and tell me when she's tightening?"

Mary set Terry on a bale of straw. She instructed him, "This mama cow is going to have her first baby. You sit there while Mommy helps Daddy. Okay?"

"Okay, Mommy," Terry said with a serious look on his face.

Mary knelt by the cow, gently stroking her muzzle and crooning, "It's all right, girl. Your baby will be here soon—oh boy, here we go, Butch, I feel her belly tightening."

As the bovine birthing drama was finishing, Terry was distracted by a shaft of sunlight. He darted off the bale of straw and followed the beam of light, slipping through the open door. Buster tagged along while Mary and Butch were engrossed in the difficult birthing process.

Terry's guardian angel followed the boy and the dog.

Always intrigued by the goldfish pond, Terry made his way to its edge. In the cumbersome snowsuit, the boy lost his balance. His bundled body broke through a thin coat of ice and splashed into the frigid water.

Buster barked wildly, running back and forth next to the pond.

Immediately, the boy's guardian angel blew warm air into every area of Terry's snowsuit to keep him afloat while keeping him warm. The toddler wasn't in danger of drowning; miraculously, he'd flipped over onto his back. Baffles in his snowsuit kept the child from sinking, but the icy water penetrated his clothing. Terry floated serenely on the pond's surface, gazing at the cloud formations in the sky.

The angel tried to communicate with Buster to get Butch or Mary. Out of desperation, the guardian nudged Buster with his foot and commanded, "Fetch Butch or Mary! Now!"

Confused, Buster looked in the angel's direction. He saw nothing but heard the command. Buster stopped barking and bolted for the open barn door. Terry's guardian maintained watch over the boy, who had started to whimper at his predicament.

Buster barked and carried on in the barn until Butch acknowledged him. "What's got you all in a dither, boy?"

Taking off his gloves and wiping his hands on an old cloth towel, Butch stepped outside and watched as Buster bolted for the goldfish pond. Looking beyond the dog, he saw a form floating on the surface of the water. Butch moved toward the pond. As he got closer, he saw it was his son. Breaking into a run, Butch called out, "Terry!"

When the toddler heard his father's voice, he began to wail.

Butch lay on his stomach and easily reached Terry with his right arm. "Hey, buddy. It's okay. Daddy's got you." Pulling Terry to the edge of the pond, Butch lifted his waterlogged son out of the water. "Well, you missed seeing a baby calf born. This is quite a pickle you got yourself into, young man. Let's get out of this wet thing and into some warm clothes. Then you can come out to the barn to see the new calf."

Terry shivered and wrapped his chubby arms around his father's neck. "Cold, Daddy."

By that time, Mary was at his side. "What on earth happened? How did he get in the pond? He was with me, right behind me, sitting on the straw bale. I didn't see him leave."

"I think the barn door was open a bit and he squeezed through it." He handed their son to Mary. "He's gotta have some warm clothes. Maybe after he's changed and warmed up, he'd like to see the calf. But I can't go through another one of these scares, Mary. First Betsy and now Terry. They might have guardian angels, but it's our responsibility to do something about this goldfish pond."

Butch paced.

Mary was hyperventilating. She nodded. "I agree!"

"Calm down, Mary. Everything is gonna be okay." In reassuring Mary, Butch reassured himself as well. "I'll find some plywood to cover this thing right now. Tomorrow morning I'll empty it and fill it in with dirt. Maybe the kids can help me take the fish down to the creek and set them free. In a few months or so I'll get some planting soil, and we'll make this thing a flower garden next spring. How about that?"

Mary took a deep calming breath and nodded in agreement. "Flowers are good." She turned and headed to the house with Terry. "Come on, bub, let's get you dried off and warmed up."

Later that evening, after the children were tucked into bed, Mary and Butch danced across the hardwood floors to the crooning of a young singer named Frank Sinatra. The couple made an effort to keep their romance alive despite their growing responsibilities.

Twenty-Three

January 1948

One day, Fred and Cora invited Butch and Mary to join them for dinner after the children were fed and put to bed. Herb was having dinner in town. The young couple came into the kitchen from the adjoining door to their apartment.

"Have a seat. Dinner's almost ready," Cora announced as she placed some serving dishes on the table.

"Can I help?" Mary asked.

"Here you go." Cora handed her a basket of homemade sliced bread.

The women sat at their places. Fred offered the blessing. Dishes were passed.

Then Fred cleared his throat. "We've bought a house in Oxford."

The sudden proclamation took Butch and Mary by surprise.

Beverly squealed, "I could hardly keep the secret anymore."

"Well, now, that is news!" Butch held his fork in midair and then put it down next to his plate. "So, are you saying you're done with farm work?"

"Yes, I'm officially retiring. However, I'll continue

with all the documentation for Cornell's co-op program. I'll continue my writing for farming magazines. I'll keep doing the radio broadcasts, as long as they'll have me. You know how much I enjoy doing those things. Beyond that, the farm is yours. If you want it."

"Do you have any doubt? Of course, I want the farm. We'll have to work out something with Mr. Bowers at the bank. Do you want to set up the meeting, Dad? Since you're retired and all, you've got a little more time."

"Sure, I'd be glad to do that. Now I'll let Mother tell you about her new house."

Cora smiled and clapped her hands. "I could hardly wait for my turn to talk. I've got to tell you about the lovely two-story home we found."

Cora's joy was contagious. Butch, Mary, and Beverly chuckled at her child-like excitement.

"First, you all know how I love the front porch of this old farmhouse. We've spent a lot of time out there over the years. I just hated the thought of leaving it." She paused. "But this new house has three porches. I can watch the sunrise, the sunset, and there will be plenty of room for the kids to play on a screened porch when it's raining."

"Tell us about the inside," Mary said as she leaned forward, cupping her chin with her hands, her elbows resting on the table.

Cora took a breath and began to describe the details that she loved about the new house. "It has transom windows and lots of built-in storage. Best of all, there's an upstairs two-bedroom apartment that we can rent out to give us an income." She again clapped her hands in excitement. "I just can't wait to hang curtains and decorate."

Fred made a show of reaching for his wallet. He

thumbed a few bills, so they flew across the table. This brought peals of laughter from the family.

"Mary, I will always be available to babysit, and if I can't, perhaps Beverly will. I don't want you to think I've abandoned you." Cora reached across the table to pat Mary's hand. "We'll only be five miles away."

Butch picked up his fork and pondered the news—news that would change his life on the farm. For so many years, he'd worked side by side with his dad. He depended not only on the extra pair of hands, but also on his father's wisdom, knowledge, and advice. It would seem odd not having him here.

"Dad, Mom, what about this house?" he asked. "Herb stays here to save money. I'm sure he's going to continue working for Lyon Brook—"

"Butch," Fred interrupted, "your mother and I thought that you and Mary would enjoy having more space to dance on Saturday nights. Nothing would have to change for Herb. Of course, if you don't want this five bedroom—"

Butch responded before his father could finish his thought. "Are you kidding? We'd love it! You know how attached we are to this house." It was Mary's turn to clap her hands with glee. Butch continued, "We've loved living in the apartment, but with only two bedrooms, it's gotten a little tight with two kids."

Mary jumped up from the table. "And I can't wait to decorate!"

Everyone dissolved into belly-shaking laughter.

Fred cleared his throat. "There is one other thing. I have talked to a young couple about renting the apartment. They don't have any children now but they plan on having a family. The income from the apartment will help you two with the added expenses of a bigger house. How does that sound?"

Butch was a bit overwhelmed at his father's forethought. "Gosh, Dad." He searched for the right words. "That's great, Mary and I appreciate it more than I can say right now." Mary got up to hug both Fred and Cora.

"So what's your timetable, Mom? Dad? When do you close? What's the estimated date for the move? I'd like to plan on getting enough hands to help with the farm work so that we're all available to help you. Mary and I have it easy, with our stuff coming through that door over there," he said, gesturing to the door that opened into the adjoining quarters.

"We close in twenty days, but Cora wants to go through the house, cleaning and finding things for me to fix before we move. I'd say we'll be moving in thirty days. Mark your calendar."

"It's a done deal, Dad. I'll line up my help and ask Randy and Jim if they can do the evening milking. As you've said hundreds of times, 'Many hands make light work.'"

Sandalphon had left his sleeping charge and crept downstairs to see what was going on. He announced to the other angels, "Everyone's life is going to change. No one knows that better than us guardians. We all need to be praying that all of it will be positive.

The next month, numerous friends and family members assembled at Lyon Brook Farm, awaiting their assignments. Fred and Cora headed up a caravan of eight pickup trucks loaded with their belongings. After driving to their new home in Oxford, they were met by Beverly and several of her friends from high school. The teens went about making up each bed as soon as the movers assembled them. It would be a godsend for the family to fall into a freshly made bed after such a busy day.

The angels had their hands full, preventing heavy furniture from being dropped on clumsy feet and nasty tumbles down a flight of stairs. The heavenly hosts made sure that all cuts, scrapes, and bruises were minor ones on that busy day. All the movers suffered muscle aches and pains, but they were shown that many hands make light work.

Cora, Mary, and Beverly prepared a buffet, which was a welcome reward for the hard work involved in the momentous move. Everyone was exhausted, but the heavy work was done. Emptying closets and other storage areas would be completed in succeeding days.

The young couple and their two children spent their last night in the adjoining apartment, where they had set up housekeeping as newlyweds. Mary remembered the day she gave birth to Betsy in the dining room. Although they needed the extra living space, Mary felt a tug at her heart in leaving their cozy first home.

The next morning, after the first milking of the day, Butch and Mary started moving their belongings into the larger part of the house. With the help of Herb and two neighbors, it was completed by lunchtime. The main house seemed to swallow their small amount of furniture. Mary looked forward to shopping flea markets and auctions to find unique accent tables for the living room. She yearned to find a piano because she had grown up in a musical home. She wanted the same for her children.

Herb snickered at the turn of events. And then his mother's words echoed in his mind. He experienced a tug of war in his heart and soul that he hadn't anticipated.

Betsy and Terry no longer had to share a small room. They each had their own spacious one. Mary looked forward to sewing pink gingham curtains for Betsy and blue plaid curtains for Terry.

Mary was excited about living there. Not only did she and Butch have more dance floor, but they also had a guest room that could be used for another child if they decided to add to their family.

Herb's room at the top of the back stairs stayed the same as when Fred and Cora lived there. It gave him easy access to the bathroom on the first floor when he got up in the wee hours of the morning to head for the barn.

Each of the children's rooms came complete with a guardian angel to watch over the youngsters as they slept. The angels knew there was danger nearby.

Twenty-Four

In August 1948 Mary told Butch she thought she might be pregnant. The following month, Doc Mayhew confirmed her suspicion. In due time—April of 1949—Judith Lynette Emig was born. The baby weighed in at eight pounds, eleven ounces. Doc allowed Butch to be by his wife's side for baby number three, as he was when Betsy was born. Judith was a beautiful baby with a mop of dark hair, who looked like her dad. In just a few days, Butch dubbed his new daughter Judy.

Mary came home after a few days of rest. She and the baby were greeted by Cora and the two older children. Betsy fell over herself to help with her baby sister. At five and a half years old, she was eager to learn diaper changing and bottle feeding. Terry was just glad that the baby wasn't interested in his toys. After a few days of pampering the new mom and cooking for Butch and his family, Cora returned home.

Life on Lyon Brook Farm returned to normal, with the exception that there was an additional family member along with an additional guardian angel. The summer of 1949 sped by with only the usual falls and cuts and scrapes that a farm family in Chenango County would expect.

A few weeks later, on a beautiful late summer day, Butch hooked up the hay wagon to one of the tractors. He began driving slowly out of the driveway toward Lyon Brook

Road. Three-year-old Terry escaped his mother's grasp and ran toward his daddy. The boy wanted to ride the tractor with his father as he'd done many times before. Distracted by the movement of his horses galloping to the fence line, Butch looked in their direction as Terry barreled toward the rolling tractor in a full-out run. Tripping over his own feet, the child fell, sliding under the empty hay wagon's dual tires. Butch felt a bump as the wagon rolled over Terry's legs.

Everything seemed to move in slow motion. Betsy stood rooted in horror on the porch, reaching her arms toward her brother. Mary ran after her son while watching the tragedy unfold. Screaming hysterically, she got her husband's attention. "Stop, Butch! Stop!"

Butch heard Mary's cry of alarm and jammed on the brakes, bringing the tractor to a stop. He saw Mary running toward the rig. Hearing her jagged scream, Butch realized in horror that the bump he'd felt was one of his children. Turning off the tractor, he jumped down to help Mary lift Terry out from under the wagon.

Moving the traumatized boy out of the dusty driveway onto the soft green grass, Mary pulled his overalls down to his ankles to assess the damage. Both parents attempted to comfort their son while they scrutinized him from top to bottom. Despite two perfect tire imprints across the tops of both of his thighs, they did not see one area of broken skin. Mary clutched the little boy to her chest. It was a miracle that his legs weren't bloodied and broken.

The boy was fast, but Terry's guardian had been faster. His angel held the bulk of the hay wagon's weight from the child's legs as it rolled over him. The tire prints were a warning to Butch, Mary, and the children that tragic accidents can happen, and sometimes guardians don't get there in time.

Through his sobs, Terry asked, "Can I have a lollypop?"

"Sure you can, honey. You've earned it. Do you feel okay?"

"Yup." The child swiped at the tears on his cheeks.

Mary put him down on the grass, pulled up his overalls, and fastened the shoulder straps.

Terry pulled away from her and ran onto the porch and into the house to await his treat.

Butch and Mary looked at each other.

"It happened so fast," Mary said. "I can't believe how quick that child is."

Butch shook his head. "He scared the livin' daylights out of me. I was sure he'd have both his legs broken. We ought to call Doc Mayhew and have him checked out to be sure."

"Okay, I'll call and take him in right away. I think it'll make us both feel better."

"I'm half afraid to get back on that tractor. My hands are shaking. But I've got to get to the Meek's farm and pick up a load of hay. Just keep the kids inside until I'm gone, okay?" Butch hesitated. "Mary, do you think it's possible that Terry has a 'Sandy'?"

"After seeing what we just saw, I wouldn't doubt it at all." Mary turned to walk into the house and get Terry's lollypop before the boy climbed onto the counter to reach the candy stash.

As the angels chuckled, their feathered wings bounced up and down. Sandy turned to one of the others. "Mary is becoming a believer, and Butch isn't far behind."

The guardian angels had their collective hands full with the free-range children and the family they had all grown to love. There was ample room for a child to roam, play, and get into trouble.

The white house, yellow barns, and outbuildings sat on a flat expanse of land. Fields of wheat, oats, and hay surrounded the property. Harvested grains were stored in silos or in the massive hayloft. Six identical, freshly painted brood houses for baby chicks formed a neat row facing the machine sheds. One of the largest outbuildings was an imposing three-story chicken house for the laying hens. When the chicks matured, they were moved to the large building and well fed to produce an abundance of fresh eggs.

Butch also raised pigs, and in his spare time, he worked with unbroken horses, training them to accept and obey a rider. He enjoyed collaborating with the agriculture experts from Cornell, as his father did. He was eager to employ the latest techniques in farming and animal husbandry. Their collaboration inspired Butch to work the long hours necessary to produce a prize-winning herd. Earning many honors for Lyon Brook Farm, Butch felt he could accomplish anything with his trusted hand Herb at his side. He was going to have to make it a point to tell Herb how much he valued him.

A quarter-mile up the dirt road, the impressive Lyon Brook Bridge stretched from a prominent point on the gorge's western side to another on the eastern side. Standing on the trestle, one could look directly into the canyon and the water below. Moss-covered stone abutments dotted the hillsides on both sides of the gorge, holding the weight of the bridge. One of those stone bases formed the retaining wall of the family's swimming hole directly below the bridge's railroad tracks.

Butch and Mary were aware of the dangers around them. They remembered the attempted sabotage of the bridge before Betsy was born. And the arsonist who tried to torch the chick houses when Betsy was an infant. Neither perpetrator had been caught. Living with a potential threat from an unknown enemy was concerning to the Emigs and each of their guardian angels.

For the moment, the heavenly host enjoyed seeing the family's happy times. At the same time, they prayed for Herb to experience a change in heart, mind, and soul.

On hot summer days, the angels watched the family swim in the creek. Butch delighted his children by diving off the stone abutment into the deepest part of the water. Their squeals echoed in the mossy glen when Butch took them for rides on his back in the water. Mary floated in an inner tube, holding baby Judy in her lap. She laughed as she watched her family frolic. It was a fun respite from the hard work of running a farm.

Twenty-Five

Betsy carried a wicker basket on her arm, as she and Terry walked to the big chicken house on a mission. "You know, Terry, someday this job will be yours. I'll prob'ly have something more important to do, like drive the tractor. But I just love gathering eggs, and I think you'll like it too."

Terry nodded. "Uh-huh. Do the chickens bite?"

The angels listened intently to the tutorial Terry was getting from his older sister.

"Not exactly. They peck you if they're in the middle of laying the egg, and you have your hand under them. You just have to watch what they're doing. Don't worry, I'll show ya." Betsy led the way to the first-floor laying parlor. She paused before going through the door.

"I'm supposed to go up the stairs to each floor, but Daddy and Herb haul those heavy bags of chicken feed and other big stuff on that elevator." She pointed to a large wooden platform with no walls. "I know it looks kinda scary, but Daddy pulls on a rope to make it go up, then he pulls another rope, and it stops. I watched him do it. One time he even let me pull the ropes."

Betsy opened the door to the first-floor laying parlor and beckoned the four-year-old to follow her. Their Buster

Brown shoes crunched on the golden straw strewn about the floor.

"See these cubbies? Each hen has her own." Betsy reached into the first cubby and slid her hand under the hen to retrieve the precious egg. Gently, she placed it in her basket. "When a hen is laying, she looks all scrunched down like we do when we're trying to poop. She makes clucking and squawking noises. So you give her time to finish what's she's doing, then sneak your hand under her to grab the egg."

After checking under every hen on the first floor, Betsy and Terry left the room, making sure the door was closed tightly.

"Do you wanna take the elevator instead of the stairs? I think I remember how Daddy did it."

Terry grinned. "Uh-huh, I wanna ride!"

They walked across the cement floor. Betsy stepped up on the wooden platform. She set down the basket of eggs and turned to her brother. "Grab my hands. I'll help you up."

Terry's chubby legs pushed off the cement as his sister pulled him onto the platform. The boy plopped down on the deck.

"Okay, Terry. You sit crisscross applesauce while I pull the rope." Terry obediently crossed his legs. Betsy reached up, grabbed the rope brake, and pulled. It released. The weighted pulley system moved the heavy platform up toward the second floor. "Yay, it worked. We're goin' up."

Terry clapped his hands with delight. "Yay, we're goin' up!"

Betsy watched as the wooden elevator deck came even with the second floor. She pulled on the rope brake. "See, Terry? We're stopped now. We can get off and get the eggs on this floor."

Picking up the full basket with one hand, Betsy took

her brother's hand. Stepping off to the second floor, Betsy put the full basket down by the door. She grabbed an empty basket before the pair entered another laying room to repeat the process.

"Terry, it's your turn to get the eggs this time."

"Will they peck me?"

"Nah, not if you're gentle. Just pet them first."

The guardians smiled as Betsy showed her brother the fine art of gathering eggs. She was unusually patient with him.

When all the floors had been visited and eggs gathered, Betsy assisted Terry onto the elevator platform. "Sit down while we go down." They rode the grain elevator to the first floor.

Terry squealed with delight.

Stepping down from the platform as it rested on the cement floor, Betsy helped her brother jump. They picked up the baskets of eggs and left the chicken house. Betsy made sure they closed the main door to keep foxes and other predators out.

"What do we do with the eggs now, Betsy?"

"We take 'em up to the main barn and the egg-cleaning room."

"What's that?" Terry asked as he followed his sister across the expansive dirt-and-stone driveway.

"Come on, I'll show you." The kids carried their baskets of eggs toward the barn.

Betsy opened the door to a small room attached to the main barn. "Hi, Mommy! Where's the baby?"

"Judy's napping while Grandma is using my sewing machine." Mary smiled at her two older children. "Betsy, do you want to show Terry what we do with the gathered eggs?"

"Yup, someday he's gonna take over my job when Daddy gives me a more fun one."

Betsy turned to her brother and instructed him on the process with her most grown-up voice. "This is where we take the eggs out of the basket and lay them on the conveyer belt. We don't do it unless Mommy is here. She runs the machine. We're not supposed to touch it. The conveyer belt pulls the eggs into the washer where brushes and water wash the eggs. Then they dry with air before they reach Mommy, and she packs them in cartons."

Terry, entranced by the whole process, turned to Betsy and asked, "Then what happens?"

"People come to our farm to buy them," Mary explained as she shut off the machine and came around the corner. She reached down to gather both children in her arms. "You guys did a great job today." Planting kisses on both their heads, she announced, "It's lunchtime; let's go." Giggling, the three raced each other to the house.

After lunch, Mary said, "It's quiet time. Betsy, you can play in your bedroom while your brother takes a nap. When you get up, we'll make a batch of cookies. How about that?"

"Oh, boy! Chocolate chip?"

"Me, too! I want chocolate chip, too," Terry squealed.

"Chocolate chip it is."

Betsy reclined on her bed with one of her favorite books. Mary settled Terry in his bed, hoping he'd nap for an hour. She felt fortunate to have some quiet time to sew. She was in the middle of a huge quilt project.

Twenty minutes later, a bedroom door opened, and four-year-old Terry held on to the railing, coming down the back stairs one step at a time. He padded across the kitchen floor and was out the door. No one saw the boy make his way to the three-story chicken house.

No one except his guardian angel.

Herb left the barn on his way to the tractor shed. He'd forgotten his mother's warning, and devious thoughts pushed their way into his mind. Today was the day he planned to start disabling the farm machinery. Hopping up on the newest tractor, Herb started it up and moved it out of the garage.

Unseen by Herb, a mighty angel stood in front of the tractor, holding up his powerful arms.

The engine shut down.

"What the...?" Herb attempted to restart the tractor, but there was silence. He didn't understand. This was the newest one, so it shouldn't be acting up. Besides, he hadn't done anything to it—yet. Dismounting, Herb lifted the engine cover.

Hearing an unfamiliar sound, Herb stopped what he was doing and listened carefully, wondering if it was an animal, maybe one of the dogs. Whatever it was, it sounded like it was in distress. He started walking toward the chicken house. The sounds seemed to be getting louder. Upon opening the door, he saw that the grain elevator was not in its place and heard a child's cry. Instinctively, he looked up. He gasped in horror.

The bottom of the platform was stopped at the second-floor level, and he saw a pair of chubby legs hanging down. They were tightly wedged between the elevator platform and the second floor.

There was only one pair of legs like that on the farm—Terry's.

Herb moaned, "Why me? Why do I have to be the one to find him?" He realized then that he had a choice. He could help the boy... or walk away and never admit that he saw or heard anything.

"That would really get to Butch," he muttered under his breath. A battle took place in Herb's heart, mind, and soul. This would be an intentionally cruel way to enact revenge. Thoughts ran through his mind. He wondered what his mother would say about that. More to the point, could he live with himself if he walked away? As if to add some urgency to Herb's decision, Terry wailed louder.

The boy's guardian angel held the elevator perfectly still with his massive wings. His angelic toes maintained a small space for Terry's legs. At the same time, the angel was trying to telepathically calm the boy, but Terry was not having any of it. The angel knew he might have to reveal himself if Herb didn't come to the boy's aid.

"How in tarnation did you get yourself in this pickle?" Herb muttered. He made a decision as he called out. "Terry, it's Herb. I'm here, buddy. I'm gonna get you down. Can you be a brave boy for me?"

"I want Mommy," Terry sobbed.

Herb responded, "I know, buddy. I'll take you to her as soon as I get you down. How did you release the brake, Terry?"

"I pulled the rope like Betsy did."

"Wow, that just shows that you're almost as tall as your sister. You are getting to be such a big boy. Listen to me; I want you to sit real still, okay? Can you do that?"

Terry was crying softly but managed to squeak out, "Uh-huh."

Reassuring him as he worked, Herb said, "You just be brave because I have to bring you down. The elevator is going to start moving now."

Herb reached up to release the brake. The elevator

began to descend. Terry cried louder as his knees passed by the rough wooden edges of the second-floor landing on the way down.

As soon as the child was within reach, Herb scooped him off the platform. "I gotcha, buddy. We're gonna go right up to the house and have your mom take a look at those legs." Terry clung to Herb's neck. The elevator proceeded to its resting position on the concrete floor.

Herb felt something move inside his chest. It was his hard heart starting to soften when he felt the child's arms around him. It was an unexpected emotion—and not at all unpleasant.

Herb calmed Terry as he inspected both his knees. He could see that they were skinned and bruised, but there wasn't much bleeding. He hoped with all his heart that the boy's legs weren't broken. Herb carried the child to the house, crooning uncharacteristically to the boy as he walked. "You are such a brave boy. I'm so proud of you. It's gonna be okay."

Mary listened to the story Herb told while carefully inspecting her son's legs. "Terry, honey, I don't know how you escaped being hurt, other than skinned knees. Let's clean your legs with some soap and water."

Terry began to fuss.

"When your boo-boos are all clean and dry, how about some Band-Aids?"

"Okay, Mommy. Will you draw on them?"

"What do you want, a doggie face?"

"Yes, with big ears."

The Band-Aids with Mary's artwork performed their magic healing. After spending some time on his mother's lap, Terry wriggled free and took off running into the living room. Kneeling on the floor, he began to play with his favorite truck.

His angel observed the child running and then kneeling on the hard floor and moved closer to the boy. He felt partially at fault for this event and prayed, *Heaven help me with future challenges! I can't turn my back for an instant or let this child out of my sight!*

"Guess his legs aren't broke," Herb announced.

"Seems unlikely," Mary responded with a sigh of relief. She turned to Herb and said, "It occurs to me you've earned a piece of warm peach pie. Would you like some coffee to go with it?"

Herb felt a smile cross his face. Warmth spread throughout his being. "Peach pie is my favorite. I'd love some and coffee's fine. Thank you, ma'am. But then I have to get back to work."

"Please call me Mary, Herb. You live here, you sit at our kitchen table, and after today, you're even more a part of the family."

Herb didn't know what to say. He hadn't been part of a family since he was eight. This was okay. This felt good. He could only manage a meager, "Thank you."

Herb's guardian glowed with thankfulness as he hovered behind his charge. Ties of bitterness and anger binding the angel's wings were loosening. One or two dropped onto the floor. The angel shook them free and kicked them away. The love that was sprinkled around Herb while helping free Terry was beginning to transform the bitter angry man. But there was still one more kernel of revenge to dissipate—the need to settle the score with Butch.

Twenty-Six

Christmas 1950

The twelve-foot Christmas tree stood in the niche created by three tall windows in Cora and Fred's Victorian style home. Clumps of tinsel were scattered at differing heights, according to the size of the grandchildren. The girls tried to straighten the strands to create a more uniform look. The boys didn't see the need.

This Christmas was unique in that all of Fred and Cora's children were home for the holidays. Butch, Mary, and their three children were the first to arrive for the day's festivities. Chet and Lorene, with their three girls, arrived minutes later. Louise, her husband Carl, and their three boys were visiting from Ithaca and staying with Fred and Cora. Cora loved having a house full of family. This year there was an extra special treat. Her youngest daughter Beverly and Bev's Air Force husband Burt were home from Texas with a month of leave.

Fred helped Cora put all the leaves in the dining room table for the adults. They did the same with a table for the children in the adjoining kitchen. High chairs were borrowed for those toddlers still using them. It was a home full of love and joy, as they gathered to celebrate the holy season.

As platters and bowls of food were passed, Mary cleared her throat. "Butch and I would like to announce that I am pregnant with baby number four." Applause erupted, interspersed with laughter and congratulations for the couple.

Beverly chimed in over the chatter of the kids' table in the kitchen. "Coincidently, Burt and I want to announce that we are expecting baby number one." Again, the family applauded. Both Butch and Burt stood up to take a bow; their wives theatrically rolled their eyes.

With ten adults and nine children sitting at two tables, Fred noted that they'd need more seating capacity the following year, if everyone came home for Christmas.

At that moment, nineteen guardian angels surrounded the family, although only Betsy knew.

Twenty-Seven

Summer 1951

Mary went into labor in the early hours of June 11, 1951. Butch and Herb finished milking the herd while Mary made a phone call to Cora to say, "It's time." Cora would stay with seven-year-old Betsy, five-year-old Terry, and two-year-old Judy until Mary's mother could get there. Between the two grandmothers, they'd have a week of childcare for the kids at home. Butch bathed while Mary finished packing her bag. They were both anxious and excited to meet this new baby. During the drive to Norwich, the couple speculated as to whether it was another boy or a third girl. Butch left Mary in the capable hands of a nurse at the emergency entrance of Chenango County Hospital while he parked the car.

Entering the hospital, Butch followed the signs to the maternity floor. He dutifully found a seat in the father's waiting room. Picking up a fishing magazine, he flipped through the pages as Mary was being checked in and examined. After a short labor, baby girl Emig was born at two o'clock, weighing seven pounds, fourteen ounces. Mary got to hold her infant briefly before the baby was taken to the nursery for the routine newborn exam and her first bath.

Butch hesitated as he entered the ward where Mary

was resting. Scanning the room, he looked for his wife and found her six beds down on the right. Her eyes were closed. She opened them as soon as she felt his presence and said, "Hi, honey, it's another girl."

"I know. Doc showed her to me before the nurse took her away. She's a cutie."

"Certainly not as big as the other three. But I can tell you from my perspective, not tiny." Mary patted her abdomen.

"Her big sisters and brother are going to be excited to meet her. I know we talked about names, but did we decide?" asked the father of four.

"I like the one we talked about last night. Do you?"

"I do. Especially the middle name Louise, after both you and my sister."

"So, it's settled. She's Gail Louise Emig," Mary proclaimed.

Butch chuckled. "You know Betsy will want to be hands-on just like she was with Judy. I think you are going to have built-in help, honey."

The couple chatted until Butch became restless.

Mary noticed. "Don't you have to get back to the farm? It's getting close to milking time."

"I wish I could stay longer, sweetie. But you're right; I need to get back. Herb and I are going to milk the herd early, so I can return for visiting hours after supper." He leaned over and kissed her lips gently. "Please rest. I love you."

"I'll try," she sighed. "They'll be bringing the baby in for feeding before I know it."

"I'll see you later. Remember, I love you." Butch waved as he exited the ward.

Mary's angel wondered if Butch had a sixth sense. Why else would Butch say "I love you" twice?

Butch hadn't been gone more than two hours when Mary began to hemorrhage. It was all hands on deck as the staff worked to save her life. Mary's rare O-negative blood type dictated that only that type be transfused, or there would be life-threatening consequences. Unfortunately, the hospital had only one bottle of O-negative blood on hand.

The anxious doctor who had come to the floor from the emergency room called the blood bank and ordered the remaining O-negative for Mary.

"I'm sending a nurse down to get it now. Have it ready," he hollered into the phone.

The normally quiet maternity floor became a beehive of activity. The nursing staff knew that Mary was fading fast. Dr. Mayhew was called back to the hospital. Having known the family since Butch was a young boy, he was sickened at the news. He feared Mary's life was hanging in the balance as he rushed from his home to the hospital.

Mary's angel prayed fervently. "Please, Almighty Father, spare this young woman's life. Her four children need their mother, and Butch would be inconsolable without his wife."

The anxious young nurse signed out the last bottle of O-negative from the blood bank and walked quickly toward the elevator. She understood the gravity of the situation. The reality that the life of a twenty-six-year-old mother of four was at stake influenced the nurse to take the stairs rather than wait for the predictably slow elevator. She burst through the stairwell door to the third floor, gasping for breath. Her heart slammed against her ribs, and perspiration ran down her back. She clutched the life-saving bottle of blood with both hands.

As she ran down the hall toward Mary's ward, the

glass bottle bobbled. She attempted to hold it tighter, but the vessel slipped from her sweaty hands.

The rest of the staff working on Mary heard the bottle hit the linoleum-covered concrete floor. Staff stepped into the hallway to see what happened. In horror, they watched as Mary Emig's one remaining lifeline spread across the floor, mixed with shards of glass.

Butch received a phone call after he finished the milking chores. "Mr. Emig, you need to come back to the hospital. Your wife has taken a turn for the worse. She's hemorrhaging."

"I'll leave now," Butch told the nurse. "I can't lose my wife," he cried out. "She's everything to me."

After hanging up the receiver, he picked it up again, asking the operator to call his parents' home. When Cora answered, she could hear the desperation in her son's voice.

"Mary's bleeding out of control. The hospital called me to come. Mary's mom will need help with the kids. You know she's not good in an emergency."

Butch ran to the barn to inform Herb that he was in charge because of the events unfolding. Butch was in such a hurry to get to the hospital that he didn't notice the color drain out of Herb's slack-jawed face.

Herb staggered to a pile of neatly folded feed bags and lowered himself to sit. He put his head in his hands. "Lord, no, not Miss Mary. She's the nicest person I know. Lord, spare Miss Mary, please!"

Herb's guardian angel came to his full height. He lifted his arms, calling out to the heavens. "Please, Lord of all, send Mary healing help and salvation. Bless and guide the hands and hearts of the medical staff caring for her. Amen."

Dr. Mayhew arrived to hear about the demise of the

last bottle of blood. "Call St. Joseph's in Syracuse to see if they have O-negative to send by courier. Stat! Get me two bottles of lactated Ringer's. Now! I want oxygen on at three liters by mask. Lay her flat and elevate her feet. Move, people! Move!"

Mary lost consciousness. Her skin was translucent, her breathing shallow.

While an angel watched over Mary's newborn baby girl, another hovered over Mary. "Heavenly Father, in your mercy, hear our prayers for this woman, a mother. We pray that you spare her life. Restore her health, oh loving Father. We lift her up to you with fervent pleading to heal her body. Amen."

Within the hour, Butch was holding his wife's pale limp hand. "Honey, don't leave us. The kids and I need you. Hang on, my princess." He'd never been so scared—scared at the prospect of losing the love of his life.

It took an hour for St Joseph's courier to arrive with all the O-negative blood they had on hand. Mary received three units of blood consecutively, rallying her vital signs.

Butch was at her side, whispering loving words of encouragement. "I'm here, princess. Remember, I signed your dance card for life, and we've got a lot of dancing to do. The kids need you. I need you."

Mary's eyes fluttered and opened. "Did you just ask me to dance?"

"I most certainly did." Butch smiled with relief.

"Is Glenn Miller here?"

"No, but as soon as you feeling like dancing, I'll get him here."

Mary smiled and squeezed her husband's hand before she dozed off again.

Butch unabashedly let the tears flow down his cheeks.

The nursing staff sent Butch home as soon as Mary's

blood pressure stabilized, and her bleeding was under control. Driving home in a trance, he murmured prayers of thanks to God for saving his wife. After parking his car, Butch staggered into the darkened kitchen and up the back stairs to his bedroom. Everyone was sleeping. Kicking his shoes off, he fell onto the bed and fell asleep immediately. He was emotionally and physically exhausted.

His slumber was interrupted off and on with nightmares of the unthinkable.

Twenty-Eight

E arlier, Herb had finished milking the herd, cleaned the barn, and put the cattle out to pasture for the night. He couldn't get Mary out of his head. He wanted to pray for her. He knew he was new at praying and certainly not eloquent. Despite those feelings, Herb lifted his face to the starlit sky and spoke from his heart.

"Lord, help," he pleaded. "Help Miss Mary. She's such a good person. Amen!" He hoped his prayer would be enough.

One more tie that bound the wings of Herb's guardian angel was loosed. As it fell to the floor, his angel observed that the affection Herb felt for one of the people who was kind to him continued to soften his hardened heart. *The man is making progress. God is good*, the guardian surmised.

Unable to go into the house and see the sad faces of the children and both their grandmothers, Herb had gone to his truck and driven toward Norwich. He didn't know where to seek solace but ended up parking in front of the Cabooze. He slid onto the nearest barstool, signaling the bartender. "I'll have whatever you have on tap."

The only other person at the bar was a man staring into his empty glass.

Herb rubbed his face with both hands. He felt like

crying, but shedding tears would be too embarrassing. He'd seen drunks crying at the bar before, and it wasn't pretty.

The other man at the bar looked over. "Rough day?" He signaled the bartender to give him a refill.

"You could say that," Herb replied.

"Drink up, it'll help," the disheveled man slurred.

"I'm not so sure." Herb took a sip of his brew.

The man held out a hand and said, "My name's Saw, short for Sawyer. My friends call me 'The Saw.'"

Herb reached out and shook the extended hand. "Herb."

"Anything you wanna talk about? I'm drunk and prob'ly won't remember nuthin' so it'll be safe with me."

"Got a real sick friend. She's one of the nicest people I know." Herb's eyes misted.

"She?"

"Yup, my boss's wife. She's been real good to me."

"Ah, she's been good to you," he leered. "Now, I get the picture."

"Get your filthy mind out of the gutter. It's not what you think. She's been very kind to me. That's all."

"Does her husband, the boss, know?"

"I assume he does. We eat at the same table every day."

"Whoa, what kind of work do you do and where?"

"I'm a hired hand on Lyon Brook Farm," Herb said, looking into the foam on top of his beer. "It's been a good deal for me."

"Sounds like you hit the big time with that job," he said sarcastically. "Where you from?"

"I told you Lyon Brook Farm. I live with the Emigs."

"Come again? You actually live with the family?"

"Yup. But things aren't so good right now because

Miss Mary's real sick and in the hospital. Butch is beside himself and left me in charge. He doesn't want to leave her side."

"Butch? Lyon Brook Farm? Is this the Emig place?"

"I already told you that. Pay attention. Why do you wanna know, anyway?"

"I know a guy who worked on the Emig farm, Paul Fisher. Know him?"

"I've met him. He worked there off and on a few years back. Not real dependable."

"My brother Buzz has a bone to pick with him."

"Oh?"

"Yeah, Buzz is in jail because that snake, Paul Fisher, ratted him out."

Herb did a double-take, giving the guy a sideways look. He started to feel uncomfortable about telling him where he worked and who he worked for. He remembered hearing about Paul being in jail and released to his older brothers' custody. He recalled that the others went to prison. "You don't say." Herb had his guard up.

"I'd like to pin Paul Fisher's ears back for what he did to my brother. I'd like to see the look in his eyes when I tell him, 'When you mess with Buzz, you get the Saw.'" Saw pounded both his fists on the bar, causing the beer glasses to bounce and slosh beer.

The bartender hurried over to wipe up the mess.

Herb's guardian angel whispered in his ear, "Go home now."

Herb heard the words. "What?" He spun around on the stool to see who was there. He didn't see anyone but Saw. Herb rubbed the back of his neck and frowned.

Saw began again, "I said I'd like to pin Paul Fisher's—"

"I heard you the first time." Herb gulped the rest of his beer and turned toward Saw. "Gotta run."

Saw narrowed his eyes and shrugged. He pondered the information Herb had given him and how he could use it to his advantage. He hoped he'd remember this evening's conversation in the morning.

Herb's angel thought about the encounter as Herb drove home. *That Saw guy has a dark spirit. He's a menace to Herb. Could he be one of the forces of evil we all sense?* The angel knew Herb had seen the man's anger and sensed some danger from him. Consequently, Herb's angel felt a need to stay close.

Twenty-Nine

Cora called family members to find places for the three older children while Mary was in the hospital. Betsy stayed with Chet and Lorene and two-year-old Judy went to Ithaca to stay with Louise and Carl. Terry stayed with Fred and Cora. Neighbors volunteered to help Herb with milking the herd both morning and evening so that Butch could get to the hospital. Everyone in the small community prayed for a complete and speedy recovery for their beloved Mary.

Unfortunately, Betsy contracted measles while living with her aunt and uncle. The child was already homesick, missing her parents and siblings. When she developed complications of pneumonia, she was tearful and bedridden. Aunt Lorene and her three girls did their best to entertain Betsy with books and puppet shows while she could not run and play. Doc Mayhew made daily house calls to check on her until he was satisfied that Betsy was on the road to recovery. The doctor forbade anyone from telling Mary how sick Betsy was. He couldn't risk his patient backsliding due to worry and anxiety.

Sandy did his best to comfort Betsy, but it just wasn't working. After consulting Archangel Michael, Sandy decided on another tactic and transformed himself.

The doorbell rang, and Lorene answered it. An older

woman in a nurse's uniform stood in front of her with a basket in her arms. She had such a kind angelic face that Lorene was instantly drawn to her.

"Hello, Mrs. Emig. I'm Mrs. Sanford. I'm a nurse. I was sent to help with Betsy. Perhaps you could use an extra pair of hands since you have three girls of your own. I can care for Betsy during the day and leave after I put her to bed. Is that acceptable to you?"

"Oh, my. How very kind, but we can't afford to pay..."

"Not to worry, I assure you it's been covered in full."

Mesmerized by the nurse's kind demeanor, Lorene admitted, "Why, yes, that would be a tremendous help. Please come in. I'll show you where Betsy is." The nurse followed Lorene to a downstairs room where a bed was pushed up against the window. The sick child watched birds at a feeder and butterflies as they visited colorful flowers in hanging pots.

Betsy looked up, and a smile spread across her face. She reached out to the nurse with one hand. "San—?"

The nurse interrupted the girl before she could finish the word. "Hello, my dear. I'll be your nurse until you're feeling better. My name is Mrs. Sanford."

"Hello," Betsy said softly.

Lorene turned toward the kitchen. "I'll go make your favorite lunch, Betsy. You tell Mrs. Sanford about your paper dolls."

"Okay, Aunt Lorene, thank you." She looked again at Mrs. Sanford, standing at the side of the bed. "Sandy?"

"Yes, Betsy, it's me. You have to call me Mrs. Sanford because I can be seen and heard by everyone now. I'm in human form. But it's our secret. I'm here to help you feel better so you can go home sooner. Do you understand?"

"Yes." Betsy reached out to take Sandy's human hand.

Mrs. Sanford went about the business of caring for the sick child. As each day passed, her aunt and uncle noticed Betsy improving in both body and spirit. The color was returning to her cheeks, and she regained strength.

Lorene told everyone who inquired about Betsy's well-being, "Mrs. Sanford has been a godsend to this family."

Little did they know that Mrs. Sanford truly was sent by God.

Mary and her baby were hospitalized for three weeks, becoming favorites of the staff. After her rest and recuperation in the hospital, Mary was discharged. Her Aunt Gertrude came to stay for as long as she was needed. One by one, her children were brought back home, making Mary one happy mama.

Butch and Fred set up a bed in the living room where Mary could spend time cuddling with Betsy, Terry, and Judy as the two older children read to her.

The Archangel watched as Mary's guardian angel cradled her in his wings, protecting her with his feathers. Choirs of angels in Heaven sang songs of praise and thanksgiving for Mary's miraculous recovery.

It was the first week of July, and Mary was still on bed rest with bathroom privileges. This particular morning she was lying in bed with her pillow covering her face. Although grateful, she struggled with so many others doing her housework and caring for her children. Mary was almost desperate to do things herself, even though she was incredibly weak. Caring for her newborn exhausted her. That, however, was one thing she insisted on doing. Mary's Aunt Gertrude was the person to get up during the night to change and bottle feed the baby. This provided her niece the opportunity to get a full night's sleep.

Mary lifted the pillow to take in the sunshine and crystal-clear blue sky of an extraordinary summer day. She sighed. "Maybe I can talk my aunt into letting me sit in a chair for a while today." Saying those words out loud brightened her spirits.

Mary's guardian angel lifted his voice to heaven. "Praise be to God for this sign that Mary is on the mend. I know that the family won't allow her to overdo it. Thank you, Lord."

Mary got up to use the bathroom, passing the black and white drawing of the bridge as she walked down the front hall. "There's something about that picture," she mused aloud.

Aunt Gertrude brought breakfast after she got back into bed. Mary gave Gail her bottle feedings throughout the day and napped when the baby napped. She didn't want to be sleepy after Butch finished with the barn chores. Ever since she got home from the hospital, she and Butch chatted and snuggled in the evening, although tonight might be different. Mary knew her husband would probably have some sparklers for the children to celebrate the holiday.

Butch and Herb had been busy planning a July 4th fireworks display as a surprise for Mary. Tonight they'd carry out their elaborate plans. They worked hard getting the barn chores and milking done early to pull off a bigger surprise than simple sparklers to delight the kids. Dusk would be upon them in a few hours, and there was still much to do.

"If we lay 'em out in the order we want to set 'em off, we'll rival the fireworks at the county fair," Butch said. He spread a plastic tarp down on the grass. The box of pyrotechnics sat on the plastic close to the house so that Mary couldn't see what they were doing.

Herb surveyed the view that Mary would have from the window beside her bed. "I think this spot in the driveway will keep the grass from catching fire and allow her to see everything. With two of us working together, we should be able to keep it organized."

Butch nodded. "I've hooked up the garden hose and filled a water bucket in case we need it. It's a good thing the kids will be inside with Mary. Can you imagine trying to do this show with three kids running around out here? I'll lay out the series of fireworks in groups, and we'll keep the rest in the box until it's time for the next series.

The two men worked side by side, setting everything up for the surprise light and sound show.

Inside the house, Fred and Cora had arrived for a visit. Cora tied the curtains back. "We understand Butch has a few fireworks for the holiday. With the curtain out of the way, you and the kids will have a front-row seat."

"I know. He told me he splurged on some sparklers for the kids and one or two boomers because he knows I love them. I think he's trying to lift my spirits."

Cora nodded. "No doubt, dear."

As Butch and Herb ate dinner and hurriedly left to go outside, Herb thought how happy he was he could do something to help cheer Mary. Dusk fell as the family gathered in the living room. One by one, the three older children climbed onto the bed. Mary sighed as she wrapped her arms around the two older children while two-year-old Judy sat in her lap. "My sweet babies, you make me so happy."

Betsy spoke up. "Mommy, you know that picture of the railroad bridge that Grandpa gave us a long time ago?"

"Yes, honey, what about it?"

"It looks like an angel's wings when he stretches them way out."

Mary gazed at the picture. "It sure does look like angel wings. Maybe it's a sign that angels are always with us. What do you think, Bets?"

"I think that's right, Mom."

"You know what, Betsy Emig? You are pretty amazing for a girl who is not yet eight years old."

"Mom, if baby Gail cries during the fireworks, I'll change her just like Aunt Gertrude showed me. I can give her a bottle too. Aunt Gertrude can watch the fireworks."

"That makes you a very helpful big sister." Mary glanced at her daughter, who was beaming with pride. Mary was grateful for Betsy's recuperation, especially after Butch told her how sick their daughter had been. She reached out to stroke Betsy's rosy cheeks and kissed the child's forehead. Mary could hardly believe that her first-born was nearly eight years old.

Terry turned toward his mother. "I'm big enough to help too, Mommy."

"I know you are. I appreciate you too, bub!"

As soon as darkness descended and the quarter moon had risen in the sky, Herb and Butch began the show with sparklers. They ran back and forth in front of the window while twirling the metal wands in their hands. The dancing antics of the two men made Fred, Cora, Gertrude, Mary, and the kids laugh and clap their hands in appreciation.

Butch touched the match to consecutive fuses and rewarded his audience with colorful starburst formations flying high into the sky.

While shooting off Roman candles one after the other, Herb didn't notice that a few sparks had dropped into the box of remaining fireworks near his feet. Suddenly, the entire carton of explosives simultaneously ignited in a spectacular show of light and sound. It was the unintentional grand finale coming out of one cardboard box.

The incident caught Herb off guard. He attempted to move the box to stop the chain reaction, but it was too late. Hot sparks singed his arms and set the front of his shirt on fire, burning his upper chest and neck. He shrieked in pain.

At first, Butch thought the man was whooping it up in the exhilaration of the moment, but when the tenor of Herb's shrieks changed, Butch grabbed the bucket and ran toward him. After dousing Herb with cold water, Butch watched as steam rose from Herb's body. The man winced in pain.

"Dear God!" Butch exclaimed. "Herb, are you all right?"

"Butch, I got burned bad."

"I can see that. Let's get your shirt off, and let me take a look." He grabbed the flashlight from his pocket. Herb painfully removed what was left of his t-shirt, and with it came a layer of skin from several spots on his chest.

"Holy cow, you've got some dandy burns, buddy. Let's get in the kitchen and put some cool wet towels on them."

With a sense of urgency, the two men moved into the house.

Mary had been thoroughly entertained as she watched Herb wildly dancing and twirling. She had no idea he was trying to avoid hot sparks and streams of burning colors. Convinced that his wild gyrations were part of the fireworks show planned for her benefit, she had convulsed with laughter. Mary held her sides while tears streamed down her cheeks at the comical sight.

When all the rockets, starbursts, twirlers, and corkscrews were extinguished, Mary watched as Butch led

Herb out of sight. She thought they were cleaning up the pyrotechnic show debris and was not aware that anything was amiss.

Butch led Herb into the kitchen where Herb perched on a stool so Butch could apply cool compresses to the affected areas. Herb was in a great deal of pain, but the sound of Mary giggling in the other room took his mind off it. Just when the men thought she'd stopped laughing, the musical peals began again. It was contagious. The children convulsed with giggles at every one of Mary's outbursts.

Both Butch and Herb smiled. "I guess she liked the show," Herb said through clenched teeth as Butch applied another cool wet towel to his chest.

"I'd say she got quite a kick out of your dance moves along with the rocket's red glare."

"If it helps her get well, then it was worth it," Herb announced.

"Thanks, Herb. I appreciate what you did and I'm real sorry you got hurt. Hold still now while I put this salve on your arms and neck. You're already starting to blister. I'm going to give Doc a call as soon as I get you bandaged up." Butch gently applied cooling burn cream to all of Herb's reddened skin, then wrapped him with gauze dressings. The top half of his body looked like a mummy. Herb drank a glass of water while Butch called Doc Mayhew.

The remaining ties that bound the wings of Herb's guardian angel were loosed that day. Herb found himself in the bosom of a family he couldn't help but like. He was beginning to forget why he was ever mad at Butch.

For that realization, all of the guardians lifted their voices in praise.

Thirty

By the end of July, Mary was back on her feet, bustling around as usual. She felt guilty every time she started to giggle when recalling the fireworks incident. The wild dancing antics of her husband and Herb so tickled her funny bone. Mary was remorseful because she initially had no idea that Herb was severely burned. She was immensely relieved Doc Mayhew came to the farm to check Herb's wounds every week.

She and Butch were talking one evening after the children were in bed. Mary put down the *Life Magazine* she was reading and turned to face her husband. "I had the strangest conversation with Doc Mayhew when he was here checking on Herb."

"Strange in what way?" Butch's brow furrowed.

"I told him that Lorene mentioned she suspected Doc was the Good Samaritan who sent a nurse to help Betsy when she had pneumonia. I thanked him for hiring her and told him how wonderful it was because we certainly couldn't afford her."

"What did he say?" Now Butch was curious.

"He said, 'Nurse? What nurse?'"

"I thought he was being funny. I said, 'You know,

Mrs. Sanford. She worked wonders with Betsy's recovery, according to Lorene.'"

"Did he remember after you were more specific?" Butch had put his farming magazine aside.

"Butch, he had the strangest expression on his face. He looked at me as if I was nuts. He told me he didn't hire a nurse and didn't know anything about it. He shook his head as he packed up his medical bag. He got in his car and left. I never did get an explanation." Unexpectedly Mary jumped up from her chair. "Betsy tells us how much Sandy helped her when she was sick. You don't suppose that Sandy was Mrs. Sanford, do you? Could it be?"

"Honey, I don't second guess anything Sandy can do." He picked up his magazine and opened it to the page he'd been reading.

"Maybe I'll talk to Betsy sometime. It really doesn't make a big difference, because we know how Sandy shelters Betsy and takes care of her. It isn't out of the realm of possibility, is it?"

"Nope," Butch replied succinctly.

The next day, Mary and Betsy were busy in the kitchen, putting together a picnic lunch. They planned to surprise Butch, who was baling hay on a nearby farm six miles up the road. The farmer had broken his leg when he stepped in a hole while chasing down a runaway calf, and all the surrounding farmers were pitching in to help. Butch knew what it was like to need help during difficult times and was grateful to be able to pay it forward.

Mary made the sandwiches while she directed Betsy to get a jar of homemade pickles for the picnic. "Betsy, I have a question. You told Dad and me that Sandy helped take care of you when you had pneumonia. Did Sandy go to Uncle

Chet and Aunt Lorene's house while they were taking care of you?"

"Yeah, he did." Betsy averted her eyes.

"I think we need a dozen sugar cookies. Would you please wrap them in waxed paper for the picnic basket?"

Betsy counted out the cookies.

"Aunt Lorene told me that a Mrs. Sanford came to help take care of you. Is that right?"

"Yeah." Betsy hesitated as she wrapped the cookies.

"Honey, was Mrs. Sanford, the nurse, really Sandy, your guardian angel? You can tell me the truth. I'm not going to be mad."

"Yeah, it was Sandy. He really did look like a lady nurse. Honest, Mom."

"I believe you, honey. It's okay. I'm happy that Sandy was there to care for you. Now let's finish getting the picnic basket ready, okay?"

"Okay." Betsy pulled the handle down on the juicer to make lemonade. Mary mixed in the correct proportions of water and sugar and stirred it vigorously before pouring the sweet drink into a gallon thermos jug.

Butch loved potato chips, and Mary had a giant tin to go in the truck. She gave Betsy and Terry each something to carry as they left the house. They were excited to surprise their dad.

"Aren't we lucky that Grandma could come to stay with your sisters so we can have a picnic with Daddy?"

"Yes, we are. Lucky, lucky, lucky!" Terry bounced up and down on the seat with each word.

Mary couldn't help but smile.

Arriving at the farm, Mary could see Butch on the tractor, baling hay in an adjacent field. She maneuvered the truck close to where he was working.

Butch looked up to see the truck approaching and spotted his two older kids waving to him. He stopped the tractor and turned it off. Walking back to the baler, he flicked the off switch so the machine could cool. He turned and strode toward his family.

"We brought a s'prise picnic, Daddy," squealed Terry.

"Okay, guys, this is great. Whaddya say we get out of the sun?" Butch led them to the shady side of the pickup truck.

"Hey, handsome, do you think you could help a gal spread out a blanket for this feast?" Mary gave Butch her most flirtatious smile while handing him a corner of the blanket.

"Hey, Daddy, here's your sandwiches," Betsy said. "I helped make them."

"Well then, I'm sure they're yummy," he replied as he sat down.

The family relaxed to enjoy their picnic in the shade of the truck. Butch savored his second sugar cookie and, soon after, felt like taking a nap in the shade. He barely noticed a soft rhythmic clicking in the distance.

Sandy observed a stealthy figure approaching the baler from the sunny side of the vehicle. In an instant, he saw a flame and then smoke coming from the hay bale sitting in the chute of the machine. The arsonist ran from the baler and disappeared over the ridge. The situation was urgent. Without fanning the flames, Sandy blew smoke in Butch's direction. He didn't need to repeat the act because Butch sat up straight.

"I smell smoke, Mary." His nostrils flared as he coughed.

Getting up, Butch ran toward the baler. He saw grey

wisps of smoke coming from the partially protruding hay bales in the machine.

Butch called over his shoulder, "Mary, do we have any water?"

"No, is something wrong?"

"The hay in the baler is on fire!"

Mary grabbed the handle of the thermos and hurried to catch up with her husband. She handed the jug to Butch, who quickly unscrewed the top and poured the sweet drink over the smoking bale. He continued to saturate the hay until it was sopping wet. Butch moved onto the next bale, which was partially visible, and soaked that one as well. The smoke died out shortly after the first bale was doused.

"It's lovely to have an unending supply of lemonade to adequately quench a fire," Sandy said to his invisible counterparts.

"Wow! That was a close one." Mary sagged against Butch's chest as she hugged her husband.

Butch rubbed her back and said, "I'm glad you made so much lemonade. Of course, you had to, considering there's four of us who love it."

Mary looked at her husband quizzically, "You know you poured more than a gallon on those bales, Butch. It just kept pouring out like the jug was bottomless."

Betsy ran to her parents. She whispered loudly, "Sandy and his friends are here to help."

Butch cocked his head. "Sandy, huh?"

Mary shrugged. "Are you surprised? We know stranger things have happened." She looked all around before saying, "Thank you, Lord, for sending Sandy and all the other angels."

The angels looked on from a distance. "Well, well,

well," Sandy said. "Looks like they're a little more than suspicious that they might have help."

"There are four of us here right now," Mary's guardian said. "I suppose you could take your pick of names to thank."

"Not many hard-working farm families living in the shadow of the Lyon Brook Bridge ever think about guardian angels in their midst. But now Butch and Mary do," Butch's guardian added.

Later that evening, Butch and Mary were dancing across the hardwood floors in the dining room to the strains of Benny Goodman's "How Long Has This Been Going On."

"I called the sheriff about that bum setting my baler on fire." Butch saw concern in Mary's eyes. "You know, this is the second time somebody's tried to destroy our property with fire."

"I know, honey." Mary's brow furrowed. "I won't ever forget the night someone tried to burn down the chick houses. And now the fire in the baler. Why on earth would someone want to do this?"

"That's a good question, Mary. Makes me wonder if someone has a beef with my dad or me."

"What did the sheriff say?"

"He made out a report and put it in our file. There's really nothing to go on. He said to tell you, the kids, and our hired hands if they see anything suspicious to call him."

"But, Butch," Mary protested, "if we see something that's not right, it could take him a half hour to get out here."

"Yeah, I told him that. He urged me to keep a loaded shotgun in the barn where the kids can't reach it—but where I can if I need it in a hurry. He also told me to teach you how to handle a shotgun."

"Does he think I might have to protect our house and the children?" Mary shuddered.

"I'm afraid so." Butch pulled his wife to him and held her tightly.

They swayed to the tune of "Someone to Watch over Me."

"Until we catch someone doing something, we don't know what they're up to. We have to be on guard."

"Butch, I have to confess, I'm shaken to my core. I don't know how to get my legs underneath me right now."

"I know it's tough, honey. Lean on me; have faith. With the help of God, we'll get through this together, just like we've always done."

Celestial beings raised their hands in supplication. "Father in Heaven, help us fight this battle. We have to be prepared. We'll always try to keep the Emig family safe from the persistent forces of evil."

Thirty-One

May 1953

After the morning milking session, Butch came into the house searching for his wife. He scratched his head while calling out for her. "Mary?"

"In here, honey," his wife answered from the living room where she was ironing her way through a pile of dresses. Big band music emanated from the radio.

"I seem to have lost one of the young pregnant cows that's due for birthing. When I called the cattle this morning, they all came down from the pasture but her."

"Do you think she could be in trouble?"

"Yeah, I think she might have had her calf and probably doesn't know what to do with it. Can you get away to take a ride in the truck with me while I look for her? With Betsy and Terry in school and not due home till three-thirty, do you think our neighbor in the apartment will watch Judy and Gail for a bit?"

Mary thought a moment. Now that Gail was almost potty-trained and Judy was almost five, they were fun to have around. "I'll run over and ask. We've become good friends; I'm sure she'll say yes. Would you get the girls' shoes and socks on? I'll be right back."

"Great, I've got shoe and sock detail covered."

The neighbor was happy to help, so Butch and Mary began their quest to find the missing cow.

Discovering the cow in a steep rock-filled area near the railroad tracks, Butch noticed that her newborn calf was lying on the grass, still covered with birth membranes. "Uh oh, not good," he said. "This cow could be dangerous. Mary, get behind me."

Mary was already out of the truck and never heard her husband's warning. Walking around the back of the vehicle, she approached the calf on the ground. The cow watched warily and began to paw the ground with her left hoof.

"Mary!" Butch called out, fear creeping into his voice. He saw his wife bend over the calf.

"She's alive and breathing," Mary hollered to him, concentrating on the newborn.

"Mary, get up and move away from the calf, slowly, honey."

Butch stood by helplessly. He had a bad feeling about this agitated mama cow. Her hoof pawed the ground. She snorted. She lowered her huge head and began to move toward Mary.

Butch yelled, "Mary, run to the truck."

Mary stood up when she heard Butch's instruction. The cow was in motion, and as Butch hollered, the animal butted Mary's body. The blow to her abdomen sent her airborne, and she landed on a rock pile.

Butch watched in horror. He heard a sickening sound as Mary's head connected with something solid. She was knocked unconscious. The cow backed off but began to paw the ground again. She lowered her head. The large mammal was preparing for another attack. By that time, Butch reached his wife. Crouching over Mary, Butch shielded her inert body. He stared down the mama cow. The creature stopped short of attacking a second time when Butch made eye contact. Inexplicably, the cow backed away as Butch cradled his injured wife in his arms.

Blood streamed down Mary's face from a cut on her head. Her eyes fluttered open, and she moaned, grabbing her abdomen. "Something I forgot to tell you, honey."

"Mary, are you okay?"

"Forgot to tell you something," Mary murmured.

Butch thought his wife was really out of it. "What?"

"I'm pregnant," Mary announced with tears rolling down her face. "Or, I was..."

"Oh, God!" Butch uttered a prayer to his Heavenly Father. "Oh, no! Oh, God, no!" He picked Mary up in his arms and headed for the truck. "We're gonna get you back home and right to bed. I'll call Doc to come as soon as possible, and I'll have Herb come up to get the calf and this cow."

Butch avoided as many bumps as he could on the way out of the rugged terrain. Mary leaned back against the seat with her eyes closed, moaning softly. Blood caked her red hair. Butch looked over at her, wishing he could go back in time. He'd do things differently. For the moment, he wanted to make Mary's pain go away. He knew the larger hurt was in both their hearts. Her head would heal, but losing a baby would always be a painful memory. He prayed.

The couple's guardian angels prayed.

Doc Mayhew arrived after Butch struggled to get Mary into the house, up the stairs, and into bed. Butch had washed the dried blood from her face and neck and attempted to clean her wound, but it only bled more. While Doc was attending his wife, Butch excused himself to check on Judy and Gail. The neighbor assured him she could keep the girls for a few more hours if need be. After he got back to his house and went upstairs to check on Doc's progress with Mary, he called his mother.

"Mom, we need you." Butch broke down. Sobbing, he explained what happened in the field. "The little girls are next door, and the big kids will be coming home from school soon."

Cora reassured him and said, "I'm on my way."

Butch wiped his tears, splashed cold water on his face, and ran up the back stairs.

Doc had scrubbed Mary's head with antiseptic and applied a dressing. Mary was resting, her red hair fanned out on the white pillowcase. Doc looked at Butch and put his finger to his lips. He ushered Butch out of the room. In the hallway, he whispered, "Let's let her sleep a while. I want you to wake her every hour, talk to her, and give her a drink of water. If she seems confused at all or vomits, call me right away."

When Cora arrived a few minutes later, Doc gave Butch instructions on wound care and signs of infection to watch for. He told them that he could not detect a fetal heartbeat. Still, with the pregnancy not being very far along, it wasn't unusual. Doc Mayhew put his arm around Butch. "Son, it's going to be a matter of time. If she's going to lose the baby, there's nothing we can do to stop it. Just say a prayer that God's will be done."

Two days later, Mary developed a fever, and her head wound looked infected. Butch took her to Doc Mayhew's office, where the doctor cleaned her wound and put her on an oral antibiotic. Within twenty-four hours, Mary broke out in angry red hives, a reaction to the medicine. Mary stopped taking it. Her freckled face was swollen, and hives on her feet made it difficult to walk. Mary needed more help than Butch alone could give. He called dependable Aunt Gertrude to come care for Mary, the children, and the house. Soon after Mary began taking an antihistamine for the hives, she started experiencing abdominal cramping and bleeding. All in all, she was physically and mentally miserable.

Lying in bed, Mary quietly recited Psalm 23. "The Lord is my shepherd, I shall not want. He makes me lie down in green pastures; leads me beside still waters; He restores my soul. He leads me in right paths for his name's sake. Even though I walk through the darkest valley, I fear no evil; for You are with me; Your rod and Your staff—they comfort me. You prepare a table before me in the presence of my enemies; You anoint my head with oil; my cup overflows. Surely goodness and mercy shall follow me all the days of my life, and I shall dwell in the house of the Lord forever."

That night Mary and Butch lost their baby.

Mary's guardian angel shed tears for the grief Butch and Mary felt as he carried their unborn child to Heaven.

Betsy and her siblings sat on the sofa in the living room as their dad and grandmother explained why their mother was resting in bed and shouldn't be disturbed. Aunt Gertrude was on her way to stay with them once again.

Cora leaned forward and said, "Mommy's going to need your help. That means doing dishes or setting the table as well as gathering eggs and other things your dad needs you to do. Betsy and Terry can help Judy and Gail pick out their clothes and get dressed. They need help tying their shoes and getting buttoned or zipped."

Butch picked Gail up and set her on his knee. "Mommy can use extra kisses. Can you do that, Gail?"

The toddler clapped her hands. "I love Mommy!"

"Judy, you can help Aunt Gertrude take Mommy her

meals on a tray. Maybe you can sing her a song. Can you do that?"

Judy nodded vigorously.

"Betsy and Terry, you'll be able to do a lot more than your younger sisters. Aunt Gertrude and I will need lots of help. Can I count on you guys?"

"Yes, Daddy." Terry fidgeted, wanting to say something, but the words didn't come out.

"Son?"

"What about the baby, Dad?"

"What exactly do you want to know, bub?"

"Was it a boy or a girl? Were we going to have a sister or a brother? Are we going to have a funeral?"

Taken aback by the questions on his son's mind, Butch looked over at his mother for answers.

She nodded and said, "Just answer them one at a time, son. I'm here."

"We don't know if it was a boy or a girl because the baby was really small." Blinking back sudden tears, Butch couldn't bring himself to mention the damage brought about by the attack. "There's not going to be a funeral because we need to concentrate on getting Mommy back on her feet. I think it would be great to pray that our baby rests in the arms of an angel in Heaven."

Smiles appeared on four sweet faces as they embraced their father's suggestion.

Balancing Gail on his knee, Butch opened his arms to gather in the three older children for a group hug. "I love you all, and Mommy loves you too. I promise you Mommy will be better in a few days." He kissed each of his children and left to work outside.

The younger girls sat on the floor to play with their dolls. Terry searched the toy closet for a bag of plastic, green army men and set up a battle on the coffee table. Betsy got up and went to the front porch swing.

Sandy perched next to Betsy. "Would you like to talk about it?"

"Why did this happen to my mom?"

Sandy suggested, "Let's take a walk." He held out his hand to the child.

Betsy put her hand in his, and the two were transported to a precipice of land, where they watched a glorious sunset. To the eyes of any onlooker, Betsy sat by herself on the front porch, swinging back and forth.

"Betsy, I've told you a lot about angels over the years, but perhaps if I explain a few more things, it'll make it easier for you to understand. Your mom's guardian is not like me. I've been assigned to you for as long as you live. I don't get called back to Heaven. Your mother's guardian travels in time and space when the Lord calls him. When that happens, for a moment he is not by your mother's side."

Betsy was mesmerized by the orange-red sun setting on the horizon in front of her. "Do you think Mom's angel wasn't there when the cow attacked her?"

"Possibly. I don't know. I do know that your mother's guardian angel has been by her side since she got hurt and will aid in her recovery."

The child gripped her guardian angel's hand tightly. "Sandy, I was scared that mom would die—almost as scared as when she was real sick after Gail was born. I love Mom so much, and I feel like I'm going to throw up when she's sick or hurt like this."

"I understand, Betsy."

"How do you understand? Do you have a mom angel?

"No, I don't have a mom angel. God made a huge number of angels at the time of creation. We don't have parents as you do. We don't marry or have children. And we don't die. We serve God and give Him glory. But here's the thing, Betsy... do you want to know a secret?"

Betsy's eyes widened, and she nodded.

"We angels have great power and intelligence—much more than humans—but we are not all-powerful or all-knowing like God. He gave all the guardian angels personalities, minds, emotions, and a will. Because of that, even though we are holy beings, we can relate well to humans. That's why I understand what you feel when you are worried or hurt."

"So guardian angels are friends and helpers and protectors but not always if they're someplace else?"

"That's the gist of it. Remember, God doesn't will bad things to happen. A guardian angel can't always prevent bad things from happening, although we often intercede at God's direction. I want you to remember that God is always present to get you through the bad times. He will never leave you."

Instantly, Sandy and Betsy returned to the rhythmically rocking porch swing. Sandy put his arm around Betsy. She laid her head on his chest, content in his serenity.

"I hope I answered all your questions, sweet girl. Look for the glory of God's creation in every sunset and each sunrise. Remember, you pray to God every day to watch over you, and He sends us."

Thirty-Two

Summer 1954

After parking his old beat-up truck on Broad Street in Norwich, Paul Fisher wandered around looking for something to do. He hadn't worked for the Emigs for ten years, but he almost wished that he still worked at the farm. He was bored out of his mind at the grocery store.

"It's all Butch's fault," he muttered to himself and to the voices in his head. "The man just couldn't tolerate my having a beer or two."

Paul heard, "You ought to make him pay."

He shook his head violently and slapped himself on the forehead. "I told you to shut up," Paul screamed at the voice in his head.

Reaching into his pocket, he ran his fingers over the smooth metal lighter. Paul opened and closed it a few times, comforted by the clicking sound. He reached back into his pocket and found some loose change and a ball of lint. Paul knew his entertainment options were limited.

Long ago, his older brothers stopped giving him money. In the far recesses of his now warped mind, Paul knew that if he'd carried his load on the Fisher farm, he'd still have some income, but since he'd gotten lazy, his brothers had fired him just like Butch Emig did. He fumed.

"Damn that Butch Emig! All this crap is because he fired me." Paul smacked his right fist into his left palm a few times. "That's the least of what I'd like to do to Butch."

Wandering down a side street, Paul came to Norwich's infamous Cabooze Bar. He probably had enough change for one beer, hardly enough to get hammered. Having heard that railroaders gathered there, Paul figured it was a safe bet that he'd find someone to buy him a beer after his change was gone.

Paul opened the door to a dark smoke-filled room. Making his way to the bar, he slid onto a wooden stool. In answer to the questioning look of the bartender, Paul said, "A bottle of Black Label." He plunked down a quarter.

In a back booth, a man pushed a Dodgers ball cap back on his head to watch Paul Fisher's every move. "There's a real rat if I ever saw one," Huck Sawyer muttered under his breath. His eyes narrowed, and his upper lip curled into a sneer. "I'd really like a piece of him. Buzz served time upstate in max at Dannemora while this weasel was free to do whatever he wanted."

Saw moved out of the booth and walked toward the bar. Taking the stool next to Paul, he asked, "Hey, kid, remember me?"

Paul looked to his left. His eyes widened first in surprise and then in fear. Moisture formed on his upper lip, and it wasn't from his beer.

"Saw? That you?"

"Yeah, you weasel, it's me."

Paul gulped. "How ya doin'?"

"Skip the small talk, bozo. Remember me saying a hundred times, 'You mess with Buzz, you get The Saw'? Remember that, you dirty rat fink?"

"Yeah, what does that have to do with me?" Paul's shirt was getting sticky with sweat.

"You betrayed my brother, and he's serving a lotta years behind bars," Saw hissed through clenched teeth. "I'm not ever going to forget what you did, and I'm watching you, Paul Fisher. I promise. I'm gonna be on you like diapers on a baby. You're gonna be sorry you ever crossed a Sawyer."

"But, I—"

Saw grabbed Paul's cheeks with one hand, squeezing until his mouth was in the shape of fish lips. "Can it, weasel boy. Save it for somebody you can con, and that's not me." Saw let go and slapped Paul's left cheek. "See ya 'round, old buddy." Saw left the bar, slamming the heavy wooden door behind him, emphasizing his threats to Paul.

Feeling a sudden urge to go to the bathroom, Paul bolted off his stool.

After leaving the bar, Paul walked up the side street onto Broad to get to his truck. He was rightfully scared. Paul had a vivid recollection of the day he testified against Saw's brother Buzz. As he walked to his truck, he was unaware of a vehicle being driven slowly down the street behind him. When Paul pulled out into traffic, he had no idea the same car was now following him home.

For weeks Saw followed Paul, getting the hang of his erratic work schedule. Saw made a note of the younger man's hangouts, routes he took, and his inexplicable stalking of Butch Emig.

It was a warm summer night when Saw watched from a distance as Paul Fisher spied on Butch and Herb through binoculars as they put their herd out to pasture after the evening milking.

Paul knew the men would be going into the house for dinner.

"Tonight's the night," one of the voices pronounced to Paul. "You'll get to even the score with Butch!"

Paul smiled to himself when the barn door closed and two figures made their way onto the wrap-around porch, where they shed their work boots before walking into the kitchen.

He started up his truck and drove up the dirt road with his headlights off.

"Well, isn't that interesting." Saw remarked to himself. "I have a gut feeling that wigged-out weasel is gonna do something bad. Guess I'll run down to the Inn on Route 12 and get me something to eat so I can track Mr. Rat Fink Fisher."

ॐ

The Emig guardian angels, alert for an attack, could feel the evil swirling around the farm and the Emig family. Archangel Michael appeared to the angels with his sword strapped to his side. "Prepare for battle, guardians. The attack is coming. Protect your charges."

The farmhouse was quiet as Mary, Butch, and the four children slept. Butch was dreaming of the Emig family reunion scheduled for the next day. There would be abundant family, food, and laughter during lawn games and swimming.

Both Butch and Mary's guardian angels hovered over the double bed, forming a protective canopy as their charges' slumber deepened. Around 3:30 a.m. Butch's angel disabled the alarm clock set for four o'clock.

At the same time, an unsettling dream had Herb tossing and turning. He woke up in a panic. His heart pounded, and sweat poured from his brow. "Wow, that was so real. I need a drink of water."

Herb slipped on his pants and t-shirt, pulled on his long socks, and padded downstairs. He ran the faucet, filling a tall glass with the cold spring water. Turning, he walked toward the large window facing the barn in time to see a dark figure sneak across the yard, slide open the barn door, and slip inside.

"What the hell?" Herb said as he set the glass on the table. He left the kitchen and put on his work boots, intending to find out who was here uninvited. As he entered the barn through the same narrow opening the intruder used, he heard the click of metal on metal echo throughout the empty milking parlor. He stood stock-still and held his breath for fear of being detected. The clicking sound stopped as the uninvited guest began to climb the wooden loft ladder built into the hay chute.

Herb's mind was racing. How could an intruder know where the ladder was? Why didn't he crash into one of the cattle stanchions or fall into the manure gutter? It was obvious the man knew his way around in this barn. Herb's brow furrowed as he thought about likely suspects. His mind churned again and he thanked God the barn was empty of cattle. It made it easier to pick up sounds. He began to think of confrontation strategy options when he was startled by footfalls in the loft above him.

Herb jumped as the first bale of hay was thrown down the chute, followed by several more. He tried to remember where Butch kept the shotgun. Moving toward the right side of the sliding barn door in the dark, Herb wished he'd thought to bring a flashlight as he approached the feed bins that held hundreds of pounds of grain for the cows. Finding the secret compartment above the built-in bins, Herb lifted the latch. He reached inside and touched the cold metal barrel of the gun. Lifting it out, he felt some measure of security—knowing it was loaded—but hoped he wouldn't have to use it.

Herb's angel arrived belatedly and wanted to reassure his charge that he had his back, but didn't want to startle him by using an audible voice—the way he had when he impersonated Herb's mother all those years ago. He settled on a brief prayer. *Lord, help me keep Herb safe and secure.*

Herb chose a vantage point where he could see the intruder when he came down the ladder. He needed to find out what this guy was up to. Herb was out of sight with his back against the feed bins when he heard another person enter the barn through the partially open door.

Herb could see a man's silhouette, and it wasn't Butch.

Herb didn't move a muscle. If the person coming through the barn door had been Butch, he could have breathed a sigh of relief. But now Herb had a new concern. He might be outnumbered.

The new trespasser quietly moved forward into the milking parlor.

Herb heard a click and saw the glow of a flashlight pointed at the stained cement floor. He wanted to scratch his head but didn't dare move a muscle, in case the second intruder was in cahoots with the first.

The whoosh of the hay bales being thrown down the chute continued until the first intruder started down the ladder to the lower level of the barn. The newer trespasser moved to his right, toward the hay chute from which the bales had been thrown.

Herb noticed that the second person didn't call out or make himself known. It could mean one of two things. Either the second person wanted to surprise the first or he was there to help the intruder and didn't need to identify himself.

Even though the initial intruder was on the ladder, the loft creaked and groaned. Herb was alarmed; he had never heard a sound quite like it. The hairs on his arms rose.

"What are you up to, rat fink?" the second trespasser asked the guy on the ladder.

Herb heard a sharp intake of breath. "Who's there?"

"Hey, Mr. Rat Fink Paul Fisher, it's your old buddy, The Saw."

Paul jumped from the ladder to the cement floor. His voice quivered with fury. "Why are you here, Satan? I told you I'd get the job done."

"Answer my question, rat!" Saw insisted as he shined the beam of his flashlight into Paul's face.

"Put that thing down," Paul said, shielding his eyes. "You're blinding me. I told you before, Satan, I'm just taking care of old business." Paul sounded defiant.

"You better get to your old business, rat fink, because it's almost dawn and someone will be bringing the cattle in for milking. So I ask you, what are you up to?"

"They told me to finish what I started," Paul insisted.

"Who told you?" Saw asked, genuinely puzzled.

"The voices, they told me..." Paul's voice trailed off as he grabbed a hay bale.

The rafters groaned and creaked.

Paul ignored Saw and began to pile bales of hay in a circle while talking to himself. "I tried to burn the chicken houses and failed. I tried destroying the baler and failed. They say I won't fail this time, Satan." Paul glared in Saw's direction while tearing one bale apart and spreading loose hay in the center of the circle.

"Stop calling me Satan, you weasel. It just so happens

160

I have some 'old business' to take care of too." Saw stepped closer to Paul.

Herb had paid close attention to Paul's confessions. Now he had a flashback to a conversation with someone called Saw. It happened one night at the Cabooze not too long ago. Saw had said he knew Paul and had no use for him. Herb shivered, realizing the confrontation could get ugly.

Saw continued to menace Paul, moving closer as he talked. "I don't have time for your nonsense, you worthless puke. I'm here to settle a score with you." With that, Saw swung his metal flashlight into Paul's face. "Remember my brother Buzz? Well, that's for him," Saw shouted as he hit Paul again.

Hearing Paul's nose crunch when the flashlight connected, Herb pushed back against the feed bin to get his legs underneath him. Suddenly, he felt strong arms around him, and someone bent over him to shelter his head. Herb was unable to move. He never had a chance to stand up and shout, "Hands up, or I'll shoot both of you."

A loud rumble shook the barn as a bloodied Paul Fisher continued to struggle with Sawyer. The rafters groaned and creaked. The loft above them split open. Heavy hay bales, splintered timbers, and broken boards spilled onto the two men and the once tidy milking parlor.

Herb's angel continued to pray, sending an unspoken message to his charge. *"Fear not, Herb. As it is written in Psalm 91, 'He who dwells in the secret place of the Most High shall abide under the shadow of the Almighty... for He shall give his angels charge over you, to keep you safe in all your ways. They shall bear you up... lest you dash your foot against a stone.'"*

Thirty-Three

A low rumble and slight vibration in the house caused Butch to roll over at 4:30 a.m. He scrunched his pillow into a ball under his head, then fell back into his dream. He was diving into the cold, refreshing water of the swimming hole underneath the Lyon Brook Bridge.

Having silenced the four o'clock alarm, Butch's guardian angel gently nudged Butch awake. He blinked twice as he tried to focus on the bedside clock.

"It's nearly five o'clock!" Butch bolted out of bed, glanced over at his wife, and said, "Good Lord, Mary! I overslept. The cows will be waiting at the barn door."

"Why didn't the alarm go off?" Mary murmured before she rolled over.

"Beats me," he answered as he threw on a t-shirt and ran down the stairs two at a time.

Mary fluffed her pillow and fell back to sleep, thinking that one of the kids would undoubtedly wake her in another hour.

Butch stood in the kitchen, throwing on the barn clothes he had hung on a hook by the door. He fastened the straps on his overalls, then quick-stepped out onto the porch where he put on his dirty work boots before taking off on the run to the barn.

Sliding the big double barn doors open, Butch took in the sight. The contents of the hayloft—all the fresh bales put in for the winter months—were strewn on the concrete barn floor where he, Herb, and his prize-winning herd would have been if his alarm had gone off earlier. Surveying the splintered wood beams and broken two by fours, Butch looked up to see the jagged hole above him. A few hay bales teetered on the edge of the fractured loft, threatening to tumble.

Remembering that he'd forgotten to check on Herb, Butch turned and ran back to the house, hoping he'd find Herb there. Torn by a sense of urgency, he took off his dirty boots, nevertheless, and left them on the stoop. Butch opened the door, rushed in, and went straight to the phone.

He didn't have to wait long before a familiar voice said, "Number, please?"

"Jenny, this is Butch." He couldn't stop his voice from quivering. "My hayloft collapsed, and I need help."

Jenny had never heard Butch so shaken. "Are you okay? The cattle? Herb?"

"I'm okay; I overslept, so I wasn't in the barn when it happened. Neither were the cattle, but I haven't found Herb yet."

"I'll call Les, Archie, Jim, and Randy to see if they can help. They may be done milking their herds by now. Don't you worry none. You just stay out of that barn till it gets stabilized. I'll call the fire department and your dad too."

"Okay, Jenny. Thanks." Butch moved past the phone and bounded up the back stairs to Herb's room. He knocked on the closed door. There was no answer. "Herb! Herb, it's Butch." There was still no answer. With the pressure of Butch's hand, the door slowly opened to reveal an empty bed. Butch gasped and began to hyperventilate.

He had to wake Mary. She had to know what was happening, but he didn't want to wake the sleeping children. He ran to his bedroom, where Mary was still sleeping. Kneeling beside the bed and gently laying his right hand on her shoulder, he whispered, "Mary, wake up. Something's happened."

His wife opened her eyes and blinked several times. "You okay? The kids? Are the kids okay?"

"We're all okay, Mary." Butch tried to control his breathing.

Mary's mind was racing. "Is it raining? I thought I heard thunder."

"No, it's not raining; something terrible happened. The hayloft collapsed, and I think Herb may be in the barn. I gotta see if I can find him. I've called for help."

Mary sat up in bed. "What? Did I hear you right? The hayloft is down? Herb? You can't find Herb?"

"If I hadn't overslept, the herd and I would be under all that rubble. I, I..." his chin started to quiver. "Mary, I don't know where to begin." His head dropped to the edge of the bed next to his wife.

They heard a siren in the distance. Butch straightened and stood up. "You better get dressed, honey. I think we're going to need lots of coffee and doughnuts—the firemen and neighbors will be here soon. Call my mom. Right now, I gotta find Herb."

Butch raced to the barn and ventured in as far he could safely go. "Herb, Herb!" he hollered. His voice was drowned out by the sirens of the Oxford fire engines coming up Lyon Brook Road. The red trucks were followed by a caravan of pickup trucks and tractors pulling wagons. The neighbors had received Jenny's message.

Butch ran out to the first fire engine. "I think Herb

Brunner is trapped in the barn. I can't find him anywhere. I can't get past the debris."

As the firemen donned their protective helmets, they approached the barn to assess the danger of a complete collapse. Butch continued calling Herb's name. In a moment of quiet, Butch heard tapping, a pause, then tapping again. Aloud, Butch translated to the firemen, "Three short taps, three long taps, three short taps."

"That's SOS!" yelled one of the firemen. "We got a survivor! Over here, men."

One of the neighbors organized the volunteers. "Form a brigade to clear these fallen bales of hay. Two guys man the wagons waiting outside the barn door and get the hay loaded. As soon as we get a full load, move the wagons around the corner to make room for the next empty wagon."

As the hay was cleared, the firemen advanced farther into the barn to remove broken timbers and splintered rafters. They braced rafters that were still intact. It was a tedious process. Someone else gave directions to form a trash pile at the edge of the dirt driveway near the chicken house. Good, usable timber, always in demand on a farm, was saved and piled on the lawn.

Butch continued to call out to Herb, not knowing if the man could hear him. "Help is on the way, buddy. You hang on. I need you."

Herb tapped out again.

The fireman proficient in Morse Code translated. "F-e-e-d-b-i-n."

Butch hollered and pointed. "The feed bin's over there. That's where he is."

Random taps began as the rescuers moved toward the area.

As the debris removal progressed, a fireman called out, "I see the top of the feed bin."

The rescuers heard Herb's muffled voice saying, "You're close. I can see the light."

The firemen worked faster. "We can see the top of your head. Are you hurt? Can you move?"

"I'm wedged in here tight. I can only move enough to tap the barrel of the shotgun with my pocket knife. I'm glad somebody out there besides me learned Morse Code as a kid."

As they got closer to Herb, one of the firemen said, "Look! There's a wooden cage holding this man in place. It's protecting his entire body."

Murmurs of those witnessing the event spread to men loading wagons outside the barn. "It's a miracle! He's alive."

Butch stood nearby, watching in awe. Herb didn't appear to have a scratch on him. The cattle were safe. He and Herb were safe. If his alarm had gone off when it was supposed to, they all would have been in the barn. He began to shake from head to toe and knew it was shock setting in. A fireman noticed and threw a blanket around Butch's shoulders.

"Sit," the fireman directed.

Butch sat on a nearby bench.

When Herb saw the first rescuer, he blurted out, "Two men are trapped over by the right hay chute."

The fireman pulled Herb to a standing position and threw a blanket over him. "Just point to where you last heard them."

Butch was dumbfounded. "What do you mean there are men by the chute? Herb, come sit with me and tell me about these others. Who are they? Why are they here?"

"Yeah, Butch, you're not gonna believe what happened and what I overheard. I had the shotgun ready and was gonna hold them at gunpoint when the barn collapsed." Herb explained what he saw from the kitchen window and what he came upon when he followed the first intruder into the barn.

"I can't believe what Paul did. That guy is a mental case." Butch shook his head. "I bet his brothers don't even know how bad it is."

"The other person is a fella named Saw," Herb explained. "He wasn't here to hurt you or the farm. He was here because he was after Paul. Seems like he had a score to settle. Speaking of settling scores, Butch, Paul is your firebug. I heard him admit it."

"I've got a pair of legs over here," one of the firemen hollered. "We need more hands to lift these timbers and bales of hay to get 'em out."

Men scrambled to the site and worked feverishly to uncover the two men. The fire chief approached as the bodies were being uncovered.

"I think we're too late, Chief," said one of the veteran firemen. "They're both in real bad shape."

The chief knelt by Paul's body and tried to find a pulse. He moved to Saw's inert form and did the same. "I don't think we could have saved them even if we'd gotten here sooner." He shook his head at the grisly scene. "You're right. I've gotta call the coroner."

Butch rubbed his hands up and down his arms, trying to get rid of the sickening chills. He pulled the blanket tighter around his shoulders but couldn't stop shaking. "It's an awful lot to stomach, Herb. It sure sounds like Paul Fisher was twisted by demons." Turning to look directly at Herb, Butch's eyes widened. "The sheriff is going to appreciate wrapping up this mystery all neat and tidy. Thank God, you heard them talking. And on another note, thank God you weren't killed. How is it that you were so protected?"

Herb rubbed his hands together in an attempt to warm them. "That's the strange thing, Butch. When the loft started to cave in, I felt wrapped up."

"Wrapped up?" Butch stared at his friend, realizing that Herb had become more than just a hired hand. Butch trusted Herb with his farm, his family, his life.

"It was as if someone twice my size wrapped giant arms around me, protecting my head and body. At some point, I blacked out until I heard you calling my name."

Butch was jolted into thinking about Betsy's angel friend Sandy. He smiled and said, "Maybe you have someone watching out for you, buddy."

Herb smiled back. "Maybe I do."

"And I'm sure glad we have you watching out for the farm. It means a lot that you would come out here to protect the property."

Extending his right hand toward Butch, Herb said, "Thanks, boss."

Butch grabbed Herb's hand and pumped it vigorously. "I'm glad you're okay. We'd hate to have anything happen to you." Butch playfully punched Herb's shoulder.

Herb laughed. "We'll rebuild in no time, Butch. You know all the neighbors will pitch in for a loft raising, and we'll be back better than ever in a couple of weeks."

Butch blinked a couple of times. "You bet, Herb. Back in the saddle, no time at all. Say, I bet the herd is at the back door, waiting. It's nearly three hours past milking time." Butch stood up, dropping the blanket that had been warming him. "I'll find out how soon we can bring some of the cows in and hook 'em up."

Herb followed suit, walking behind Butch to gather the equipment.

As he walked, Herb realized he was in no hurry to leave Lyon Brook Farm, even though he'd been saving money to buy his own farm for years.

Butch's guardian pondered a recurring theme among the angels. *In Chenango County, New York, one hard-working farm family and their hired hand believe they have experienced the protection of guardian angels. And they'd be correct.*

Thirty-Four

The fire chief took off his helmet as he left the chaotic scene in the barn and walked to the house. He knocked on the kitchen door to ask Mary if he could use the phone. After removing his boots, the man stepped inside. Cora and Mary were overseeing breakfast for the kids.

Mary couldn't help but overhear the fire chief ask the switchboard operator to send the coroner to their farm. After a sharp intake of breath, she bolted toward the door and ran out to the barn. Spotting her husband in the doorway to the milking parlor, she yelled, "Honey, is Herb okay?"

When she reached Butch, she threw her arms around his neck. She looked over her husband's shoulder and saw a disheveled, dusty Herb picking straw from his hair. Immediately, she left her life-long dance partner to wrap her arms around Herb's neck.

"Oh, thank God you're okay. I was so worried. Are you hurt?"

Both Butch and Herb's faces were wreathed in smiles at the obvious affection she had for the man.

"Mary, calm down. You'll have people talking," Butch admonished.

Herb blushed and stammered, "I'm fine, Miss Mary. Not a scratch."

"It's a story he'll have to tell you later. The bodies have to be removed from the barn before we can do anything more." Butch moved toward the chief to discuss a process he thought of for making the north end of the barn safe enough to milk the herd.

"Bodies?" Mary asked, "Dead bodies? More than one? Who died in our barn?"

Herb looked at Butch, who nodded.

"Mary, come sit on the porch, and I'll tell you everything while Butch is talking with the chief." They moved across the lawn to the wooden Adirondack chairs on the porch outside the kitchen, where Herb told Mary his story.

"Chief, I gotta get my herd milked," Butch pleaded.

The fire chief said, "We're just about finished up with the reinforcement beams. As soon as I get the all-clear sign, I'll let you know. It shouldn't be much longer, maybe twenty or thirty minutes. We want you and the cows to be safe."

The coroner arrived along with two hearses to take the bodies of Paul Fisher and Huck Sawyer. The Fisher family had been notified, since Randy and Jim were present at the scene. The Sheriff's Department was looking into the next of kin for Sawyer.

While the firemen worked to put the final support beams in place, Butch and Herb cordoned off the barnyard into incoming and outgoing lanes.

"Do you have enough rope over there?" Butch asked Herb.

"Yup, this was a good idea to funnel the cows into the barn in one lane and out the other. Did you notice that the neighbors have already covered the hay wagons with tarps to protect the bales? They moved the wagons alongside the barn for easy access for us. These guys have been a godsend."

"They sure have. I don't know how I'll ever be able to thank them. I guess they know we'd do the same. We have in the past, and we will in the future. That's just what good neighbors do."

Inside the house, Mary and Cora were joined by a few neighbor women. Together, they had made several pots of strong coffee and dozens of doughnuts. The four Emig children helped to roll them in sugar and piled the confections on plates. The ladies carried everything to the tables set up on the porch. Workers responded to the dinner bell to grab a coffee and a sweet treat without having to remove their boots.

Betsy and Terry sidled up to their mother as she was pouring coffee. "Mom, does this mean we're not having the family reunion?"

"Yes, I'm afraid it does—the emergency in the barn kind of canceled those plans for us. I'm sorry. I know you two were looking forward to spending time with your cousins."

Both kids nodded somberly. Mary said, "Hey, kids, go ask Grandma if there are more donuts that need to be sugared. You're the experts."

Betsy and Terry jumped at that suggestion; it meant they could munch on the broken donut pieces that their grandma called rejects.

Inside the barn, Butch stroked his chin while he thought. "Herb, I guess that with the loft empty, the firemen will be placing more support beams. We should be able to use ten stanchions on either side of the main aisle to milk the cows. I figure it'll take about ten to twelve minutes to milk each group of ten."

"With this many hands to clean udders and distribute hay to forty head of cattle, it'll go faster," Herb said. "We could have everyone pitch in to massage udder balm after milking and be done in under an hour."

"What a blessing to have all the help," Butch remarked as he and Herb joined the others for coffee and a doughnut. Taking a break felt good, but both men were anxious to get the herd milked and put back out to pasture. Fatigue had not yet settled in.

Word of a family needing help had traveled fast in the small tightly-knit community. Neighbors, friends, and community leaders offered support unparalleled in larger cities. The kindness of mankind gave the angel community great joy.

By the time Butch sat down for a late lunch with his wife, there was a plan for the lumber mill to deliver supplies needed to rebuild the loft. Friends and neighbors had volunteered to help with both construction and daily milking until the loft was completed. The herd had been taken care of, and the Emig's banker had called to sympathize on the unfortunate events. He assured Butch that the money was there for whatever repairs needed to be done.

Mary sat on the porch beside her husband. "We are so blessed, aren't we?"

"Ayuh, we are. Too bad it takes a tragedy to show us that. I know it's early in the day but, Princess Mary, may I have this dance?"

Mary smiled and nodded, her red curls falling across her forehead. "Why, of course. What music is your pleasure, my love?"

"How about Glenn Miller's 'In the Mood'?"

"One of my favorites." She grabbed his hand and pulled him into the dining room, where she put a record on the Victrola. They moved a few chairs to give themselves enough space to twirl, jump, and jive to the music.

Sandy and the other guardians gathered outside on the porch, where Sandy reminded the angels of the words in Jeremiah 31:13: "'Then shall the young women rejoice in the dance and the young men and the old shall be merry. I will turn their mourning into joy, I will comfort them, and give them gladness for sorrow.' Doesn't it gladden your hearts to see this couple thankful despite the misfortune and tragedy?"

Thirty-Five

The Emig family gathered for their weekly Sunday dinner at Fred and Cora's home. Family members and Herb filled the dining room as they held hands to pray. Fred gestured to everyone to bow their heads.

"Heavenly Father, bless all of us gathered here today, and those family members who cannot be with us. We ask that You bless this food for our nourishment and us to Your service. Amen."

Conversations and laughter erupted as the food was passed and mothers fixed plates for small children. When everyone had been served, chatter ceased. The clinking of silverware signaled that each family member was busy tasting the meticulously prepared food.

Fred finished chewing and paused to reflect. "Well, this has been some year, hasn't it? Who would have thought that one of our neighbors on Lyon Brook Road would be a firebug?" Murmurs of affirmation resounded around the table. "Butch, is everything back to normal in the barn?"

"Yes, Dad." He nodded at Herb across the table. "We're finally back into the swing of things, the cows are producing record amounts of milk, and things couldn't be better."

"It's November and hunting season is right around

the corner. Are either you or Herb planning on hunting this deer season, Butch?" Fred pointed with his knife at the other men around the table. "Chet, Carl, how about you two? Going hunting?"

"I know I am," Butch answered. "We count on having venison in the freezer every year. I'm just going out into the woods on our property where I put out salt licks. I know the whitetails are out there. I look forward to Mary cooking venison."

Herb chimed in, "I plan on going until I bag one to contribute to the freezer. I like Mary's cooking too."

Mary blushed at the compliment. Cora smiled, remembering all the cooking lessons she gave Mary while living on the farm. She had done her job well for her son to rave about his wife's culinary skills. Cora and Mary shared a glance as Cora winked.

Both Chet and Carl admitted that they wouldn't be hunting.

"It's going into our busiest car-buying season, so I'm hesitant to take any days off," Chet reminded everyone.

"Butch, have you posted 'No Trespassing' signs around the farm? Can't have hunters mistaking the cows for deer," Fred said. "You just never know what the city slickers will shoot at during hunting season, and we gotta keep our cows safe."

"Yeah, I did, Dad. Posted signs everywhere." Butch hoped he had put up enough because hunting season would begin the next day at dawn.

On Monday, Butch and Herb got used to hearing sporadic gunfire throughout the day. Hunters walked all along the property adjacent to their land. Neighbors reassured Butch that the only people hunting on their properties were family members. But Butch didn't worry about his neighbors as much as he worried about the novices and inconsiderate hunters from Binghamton, Syracuse, or New York City. Those wild cards descended on the plentiful deer herds in the central part of the state like locusts.

One week later, Butch and Herb began to call the cattle at four o'clock in the afternoon. The cows had been out to pasture, and it was time for evening milking. Instead of seeing the entire herd come down the gently sloping hillsides toward the barn, they saw only twenty-three cows moving toward them as dusk was upon them.

"That's only part of our herd," Butch said. "Where the blazes are the rest?"

"Good question. It's hunting season, so I think we should go look after we put these cattle into stanchions. I'll get the truck and some flashlights while you secure the cows," Herb said. "Meet you in the driveway."

Butch finished and grabbed a barn coat. He stepped outside, dreading what they might find.

The angels joined the men in silent prayer, accompanying them in the truck to scour the pastures in search of the missing dairy cows.

Reaching the rocky land at the outermost edge of Emig property, the two men hadn't found any of the missing cows.

"Well, I'll be!" Butch exclaimed as they came upon an open gate. "This leads to the land owned by the railroad. We had trespassers." He threw the truck into park, pulled on the emergency brake, and jumped out.

Herb followed. "Butch, take this flashlight. Why don't we split up to cover more ground?"

"Good idea. Drive whatever cattle you find back toward the gate and pray that a train doesn't come. Let's start calling them."

The two men took off to run alongside the tracks, calling, "Ca Boss, Ca Boss."

Butch was the first to find some of his prize Ayrshire bovines lumbering along a flat strip of land. They had been grazing on the tall weeds on either side of the railroad tracks. Others were trying to walk across the tracks to get to the grass. None of the cows had wandered onto the bridge over the gorge. Butch shuddered at the thought.

The cows heard the men calling. They looked at the beams from the flashlights, then turned and slowly started moving toward the men. Butch grabbed two by the halters to lead them back across the tracks toward the open gate. Crossing the rails, stepping in between railroad ties, and walking on coarse uneven gravel was a difficult task with two cows in tow. At the same time, Butch's head was on a swivel, watching and listening for a train in the distance. He led several cows across the tracks, herding them through the open gate and returning to the tracks before hearing the train whistle.

The rails were lightly humming. The train would be upon them in a few minutes.

Butch felt his pulse quicken. His breath was coming faster as he tried to hurry his cows along. With a few more bovines to bring back across the tracks, time was of the essence.

The animals noticed the urgency in Butch's voice. They, too, heard the train whistle and could feel the vibration of the rails. One of the cows mooed in anguish, having wedged her hoof between the railroad ties.

The whistle sounded again.

Butch saw Herb with several cows in tow coming from the opposite direction. Their heavy milk-laden udders swayed back and forth. As Herb hustled them through the gate, Butch beckoned him for help.

"I've got a hoof stuck here. Gimme a hand, Herb. Between the two of us, maybe we can keep her from panicking and breaking a leg."

Both men supported the massive animal's left front leg as they maneuvered it to release the hoof. The whistle sounded louder; the train was getting closer.

Butch paused, looked heavenward, and prayed aloud, "Lord, we need help. I beg you."

Butch's guardian angel said to Herb's angel, "I'll calm the frightened animal while stretching the ties to release the trapped hoof. And you help the others cross the tracks and get through the open gate to join the herd. Now to get these two men to remove themselves from danger."

The angels used their wings to create a strong wind as Butch and Herb sprinted behind the freed cow toward the open gate. Butch pointed over his shoulder. "Herb, I can see the headlight on the train. I just hate it when this happens."

Herb couldn't help but laugh at Butch's attempt at levity but sobered when he thought about an unpleasant, criminal incident on these same tracks—an incident that had put his boss's life in danger. Trying to match Butch's mood, he said, "Butch, the cows are starting to run. I'll do my best to 'steer' them in the right direction."

"Okay, okay, you're real funny tonight, Herbster. Let's get moo-ving."

The two men ran with the rest of the herd, slapping them on the hindquarters as the train started crossing the bridge over the gorge.

"Hurry, bossy! Herb, go, go, go!"

The conductor blasted the train's whistle to clear the tracks.

With both men and seventeen cows out of immediate danger, the procession gathered on Emig land. The cows grazed on grasses poking up from the light snow cover. Butch doubled back to close the gate. He feigned collapse, lying on the cold hard ground. A cow approached him and licked the salt off his sweaty face. He laughed, then got up, swatting a few cows on their rumps to get them moving down the hill toward the familiar yellow barn. He and Herb got in the truck and turned on the headlights and the heater. They rubbed their cold hands together as the lights pointed the way home for the lumbering cattle ahead of them.

Herb pointed to one of them. "Butch, she's limping." As if on cue, the cow began to bleat with every wobbly step. It took thirty minutes for the jittery cattle to make it to the barnyard. The two men ushered every last straggler of the prize-winning herd inside the barn.

The cows systematically went to their assigned stanchions to drink the fresh cold water pumped into each elevated water bowl. The hay in each food trough was saturated with blackstrap molasses. Both Butch and Herb knew their primary goal was to get the herd calmed down and back into their regular routine as quickly as possible. Butch turned the barn radio on to a station playing soothing music. They set about washing each animal's udder with warm soapy water and a soft cloth. One by one, the cows were hooked up to the milking machines as they ate and drank. When the process was complete, the milking machinery was washed and dried. Herb and Butch could finally take a breath.

"You know, I sure hope the scare of running from the train doesn't affect these beautiful cows," Butch mused aloud.

"Time will tell," Herb replied, hoping that their

milk production didn't drop off. That, he knew, would be devastating to the Emig's finances. In the next minute, a thought steeped with guilt percolated in Herb's mind. He wondered if he should fess up to being the man who tried to blow up the railroad bridge. Herb knew he'd better think long and hard about confessing. It could change everything, even though he knew he was a different man now.

Back at the truck, Herb's guardian voiced his concern to Butch's angel. "Milk production is a dairy farm's lifeblood. We need to lift this herd up in prayer. We need to support these two, especially Herb. He's having quite an internal struggle. The future might be uncertain for both of these men."

"I've gotta go back to that upper gate with some sturdier chains and padlocks. We have to make sure no one can trespass again," Butch said. "I shudder to think what would have happened if we hadn't been able to get the cattle back onto our land when we did. Sure as shootin' the train would have killed or injured most of those cows." Butch talked to Herb's back as they completed the morning barn chores.

Herb turned around, nodding his head. "I'll help you reinforce the gate as soon as we finish up here. With this cold snap, we're going to leave the girls in the barn, right?"

"Right. After yesterday's excitement, I'd like to give them a day of rest and pampering. The milk production was down a bit this morning, so I'd like to continue putting molasses on every bit of hay they get."

Herb could see the worry etched into Butch's face. His gut went into spasm.

The two men got into the pickup and headed to

the perimeter of Emig land with their chains and padlocks. Butch had already called the sheriff's office and adjacent neighbors to report the trespassers.

That evening Herb and Butch prepared to milk the herd. As they gently washed the udders of the traumatized cows, the men couldn't help but notice that they weren't as full of milk as usual. The men measured the amount extracted from each cow with sinking hearts, noting it on clipboards hanging at each stanchion.

Butch signaled Herb that he was going to the house for a few minutes. After taking off his boots on the porch, he walked through the kitchen door and went straight to the phone. "Jenny, can you get Doc Langman for me?"

"Sure, Butch, one moment, please."

After a lengthy conversation with the veterinarian, Butch hung up the phone and returned to the barn.

Herb looked at Butch as he walked through the door. From the look on his face, Herb knew the news wasn't going to be encouraging.

"I called Doc Langman," Butch said as he jammed his hands inside the front of his coveralls.

"And?" Herb prompted.

"I took some notes. He agreed with the steps we've taken to boost their nutritional status, keep them calm, and watch for milk production trends, but he wants us to consider others." Butch turned and walked into the cold storage room.

Herb knew his boss was upset. He'd be distraught, too, if it was his herd that was affected. He knew Butch just needed a minute.

When he got himself together, Butch emerged, holding a clipboard to his chest. "We've got our work cut out for us for the next four months, Herb. It's not going to be easy. The trauma these cows experienced will take a toll. To top it off, the vet says some of them may have eaten toxic weeds, which will ruin their milk. We'll be able to smell it and taste it. If I had those trespassers in front of me right now, I'd gladly horsewhip them for leaving that gate open."

Herb nodded in agreement, "I'd be right there with you, Butch."

Thirty-Six

F ive months later, the herd was whittled down to two-thirds of what it once was. Many cows had been sold off for meat. The task ahead was to rebuild. But that took a lot of money—money that Butch didn't have.

After the morning milking, while Herb was busy cleaning up in the barn, Butch walked toward the house, thinking about his lost revenues from decreased milk production. He knew he couldn't make it up from the sale of eggs, grains, or hogs and was afraid he wouldn't be able to feed his family, pay Herb, and stay on top of mounting bills.

Butch's guardian hovered nearby. *I'll spend time in prayer, and with the help of the Lord, we can show Butch the way. As scripture says in Jeremiah 29:11: For surely I know the plans I have for you, says the Lord, plans for your welfare and not for harm, to give you a future with hope.*

That evening, Butch was reading the *Norwich Sun*. A Help Wanted advertisement caught his attention. The ad was appealing, and Butch was desperate. He called the telephone number and scheduled an interview. Within two weeks, Butch got an offer to represent Farm Bureau Life Insurance Company as a salesman. He accepted the offer. With his reputation as an award-winning farmer in the tri-county area, Butch was a desirable commodity. He was a well-spoken, good looking young man who presented an impressive contact list. His bosses liked the total package. Classwork and field training, followed by exams, took place over the next few months. Butch did well. Mary bought him a smart leather briefcase and a case of black pens as a graduation gift. She supported his efforts and wanted more than anything for him to succeed.

Herb took complete responsibility for the farm while Butch studied. The reliable and indispensable hired man kept the farm running while Butch sold life insurance from door to door. Butch helped with the early morning milking and tried his best to be home each evening for the evening chores. It all seemed to work until one day it didn't.

"Mary, I feel like I'm burning the candle at both ends." It was eight o'clock, and he was exhausted as he plopped into his chair for dinner. The younger children were in bed, and the two older ones were getting ready for bed.

Mary put a bowl of beef stew in front of her husband as she sat down beside him. "I've seen the worry lines in your face, honey. And I know you're doing a lot of tossing and turning at night," she said, stroking his arm.

"I can't turn my brain off when I go to bed. I'm worrying about the farm and doing this insurance stuff all night long." He picked up his spoon and scooped up a piece of potato covered in thick brown gravy. "Wow, this smells good." He seemed to relax with each mouthful of the hearty homemade stew. "Tastes good too."

Mary smiled at the compliment.

"I've been doing some serious thinking about selling the farm." Butch searched his wife's eyes for approval.

"Really?" Mary's eyebrows rose, and she put down her knife and fork. She studied her husband. "Are you sure you're ready to give up farming and walk away after all these years?"

He looked out the picture window into the darkness of the night. He knew what was out there: green pastures, barns, and chicken houses, not to mention all the animals and farm machinery. All of it had consumed his life since he'd been a small boy. He knew nothing different.

Butch sighed. "I need to talk to Mom and Dad about this. If we're going to survive, I've got to make some changes. With God's help, if everything works out, I'll be content to move on."

Butch resumed eating while Mary sat in silence.

Finally she said, "Let's call your dad in the morning to see if he has time to see us. He's a smart thoughtful man. He may have some ideas you haven't considered."

Guardian angels hovered nearby, hearing the conversation. Lifting their voices, the angels prayed to the Lord for a viable plan to become apparent.

༒

When Butch and Mary arrived at Fred and Cora's home the next morning, they held hands as they walked to the front door. Gail bounced ahead of them, excited to get to Grandma's toy box. She played there while the grownups talked. All the other children were in school.

Once inside and seated around the dining room table, Fred listened as Butch and Mary laid out their detailed plan. Nodding every now and then, Fred looked over Butch's handwritten T-chart in front of him. The "pros" were on one side of the paper; the "cons" were on the other side.

"This chart looks like you've been quite thoughtful about the decision you have before you as a family. Under the circumstances, I'm not surprised at the option under consideration. Neither of you could have predicted the turn of events that led you down this path. Have you talked to any interested parties yet?"

"Only in generalities, Butch said. "We wanted to run everything by you first."

The two couples discussed every option and scenario over fresh-perked coffee and cake right out of the oven.

Fred studied the faces of his son and daughter-in-law. "I suppose the next step would be talking specifics with a buyer or buyers."

"I suppose you're right, Dad." Butch sat back, and for the first time in a long time, he relaxed, having reconciled this emotional decision in his mind.

The angels had heard Butch's prayers at night and as he worked during the day. He prayed to find someone who loved the land and Lyon Brook Farm as much as he did. The angels prayed for the same thing.

Cora said, "In all of this discussion, I've neglected to ask if you've thought about another place to live."

"It's funny you ask, Mom. I was mentioning my plans to Doc Langman. He and Cathy are building a new house and vet clinic. They're going to look for a tenant for their old house. I told him, 'Look no more, we'll take it.'" Butch laughed. "Can you believe it? It's almost as if God planned it that way."

Cora clapped her hands. "That puts my grandchildren just across town from us. I'm delighted."

Mary leaned over and gave her husband a hug. "We'd better be going. The kids will be home from school soon, and I want to stop by the grocery store to get some packing boxes. I'll need to start cleaning out closets and cupboards."

The couple said goodbye and drove toward their farm, lost in thoughts of their future. After crossing the bridge over the Chenango River, they followed the winding road that meandered past pastures and grain fields. As they turned down the familiar dirt road, they looked up at the imposing Lyon Brook Bridge. It had stood guard over the family's land and home since before they were born. They were going to miss all of this.

The angels agreed.

Thirty-Seven

Herb lay in bed with his hands behind his head, staring at the ceiling. He was trying to fathom what it would be like not living on this farm, in this house. His heart skipped a beat when he remembered the words Butch uttered a few weeks back. "Herb, I have to sell the farm. I can't make enough without working another job, and it's taking a toll on all of us."

Remembering Butch's burdensome words, Herb wanted to throw up. He'd thought of little else since that conversation. He got out of bed and went to his dresser to retrieve his savings account book. Opening the little blue book, Herb studied the balance. Five thousand dollars wasn't enough to even consider buying a farm. He'd always been a penny pincher, but couldn't save much on a hired hand's salary. He knew he had to stay busy today, or thoughts of leaving Lyon Brook Farm would overwhelm him.

He got up, dressed, and went downstairs to join Butch for breakfast.

"Good morning, Herb," said Mary.

"Morning, Miss Mary." Herb grabbed a mug and poured himself a coffee before he sat across from Butch.

"You got mail yesterday, Herb." Butch gestured to an envelope placed face down on the table next to Herb's plate.

"Sorry I didn't give it to you sooner, but it was mixed up with my mail on the desk." Butch pointed over his shoulder to the old rolltop in the corner, strewn with papers. "I don't know how I find anything over there," he said.

Herb picked up the envelope, wondering who could have sent him a letter. He turned it over to see the name and address of an attorney in Syracuse. His heart rate increased, and his palms got sweaty as he thought about a past life he'd rather forget—a past life Butch didn't know anything about. Dropping the envelope back on the table, Herb studied a pattern of loose coffee grounds floating on the top of the cream he had just added to his cup.

"Aren't you gonna open your mail?" Butch asked.

"Yeah, later." Herb changed the subject. "I think I'm gonna help myself to some biscuits and gravy first. I'm kind of hungry."

"Well, all right then, I hear you on that one." Butch took two biscuits and passed the plate to Herb. The men ate in silence.

The sun was coming up, signaling milking time. Herb picked up the envelope. He folded it in half and stuffed it in his overall pocket. "Let's see to those cows," he said as he headed outside.

After Butch and Herb finished milking the cows, they put them out to pasture. For the next few hours, they worked side by side cleaning up the barn, loading the manure spreader, and putting down fresh hay for the cattle. Both double barn doors were open to the sunshine and fresh air. The old wooden radio was tuned to a station playing Big Band music.

Herb was deep in thought when Butch waved at him from the other end of the barn. Over the sound of Benny Goodman, the King of Swing, Butch hollered, "Let's take a break. Meet me on the porch. I'll bring coffee."

Herb broke out in a sweat. "Wait, Butch. There's something I need to get off my chest." He'd been thinking long and hard about telling Butch about his past. Now he needed to be honest about why he'd come here ten years ago. He wondered if his friendship with Butch was solid enough to withstand the brutal truth. Certainly, he had proved his loyalty and trustworthiness over time. He and Butch had developed a brotherly bond; he felt it. But he also felt a specter of doubt looming over him. He pulled a handkerchief out of his back pocket and wiped his brow. "And I need to tell you before I open that letter I got. It's from a lawyer."

Butch could see sweat forming on Herb's forehead and upper lip. "Herb, it's me. What do you have to say that's got you so nervous?"

"It's just that I... I have something I need to confess. Uh, you know the man I am now, but I wasn't always a good guy."

"Hey, Herb, I did some dumb stuff as a kid too."

"Well, I did some dumb stuff and some horrible stuff. Before I came to work for you, I was living and working in Ithaca."

"Yeah, I remember—"

"Well, I went to Ithaca to get out of town," Herb interrupted. "Because the police were looking for me for something I did. Something terrible."

Butch took a step forward. "Herb? What did you do?"

"Oh God, Butch... I'm the stupid guy that hit Randy Fisher over the head and tried to blow up the Lyon Brook Bridge." Herb took a deep breath. "It's eaten at me all these years, but that's not the worst part."

Butch scowled. "What's the worst part, Herb? What

could be worse than hitting Randy with a bat?"

"The worst part..." Herb broke down, sobbing loudly. His shoulders shook. Lifting his tear-streaked face, Herb said, "Revenge drove me. It was all I thought about. I wanted to get back at the railroad for firing me by blowing up the damn bridge. But the worst part"—he paused to take a ragged breath—"the worst part was that my anger shifted toward you for stopping me. Instead of being disgusted with my actions, I felt like I needed to get even with you." With a loud honk, Herb blew his nose on his handkerchief.

"Is that why you applied for the hired-hand position when you got back from Ithaca?"

"Yup, it's the only reason. I was on my best behavior because I wanted to get in good with you." Herb hung his head in shame. "But you and Mary—and Fred and Cora—were so good to me from that first day..."

"Yeah, you became part of the family."

"Butch, everyone welcomed me with open arms and gave me something I never had—acceptance. The kids touched my heart, you all trusted me, and it changed me. It made me different. You made me a better man."

"You know, Herb, God works in mysterious ways." Butch fished around in his overall pockets for something. Checking one pocket and then another, he pulled out a small jackknife and tossed it to Herb.

"I think this might belong to you," Butch said with a grim twist to his mouth.

"It looks just like a knife my mom gave me when I was eight. I lost mine years ago. I scratched my initials on the side." He turned the knife over to see HB crudely engraved in the metal. "Oh, my Lord, it's mine." Herb looked up at Butch. "How? Where?"

"I found it on the railroad bridge that night, right

next to some dynamite that was tied to the structure."

Herb stared at his friend. "You knew it was me?"

"I suspected."

"And you kept me around?"

"Yeah, I wanted to keep my eye on you." Butch grinned slowly. "And then you kind of grew on me."

Herb couldn't process his friend's facial expression. "Butch, this knife is evidence,"

"Who's to say, Herb? It's not really evidence. We don't know how or when it ended up on the tracks almost a dozen years ago. And even though Randy is fine now, he doesn't remember a thing. Besides, if I hadn't found the knife I wouldn't have been able to cut the dynamite charges off the bridge so quickly..."

"But... but what are you gonna do?"

"What am I going to do? I found a knife you lost, and I'm giving it back to you. The case was closed years ago because of a lack of evidence. The sheriff told me that himself, Herb. In my eyes, you've redeemed yourself a hundred times over for a reckless foolish act a long time ago. Besides, I checked this fact and the statute of limitations on assault and battery in this state is long over."

Herb looked confused. "Then what is this letter about?" he said, fishing the envelope from his pocket.

"I don't know," said Butch. "But whatever it is, we're here to help you get through it. Let's take that break and find out what it is."

Herb walked to the sink and scrubbed his hands and forearms with Lava soap and hot water. He dried off with a clean towel before walking toward the house, where Butch awaited him at the picnic table on the porch.

The angels remained near the barn in the morning sunshine. One turned to the other. "Watching the blessing of forgiveness and redemption unfold is always satisfying. Praise be to God!"

"We lucked out," Butch told Herb. "Mary was just taking some blueberry muffins out of the oven. I snagged a couple." Butch pushed a plate with muffins across the table. Mary came out with the coffee and fixings.

"Oh, man. It's hard to keep my girlish figure around here," Herb joked. He didn't realize it, but Butch had lifted a huge weight from his shoulders.

Herb took his mail out of his pocket and slid his knife under the loose end of the flap, opening what could be a Pandora's Box. He pulled out an official-looking typewritten letter and began to read. Butch and Mary watched, transfixed at Herb's changing facial expressions.

Herb was silent. Then he re-read the letter and looked up at Butch. "Do you have an offer on the farm yet?"

Butch looked surprised. "Well, I've been talking with someone interested in our co-op arrangement with Cornell. We're in the early stages, but I think he's got the money. Why?"

"I've got the money, Butch! I want to buy Lyon Brook Farm! You know how much I love this place."

"What in tarnation are you talking about, Herb? Did you find a money tree?"

"No, it fell out of this envelope. I've inherited a bunch of money from my mother."

"I thought your mother left you years ago. What in the world are you talking about?"

"According to this attorney, Mr. Posefsky, my mother was a rich woman when she died." Herb read from the letter, "'Mr. Herbert Brunner, you are Twila Brunner

Mantz's only heir.'" Herb put the letter down and looked at Butch, "Obviously, my mother remarried. I never knew what happened to her. I suspected she was trying to get away from my abusive father; she must have divorced him." Picking up the letter, he continued to read and summarize. "'She married William Mantz, who pre-deceased her. Mr. Mantz had an extensive collection of antique tractors. He also owned three hundred acres of prime land around Oneida Lake, near Syracuse.'"

Herb had to stop reading because he could no longer see the words on the page through his tears. He put the letter down and wiped his eyes with the back of his hands.

Taking a deep breath, Herb looked across the table. "Butch, all of that stuff is in my mother's estate. I want to buy Lyon Brook Farm if you can hold on until the estate is settled."

Mary pulled a floral handkerchief out of her apron pocket to wipe the tears streaming down her cheeks. Butch sat at the table with his mouth open.

Herb continued. "It looks like I'm going to have enough money to buy the farm and enough operating capital to rebuild the herd."

A chorus of praise emanated from the angels who now surrounded the three. This was a joyous solution that no one had expected.

Butch took a sip of his coffee. "I wonder how the lawyer found you."

"He says here that he tracked me from my driver's license, which lists this address." Herb looked down at the letter, reading through the information. "He says Mom told him she didn't try to find me because she was afraid my father would hurt me if she had any contact with me. The only way Dad let her go and gave her a divorce was if she promised not to take me with her or ever come back for me. If she did, he told her he would track us down and kill us both. She was terrified of him. I get that." Herb read more. "I have to contact Mr. Posefsky to set up an appointment to sign papers. Decisions have to be made on what to do with the properties, the antique tractors, and other stuff."

Butch wiped his mouth with the back of his hand. "I would suggest that you take someone you trust with you to this appointment. Making a lot of important decisions like that can be overwhelming. Besides, if there are household furnishings involved, you might want to hang on to them. Have you thought about furnishing this big house?"

Herb's eyes widened. "Good grief! You're right. No, I didn't give it one thought. I only thought of the farm and farming, not living in the house by myself. It's kind of overwhelming and all. Maybe I'd be better off staying in the apartment and renting out the house. Whaddya think, Butch?"

"That's what I'd do. Of course, you may not be single forever, especially when the women of Chenango County discover that you've inherited a lot of money. But you could live in the apartment until it got too small for your family, like we did.."

"Would you go with me to Syracuse, Butch? I trust your judgment. I can't think of anyone else I'd want by my side. Do you think we can swing that?"

"I'm honored, Herb. And I think we can work it out. We'll get the milking done early tomorrow, take off for Syracuse, get your business done, and return in time for the evening chores." Butch got up from the picnic table and punched Herb's shoulder. "We've got work to finish up before you call that lawyer about our trip to Syracuse, Herb. Let's get to it."

Thirty-Eight

Herb and Butch left the farm at seven o'clock in the morning. They planned to stop for breakfast before meeting the attorney handling Twila Mantz's estate.

Finding a diner on Main Street, they were seated and given menus. Both men knew what they wanted and placed their breakfast order. When the platters arrived, Herb eyed his cinnamon toast before biting into it.

"I'd like to see my mother's house, the antique tractor collection, and the property near Oneida Lake if possible."

"Sure. If we need to, I'll call Randy or Jim to see if they can milk our herd tonight. It's not like we have a full house right now," Butch replied.

"I appreciate that, Butch. I'm glad you're here to keep my head straight, but if we can get it all done today, I'd like to."

The attorney's office opened at nine o'clock, and Herb was the lawyer's first client. After signing necessary papers to probate the will, Mr. Posefsky handed Herb two sets of keys. "Your mother's house has been unoccupied for several months, so don't be surprised at cobwebs." Offering a piece of paper, he added, "I wrote the address and directions to the house on one side and the directions to the lake property on the reverse. You'll note that the keys are labeled; one set

197

is for the house, the other for the barn where the tractors are stored. Don't lose those keys. They're the only ones I have right now. I was planning to go to the locksmith and have another set made, just didn't get there. I'll be in the office until five-thirty if you want to drop off the keys before returning to Norwich."

Herb and Butch thanked Mr. Posefsky. "I'll be sure to get them back before you close," offered Herb.

Herb recited the directions for Butch, who found Twila's home without any problem. After pulling into the driveway, both men sat and stared at the beautiful two-story Victorian home with its spectacular landscaping and perfectly groomed grounds.

"Wow! I never... did you ever... will you look at this?" Herb stammered.

They got out of the car, walked up the sidewalk to the front porch, and put the key in the front door. As soon as the door opened, revealing a large foyer featuring a grand staircase and formal chandelier, Herb immediately felt out of place.

"Wow," Butch exclaimed as he took it all in. "You'll want to hang on to a lot of this stuff for your own home, Herb."

Herb looked around. Although he'd hadn't lived under the same roof with his mother for decades, he saw his mother's favorite colors everywhere. "You're right, Butch. I do want to keep it. She was a classy lady despite our circumstances. What I can't use right now can go into storage."

Walking through each room—touching wood, running his hand over upholstery, and seeing the latest appliances in the modern kitchen—Herb marveled at his blessings. "Butch, is this real? Are we in my mother's house with all her stuff that I inherited?"

"Yup, we are. And yes, you did inherit it. But I don't blame you for wanting to pinch yourself. This has happened so fast. And this"—he waved his arm to encompass everything in their vision—"is so darn ritzy. It's hard to digest it all."

"I only wish I had known back then why she left. I would have found her somehow, dad or no dad. I'm glad to have her things, but I regret that I never got to see her again," Herb said.

They heard someone coming in the front door, so they walked out into the foyer to investigate. An older woman with a full market basket over her arm approached them.

"Hello, I'm a friend of Twila's. My name's Thelma. I saw the car in the driveway and thought I'd bring lunch."

"That's very nice of you, but we were going to eat at the diner on Main Street where we had breakfast. We don't want to make a mess."

"Nonsense," the woman answered. "I'll have this ready in a few minutes. You go about your business."

She walked past Herb on her way to the refrigerator. He was caught off guard by a familiar scent. Instantly, he was pulled back to his childhood with a memory of his mother sitting next to him on his bed as she read him a story. Herb followed the woman toward the kitchen. He paused in the doorway and looked at her. She lifted her eyes from the bread she was slicing and gave him a wink.

Despite the chills running down his spine, Herb turned to follow Butch to the ornate curved stairway as Butch was saying something. "... and you know, it'll be nice for you to finally have a bigger bed."

"Huh?"

"I said, with what I think we'll find up here, you'll have a complete bedroom set, and it would be nice for you to have a bigger bed."

As they stepped into the first bedroom, Herb nodded. "Yup, it sure will be nice."

After walking through the entire home, they returned to the kitchen where bratwurst on Kaiser rolls waited for them on the kitchen table. Thelma poured fresh-squeezed lemonade into tall glasses and placed some freshly baked cookies on the table. "Those are for dessert after you eat your sandwiches." She emphasized the "after."

Herb mused aloud, "My favorite thing to eat when I was a kid was bratwurst on a Kaiser roll, and I love fresh-squeezed lemonade. My mom used to make this lunch for me when I was a boy." Despite the lump forming in his throat, he bit into his sandwich. He couldn't take his eyes off Thelma.

The old lady met his gaze and said, "I know; she told me."

Herb cleared his throat. "Won't you join us?" He had so many questions for her.

"No, thank you. I best be on my way as soon as you're finished and after I straighten up here. Twila would just hate us leaving a mess."

The two men finished lunch, including every last cookie.

"Thelma, that was delicious! Better than any diner," Herb declared.

Butch carried their dishes to the sink and put them in the warm, sudsy water while Herb wiped off the table and countertops. They thanked her for her hospitality and walked toward the grand hallway and the front door.

Thelma caught Herb's eye at the last moment. "I'm glad you got your knife back."

Herb faltered but continued following Butch. He stopped and turned back toward the kitchen. "I better check to see if she has a key to lock up since we're leaving."

Suddenly, Herb was struck by Thelma's last comment. How in the world had she known he got his knife back? And how did she know it was ever lost?

Herb walked into the kitchen and found it spotless. The woman wasn't there, so he called out, "Hello?"

Butch answered. "Yeah, hello, I'm out by the front door."

Herb called out again, "Hello? Thelma, are you here?"

Butch appeared. "Are you talking to me?"

"No, I was calling Thelma, the lady who just brought us lunch. Did she walk past you?"

"No."

"Well, did you see her go out the back door?" Herb asked.

"No, but we didn't unlock the back door. The front door is the only one we used."

"She's gone, Butch. Like she was never here. She smelled like my mom, waited on us like my mom, and made my favorite lunch. What on earth is going on?"

Butch scratched his head as a revelation percolated through his brain. "Maybe she wasn't of this earth, Herb."

"What the heck does that mean?" Herb was getting flustered.

"Maybe she was an angel," Butch offered. "Stranger things have happened."

"Butch, she knew I got my knife back—the one my mother gave me. How did she know that?"

"Angels know stuff, Herb. I'm more convinced than ever that you have a guardian watching out for you."

The two guardians looked at each other and winked before lifting their voices to Heaven. They called these visits angel sightings and knew the events could bring peace and comfort to loved ones left on Earth. They had wanted Herb to feel his mother's essence. It was apparent that he did.

As unsettled as Herb felt, he and Butch had much more to accomplish in a short amount of time.

"I can't wait to see what's in the barn," Herb said as he inserted the key into the padlock. They pushed the door open and found an impressive array of antique tractors.

"Holy cow!" Herb scratched the back of his neck and said to Butch, "Can you believe this?"

Walking the length of the barn, they counted the tractors, noting each make and model. After they completed the inventory, they locked the barn, got in the car, and drove toward the lake, searching for acreage that now belonged to Herb.

Standing on the shore of Oneida Lake, Herb turned to Butch. "I have to be dreaming. This whole day has been so hard to digest. After years of scratching to make a living, I find out that I'm the owner of all this..." He put his hands over his eyes to hide the tears. "And there's nothing my dad can do about it now, even if he's still alive."

Butch patted his friend on the back. "I know how much you're able to appreciate all this, Herb. Maybe if it had happened sooner, you would have reacted differently."

The men walked the waterfront and were struck by the view. Herb crossed his arms and announced, "This is the view I want from my deck. I guess we'll have to tell the lawyer I want an acre for myself."

"I reckon you'll have to have it surveyed, but Mr.

Posefsky can guide you there." Butch continued, "This has been some crazy day, buddy. I get it. It's a lot to process, but it's a shame your mother can't see what a life-changing gift she left you."

Herb nodded, "Yup, that's for sure. Hey, we'd better get moving to drop those keys off."

Herb's angel pondered the ways of God. *Who says Twila can't see what she's done for the son she had to abandon all those years ago? Our Lord can do anything. She was a faithful, God-fearing woman.*

"Think you can direct me back to the lawyer's office and home again?" Butch had a smirk on his face as he looked at Herb.

"I sure can. Got the directions right here. Let's get moving."

After dropping the keys at the lawyer's office, Herb sat in the passenger seat while Butch drove them back to Lyon Brook Farm. Herb scribbled a list of questions on a piece of paper. Butch concentrated on the road.

Riding on top of the vehicle, the two guardians had their heads together. Herb's angel said, "If Herb had any idea what a tidy sum he was going receive, it would be overwhelming. Getting proceeds from gradual sales is going to give him a chance to feel rich in increments."

Butch's angel responded, "More important than the inheritance is the strengthened bond between the two men on this trip. I'm so pleased to see them share another celestial experience."

Twila's attorney contacted a realtor to make arrangements for the sale of all the property except for Herb's plot. He hired an auctioneer who specialized in antiques to set up the tractor sale. As for the contents of the house, Herb wanted everything in storage except what he decided to move to the farm. The rest he'd figure out later. He did not want to make any rash decisions regarding his mother's belongings.

Six weeks later, the final papers were signed, transferring ownership of Lyon Brook Farm from Butch and Mary Emig to Herb Brunner.

"You know there's no hurry for you to move out of the house, right? You never said when Doc Langman's place would be ready for you," Herb commented.

Butch had both his hands shoved into his pants pockets as the two men walked toward Herb's shiny new Ford truck. Mary had signed the papers the day before so she could be with the children while Butch signed them today.

"It's ready now," Butch said to his friend. "The painting and cleaning are done, and we'll start to move next week, one load at a time. I've got a couple of pickup trucks lined up."

"You can use mine too," Herb offered.

"Well, I hesitated to ask because it's so new and shiny, and I'd feel bad if something happened."

"Hey, I'm Mr. Moneybags now. If it gets scratched I'll use it as a work truck and buy myself a new one." Looking at Butch through the cab of the shiny truck that still smelled new, both burst out laughing as they stepped on the running boards to get into their seats. The two men simultaneously shut their doors.

Butch needed the laugh. It was a somber day. He no longer owned Lyon Brook Farm.

Herb read his former boss's mind. He knew this was hard for Butch. Changing the subject, he said, "My attorney tells me there's a For Sale sign on my mom's house, and the tractor auction was successful. The money should be in my bank account any day now. And at the lake, the surveyors have stakes marking my acre of land. I found a builder from North Syracuse and gave him a call. He's got plans for a new design he called an A-frame. It's popular right now. I'm kinda interested in seeing what it looks like."

"That sounds great. I'd like to see those plans too." Butch grinned and added, "Mr. Moneybags." They both burst out laughing. Herb turned left, crossed over the Chenango River, and continued on a back road to the farm.

"I hope you and the family feel free to come to the lake as often as you can make it. You know I'd love to have you visit anytime."

"We know, Herb. I appreciate the invitation. I'm not one to pass up the chance for some good fishing, and the kids always love playing in the water."

"I've made arrangements with a moving company to have some of Mom's furniture delivered to the farm. What I don't use in the apartment, I'll be storing in the attic." Herb kept his eyes on the narrow road.

"It's nice-looking, good-quality stuff," Butch acknowledged.

"Did I tell you I interviewed a farm manager?"

"No, I don't think so. If you did, I was so busy I missed it. You can afford to have full-time help. It's a good idea." Butch stared straight ahead as they made another left turn onto the dirt road leading to Lyon Brook Farm.

"Yeah, he's married with three kids in high school. I offered to rent him the farmhouse. I'll be traveling around to different cattle auctions looking for some prize-winning Ayrshires to grow the herd. As the numbers increase, I may have to hire another hand."

Butch nodded his approval.

"Gotta tell you, Butch, I love being included with you, Mary, and the kids in family Sunday dinners with Cora and Fred. I get to see them, Chet and his family, and get caught up with what's happening with his girls. They're growing like weeds."

"They like seeing you too, Herb. After we move into town, it'll be good for us to catch up and hear what's happening on the farm."

The truck stopped in the driveway, and the two men got out as the swirling dust settled, slightly dulling the shine on Herb's new vehicle. Butch closed the door and walked up the porch steps as Herb walked around to the attached apartment. Butch couldn't help but think how much he was going to miss Herb. He'd have no one to talk to or joke with when he was on the road selling insurance.

A few days later, Butch, Mary, and the four children started moving their belongings from the farm into Doc Langman's Victorian house. Even though the property was within the town limits, it had a barn and pasture land with plenty of room for a garden. Mary brought along several hens and a rooster to provide a steady supply of fresh eggs. Having access to homegrown food was a hard habit to break. After a busy week on the road, Butch enjoyed roaming the pasture land behind the barn.

"You know the old saying, 'You can take the boy out of the farm, but you can't take the farm out of the boy,'" Butch's guardian said to the rest of the angels.

Betsy and Terry were allowed to walk or ride their bicycles a mile to visit their grandparents. It was an extra treat when Mary allowed them to stop at the corner soda fountain for a ten-cent root beer float. The two older kids had to keep this a secret from their younger siblings who weren't old enough to walk that far.

Butch enjoyed his work as an insurance salesman. At the end of 1955, he was offered a promotion with a transfer, requiring a move to Southeastern Pennsylvania. Leaving their beloved extended family in New York was a situation they never thought they'd have to address.

"Mary, this is a big promotion with a future," Butch explained. "Area sales managers have a shot at the district sales manager job and on up the ladder. It means more income for the family."

With tears in her eyes, Mary agreed. "Whither thou goest I will go; and where thou lodgest, I will lodge, my love."

Butch leaned over to kiss her on the cheek. "You are and always will be my princess."

Mary's guardian wept at the recitation of Ruth 1:16, thinking it was fitting for the love he saw with this couple.

Betsy was crushed to think of leaving her cousins and school friends.

Sandalphon gathered the guardians together. "I've received a message from the archangel. It is from 1 Peter 5:8: 'Be sober, be vigilant; because your adversary the devil, as a roaring lion, walks about, seeking whom he may devour.'"

Thirty-Nine

Summer 1956

After school was out, the couple began making plans for the long-distance move to Pennsylvania Dutch country outside of Allentown. As the day approached, the mood at Sunday dinners became more somber. Butch and Mary promised to make the four-hour trip back to Oxford often, stipulating that the rest of the family also make the trip to visit them.

Butch laid a guilt trip on his parents and siblings. "After all," he reasoned, "we're the ones with four kids."

By midsummer, Butch and Mary had not yet found a place for their large brood to live. House hunting was relegated to weekends, and the pressure to find a place was building. Each time Butch and Mary returned, the children had the same questions.

"Did you find a house?"

"Does it have a swimming pool?"

"Am I gonna have my own bedroom?"

When the couple returned from their third trip, they picked up the children from Fred and Cora's and gave them each a Tootsie Pop. It was hoped the chewy suckers would slow down the questioning until they reached their home on the other side of town.

"Did you find us a place to live this time?" Betsy asked as they all stood on the sidewalk before going to the front door. Terry, Judy, and Gail stood next to their big sister, waiting for an answer.

Mary opened the front door to usher her family inside.

"We looked at a lot of places. I can't really remember them all." Butch searched the ceiling for an answer while Mary clattered pots and pans around in the kitchen.

"But Dad, we have to have a place to live before school starts. Where is the mover gonna put all our stuff?" Terry whined.

"Maybe by the time the movers are here, we'll be able to tell them where to take our stuff, your games, and your toys," Butch answered. He turned away from his kids, ostensibly to sneeze. "Mother, what do you think?" He caught Mary's eye with a wink.

"I think we will be fine, and the movers are going to know exactly where to go when the time comes. Don't worry, kids. You will have a place to lay your heads." She wrapped her arms around her four children, kissing each on the head. "I'll bet the chickens are out of feed. Who wants to check?" Three hands went up. The three older kids raced each other to the barn as five-year-old Gail scampered to the toy box in the playroom.

Butch burst out laughing. Mary turned to him and scolded, "You are mean."

"I want it to be a surprise," he said with his arms wide, palms up. "I want the kids to be excited when moving day comes."

"You're worse than a kid yourself," Mary said, swatting at him with the skirt of her apron as she walked to the sink.

A few weeks later, the family drove out of Oxford behind a moving truck, headed toward their new home. The children had no idea what awaited them.

While the younger children were playing or sleeping on the long car ride, thirteen-year-old Betsy looked at the scenery and read highway signs. Almost four hours later, she read one that said, Allentown 15 Miles. She noticed her parents were giggling and the car had turned off the main highway. They were now traveling a curvy country road through a lush valley.

Butch slowed before he turned into a narrow dirt driveway lined with weeping willow trees. Proceeding cautiously across a flat wooden bridge, Butch brought the car to a stop.

"I think we're lost," he announced. "I'm going to ask for directions at this house. It's been a long trip, so why don't you all get out and stretch your legs." The family piled out of the car one after the other. Like a pied piper, Butch led his wife and children across an expansive lawn before approaching a large in-ground swimming pool.

"Look, Betsy, how pretty." Mary pointed out a lovely rock garden bursting with colorful flowers and ferns.

"Daddy, won't these people mind us walking around their yard?" Terry asked.

"I don't know, son. Maybe we should ask." He went to the front door. While making a show of knocking, Butch slipped a key in the lock, turned it, and opened the door.

His daughters squealed, "Daddy, don't!"

"Why is Dad walking into somebody's house?" Betsy asked her mother.

Butch turned toward his family and held out his arms. "Welcome to The Briar Patch. This is your new home, kids." His four children were in wide-eyed shock.

"It's ours?" five-year-old Gail asked.

"What's a Briar Patch?" Judy asked.

"Yup, all ours. The Briar Patch is the name of this property, and your mom and I kinda like it," Butch answered.

All four kids jumped up and down and screamed with delight. They ran around the pool and back and forth across the patio.

Finally, Betsy asked, "Really and truly? Are we going to live here? Is this our house?"

"Yes, it's our house, and we are going to live here. We have apple and cherry trees, berry bushes, and a big garden." Mary said. "Just think of the fruit pies we'll have."

"Just think of this swimming pool!" Terry yelled, just as the big yellow moving truck pulled into the driveway. The rest of the day was a blur of boxes and furniture. Mary stood in the kitchen like a traffic cop, directing movers upstairs, downstairs, and to the sunporch. She was only lacking the uniform and a whistle.

Betsy gathered her siblings to explore the three acres of fruit and nut trees, the underground spring, and the crayfish in the creek. They gathered wildflowers to present to their mother and smooth rocks for their dad to use as paperweights in his office. Terry found a tree for climbing and planned to ask his dad if he could build him a treehouse just like the one they'd had on the farm. It was a good day for the children, and they slept soundly that night, knowing that it would still be there when they woke up.

The guardian angels also had a busy day keeping up with four kids running in different directions. Fortunately, no one fell in the water or so much as skinned a knee. At least they didn't have to worry about runaway horses or kicking cows. The dangers here would be different.

The following Monday morning, Mary took each of

the children to school. Betsy was in eighth grade at the high school, which started earlier than the elementary schools. With all the younger kids in tow, Mary took Betsy into the school office to register. Betsy fidgeted and bit her lip. The office person issued the visibly nervous thirteen-year-old a locker, a schedule, and a homeroom assignment. Mary swallowed a lump in her throat as she watched Betsy being ushered away by a secretary.

"I'll see you later this afternoon, honey," Mary called out to her daughter.

Betsy lifted her hand in acknowledgment.

Mary drove another eight miles to take Terry, Judy, and Gail to their school. Before she left the school, she saw that they were settled in their sixth, second, and kindergarten classrooms.

When Mary pulled into the driveway of her new home, she realized that she actually had some time to herself, for the first time in thirteen years. Singing softly under her breath, she tackled the moving boxes stacked around the sunporch. Talking to herself out loud, since there was no one else in the house, she gave herself a goal. "I'll try to get half a dozen boxes emptied and put away before the kids come home from school."

She sliced through the tape to open the first box. Carefully removing the packing paper, Mary discovered the black-and-white framed drawing of the Lyon Brook Bridge.

"This is perfect!" she exclaimed. "Butch will be so surprised when he comes home." She went to the toolbox for a hammer and a nail to hang the picture. Admiring her choice of placement near her husband's desk, Mary smiled. "What great memories this has for him. I love it here." She clapped her hands and resumed singing.

Meanwhile, back at the high school, Betsy's fears

were calmed when she was taken under the collective wing of some of her classmates. They were fascinated by her distinctive New York accent. She was Betsy Emig, and for those who couldn't remember her name, she was the "new girl."

Sandy laughed and shrugged his shoulders, moving his big wings up and down. Watching Sandy made Betsy laugh. Having her guardian angel nearby gave her a modicum of confidence, even though they couldn't talk because of the scrutiny Betsy was under. One of her classmates was always at her side, showing Betsy around the labyrinth of hallways.

When classes were dismissed at three o'clock, someone helped her find Bus #6 in a long line of yellow vehicles parked outside.

The remainder of 1956 held promise for the family despite the ups and downs of moving from one locale to another. Starting a new school in September had been a big adjustment for the kids. But the most significant adjustment came in late November when Mary discovered she was pregnant again.

The angels prepared to welcome another child and another guardian angel.

Forty

April 1957

Butch walked across the lawn to the mailbox at the edge of the road. He reached inside to find bills, advertisements, and a thick letter bearing his parents' return address. He ripped open the envelope on his way back to the house, unfolding the first of many pages. Butch loved reading his folks' chatty letters about his siblings, what was happening in and around Chenango County, and how his friend Herb was doing. He was happy to know Herb was in the Emig family's loving arms at their Sunday dinners. In turn, Herb loved and treated both Fred and Cora as the parents he always wanted.

Butch read through the family news and came to a paragraph that stopped him in his tracks. He re-read his mother's neat handwritten passage: "The O & W Railroad went bankrupt this year. The trains aren't running, and their tracks have been abandoned as of March 29, 1957. We won't have any more trains crossing the Lyon Brook Bridge." Butch couldn't believe what he was reading. Those tracks had been used since the late 1800s. The bridge over the Lyon Brook Gorge was an engineering feat that had drawn onlookers from miles around.

He sighed, thinking how grateful he was for the

drawing of the bridge that hung on the wall next to his desk. It was a piece of history. His vivid recollection of the swimming hole in the creek near the supporting piers brought a fleeting smile to his face. There was something special about the clear mountain water cooling him off on a hot summer day.

Butch walked into the house and called to Mary. "Mom sent a letter. You gotta hear the news." His very pregnant wife appeared with a dust mop in her hand. He read the letter from the beginning then looked up at Mary. "You're not gonna believe this next part. 'We are thinking about selling this wonderful home in New York to move to Florida, somewhere near your sister Louise.'"

"What?" Mary asked incredulously.

"Well, now that I think about it, I can see why. A few years back, Carl accepted a job in Lakeland. With Louise and the boys down there, it makes sense for Mom and Dad to consider the move. Chet and Lorene are the only family they have left in Oxford. Chet works long hours six days a week, and Mom and Dad are not getting any younger."

"I get it," Mary said as she fingered the ruffle on her floral apron, "They're both in precarious health. The warmer climate will help them feel better, and maybe live longer."

Even so, the news that his parents were likely to leave Oxford stunned him. They would be far away and not so easy to visit. He was comforted by the knowledge that his older sister would watch over them like a mother hen.

Butch finished reading the last paragraph of the letter where Cora inquired how Mary's pregnancy was progressing. He turned to his wife. "We'll have to call them on Friday night as soon as the rates drop."

He thought about Herb's attachment to his mother and father. After Cora and Fred's move, Sunday dinners would likely end. Butch knew it would be difficult for Herb. A weekend phone call to his buddy was due too. They'd be able to talk about all the changes taking place.

Sandalphon and the other guardians gathered by the pool to receive instructions from Archangel Michael. "One certainty of human life is that change is constant. And to be sure, this family will experience some drastic changes over the next few years. I can't emphasize enough that each of us needs to stay on our toes. Do not be lulled into a false sense of security, angels."

The month of June brought a flurry of travel.

Terry and Judy reluctantly said good-bye to the rest of their family before getting in the back seat of Fred and Cora's car.

"Be good for Grandma and Grandpa," Mary said as she hugged and kissed her two middle children. "Just think of the surprise you'll have when you come home, a new baby brother or sister."

Terry looked up at his mother. "Why does Betsy get to stay with you, Mom?"

"She's going to be taking care of Gail and helping me when I get home from the hospital. Don't worry, sweetheart, you'll be back home before you know it."

Butch reached into the back seat to ruffle the hair on two heads. "I'm counting on you two to have fun with your cousins in Oxford. Give everyone big hugs from us, will you? And don't forget to mind your Ps and Qs!"

Terry and Judy solemnly nodded as the car door closed. Fred and Cora drove out of the parking lot as the two children's faces pressed against the windows.

Butch, Mary, Betsy, and Gail waved until they were out of sight before they got into their car to return to their country home nestled in the valley. All four of them were weary from driving. It was the day after Gail's sixth birthday party. Between preparing for the party and this trip, Mary's back was aching, and her feet were swollen.

Butch helped Betsy make baking powder biscuits after they got home. Mary sat at the table cutting up fresh strawberries for shortcake. It was going to be an easy summer night's supper.

The four of them ate on the sun porch.

Betsy said to her mother, "Sandy tells me you'll need a pink blanket."

Butch said, "It doesn't surprise me. Terry and I are already outnumbered."

Gail gazed studiously at her mother. "Mommy, what if you have a monkey?"

Butch nearly spit out his mouthful of biscuit.

Mary giggled at the vision of a primate making an appearance in the delivery room. Wiping the tears from her eyes, she answered her youngest daughter. "Monkeys don't run in the family, honey. You're going to be a big sister to a baby boy or a baby girl. Won't that be fun?"

Gail nodded. "Uh-huh, will I be able to feed the baby?"

"Yes, you can help. Now, how about finishing your shortcake?" Mary picked up her spoon as a good example. Suddenly, the utensil stopped midway between her bowl and her mouth as she gasped, "Uh oh!"

"What, uh oh?" Butch asked as he saw the startled expression on his wife's face.

"My water just broke."

"Oh, oh, oh," Butch said as he pushed back his chair to stand up. "What do you want me to do?" Butch was flustered, thinking of their last delivery when Mary nearly died afterward.

"Get some towels and grab a few newspapers off of

the pile by the washing machine to soak up the water on the floor," Mary instructed. "Betsy, take Gail to the playroom with her new doll and her *Cat in the Hat* book. Tell her you'll be back in a few minutes after you help Dad get me in the car."

Betsy did as she was told, ushering her sister out the door and to the other room. "But, Betsy, why can't I help Mommy too?" Gail whined.

"Because your new baby doll has to have her diaper changed, and I think it's time for a bottle before her nap. What do you think? I promise I'll come back to check on you in a few minutes, okay? I promise I'll tiptoe, so I don't wake your baby."

"Uh-huh, she's hungry. I can tell." Gail cuddled her new doll before laying her down to change the dolly's diaper.

"You are such a good little mommy," Betsy said as she turned to leave.

The teen spoke softly under her breath as she scurried back to help her parents. "Sandy, please tell me this situation is going to be okay. I'm scared."

"Betsy, I can assure you that both your parents' guardians are with them right now. They aren't leaving for another assignment until everything is back to normal. You're not only getting another sibling, but another angel joins the crew already here. That new baby is not coming alone." He had a wide grin on his face.

Feeling a little better, Betsy rounded the corner to see her dad steering Mary through the kitchen into the garage.

"Help me get your mother to the car, Bets. We'll need more towels and newspaper for the seat of the car. We've got to get going to the hospital."

Mary looked at her teen daughter and said, "Some

white vinegar and water will clean up the mess on the floor. Thanks, honey."

Betsy tucked a towel in between her mother's legs, and giving her a kiss on the cheek, whispered, "Mom, don't worry. Sandy told me you and the baby will both be fine." She closed her mother's door.

Gravel and dirt kicked into the air as the sedan sped out of the driveway.

Butch glanced over at his wife, "Hang on, Mary. The hospital's fourteen miles away. I'm hoping I can drive fast enough to pick up a state trooper to lead the way with a siren."

Mary leaned her head back, and her hands grasped her huge belly. Taking deep slow breaths, in through her nose and out through her mouth, she grimaced.

"How are the pains, honey?" Butch asked, glancing at her sideways.

"They're coming one right after the other. I'm trying to slow them down with my breathing, but I don't think it's working."

Butch glanced at the speedometer. The needle hovered around eighty miles per hour—not a state trooper in sight. Once in the city limits, Butch slowed some. He finally drove into the emergency entrance of Allentown General Hospital.

Butch put the car in park, then hopped out and ran to Mary's side of the car. As he opened her door, he realized he needed help. "Let me get a wheelchair, honey. I'll be right back."

Butch ran through the automatic sliding doors and grabbed a wheelchair while yelling, "Help! I need help. My wife's having a baby."

A nurse appeared around the corner in a fast walk.

Showing up at Butch's side to assist Mary in getting to the chair, she asked, "First baby?"

"No, fifth baby, sixth pregnancy."

"How far apart are the pains?"

"Every two minutes," Mary gasped.

"Oh Lordy, you're getting ready to pop this thing out, aren't you, honey?" The nurse pushed Mary through the doors and took off running down the hall shouting something to others that Butch couldn't decipher.

"I'll be right there, Mary." The elevator door closed. "Just as soon as I move the car," he said to an empty hallway. Butch parked across the street and ran back to the hospital. Walking into the labor and delivery waiting room staffed by a volunteer, he announced, "I'm Butch Emig; my wife Mary was just brought in."

"They'll be out to talk to you in a jiffy, Mr. Emig." The white-haired woman gestured to a row of chairs. "Have a seat. There's lots of magazines."

Butch grabbed a magazine and was about to sit when the door to the inner sanctum opened.

A woman in scrubs walked out. "Mr. Emig?"

"Yes?" Butch moved toward her.

"I'm Dr. Johnson. You have a beautiful baby girl. She weighs seven pounds, eight ounces."

"Whoa, that was fast. How's Mary?" Butch asked with worry etched into his face.

"Yes, it was fast. We got her on the table, and the baby delivered into my catcher's mitt. They're both doing great." The doctor laughed. "One of the fastest I've ever had. I know what happened with the last birth, and I can tell you there's no sign of abnormal bleeding. She should be able to go home in five days if all continues to go well."

A sigh of relief escaped from Butch as he allowed his

shoulders to relax. "Thank you, Doctor, thank you. When can I see them?"

"I'll have the nurse come and get you as soon as they get Mary settled. The baby is getting her first bath. You'll be able to watch through the nursery window."

Butch walked to the nearest chair and sat down. He said a few words of thanksgiving before noticing that the *Field and Stream* magazine he'd picked up minutes earlier was crumpled up in his clenched fist. He let it drop onto a nearby table as he rubbed both arms and rotated his shoulders.

His guardian hovered nearby, wishing Butch had the same gift that Betsy had. He would tell Butch, *Fear not, her guardian is at her side and has been from the beginning. She's resting in his arms and able to sleep. And by the way, you didn't need a state trooper to guide you today. You were traveling on the wings of angels.*

Mary opened her eyes when she felt someone take her hand a short time later. Butch kissed her cheek. "Good job, honey. I saw our baby in the nursery. She's a keeper."

Mary smiled. "I know. I held her for a few minutes before they took her away. She looks so tiny compared to our other kids when they were born. Boy, am I hungry. I asked the nurse for a cheeseburger and French fries. She said she'd see what she could do. That probably means I'm going to get Jell-O and graham crackers."

Butch laughed. He was glad to see her sense of humor intact. "Did we decide on a name?"

"I think we both like Joni, after your favorite singer Joni James. All the other girls have a middle name that starts with L. Do you like Joni Lynn?" She studied his face as he pondered the name.

"Sounds good to me. Joni Lynn, it is. I'll be able to tell Betsy Lee and Gail Louise when I get home. And then I'll call and tell Terry and Judith Lynette. I was going to stop at the farmers' market to get a watermelon so we could celebrate birthdays."

"Birthdays?" Mary tilted her head.

"Joni's birthday today and Gail's birthday yesterday. Gail turned six."

"Oh, goodness. For a minute, I forgot. What's wrong with me?"

Butch laughed, "Need I tell you how busy today was?"

The couple chatted until Mary's eyelids grew heavy. Butch kissed her on the cheek and got up to leave.

"I've got to get home to milk the cows," Butch said in jest. The couple simultaneously burst into giggles.

"No more rushing home to do that. It's a hard habit to break, isn't it?" Mary observed.

"It's getting better. Thinking of the farm reminds me I've got to call Herb tonight to tell him the news. That is, after I talk to our parents and children." He stood up, bent over, and kissed her gently on the lips. "Good night, princess. Sleep well, and rest up. We can't wait to get you back home."

"Good night, honey. I'll see you tomorrow." Mary closed her eyes again.

As Butch walked to the parking lot, he thought about what a day it had been. He was glad the baby wasn't born on the way to the hospital. He drove a block to the farmer's market to get a watermelon.

Later, the new guardian angel joined the others. The angels sang Psalm 128: 1-4: "Happy is everyone who fears the Lord, who walks in His ways. You shall eat the fruit of the labor of your hands; you shall be happy, and it shall go well with you. Your wife will be like a fruitful vine within your house; your children will be like olive shoots around your table. Thus shall the man be blessed who fears the Lord."

Forty-One

Late Spring 1961

Four years later, Mary and Butch relaxed on the poolside patio. Joni, wearing a bright orange life jacket, played in the swimming pool while her parents looked on.

"That beautiful child has been such a blessing to me with the older kids always in school or doing things with their friends," Mary said, pointing to the tiny brown-eyed brunette toddler. "I can't even wrap my head around the fact that Betsy graduates this month and leaves for college in less than three months. It'll seem odd without her around the house and at the dinner table."

"It'll be Terry's turn in two years." Butch shifted in his red metal lawn chair as Mary lifted her sunglasses to wipe a stray tear. He was fully aware his children would leave home for school, jobs, and marriage. "By the way, Herb said in his last letter that they still haven't torn down the railroad trestle over the gorge after the scrap train removed all the rails a few years back."

"How are things going for him and Corinne?"

"Well, their boy is two, and Herb informed me that the second baby is due in November."

"I'm so excited for them. That's great news. Have

they thought about moving out of the apartment into the main house for more room?"

"Yes, as a matter of fact, Herb told me he and his manager will swap places. The manager's kids are grown and gone now. They're just going to move one room at a time from the apartment to the house. Oh, he had big news. He bought Archie Meek's place."

"He did? Wow! How is he going to manage all that land?"

"With a bunch of new equipment. He replaced all the old machinery with the latest models and whatever new toys struck his fancy." Butch laughed at the vision. "He has the money to be a gentleman farmer. He's hired another manager, this one for the Meek place. And he locked in another five-year contract with Cornell University. It's a good thing for Lyon Brook Enterprises. I couldn't be happier for him."

"Considering what a rough start he had in life, it's a blessing to see him now," Mary said.

"I remember worrying about finding someone who'd grow to love the farm as much as I did. He was an answer to prayer for all of us." Butch lifted his sunglasses to gaze at Mary. "How likely was it that Herb Brunner, the man who tried to blow up the Lyon Brook Bridge, would be the one to buy the farm? God works wonders, doesn't He?"

"It's amazing, honey." Mary grabbed a towel to wrap around Joni, who had climbed out of the pool.

Joni squealed and pointed at the yellow school bus stopping in front of the mailbox. "Judy and Gail are home, Mommy."

Mary waved at her two girls as they scurried across the lawn. "Can we go swimming, Mom?" Ten-year-old Gail asked before Judy could get the words out.

"Sure. Then it's homework for both of you while I fix dinner. Go get your bathing suits on."

Butch looked at his wife. "It's amazing."

"What exactly?" Mary turned her head as she hung Joni's life jacket on the back of the chair to dry.

"How much our kids have grown. How fast the years fly by. It seems like yesterday that we were just two kids starting out in life—and now our oldest will be leaving for college, and our baby will start kindergarten in September."

The couple heard the sound of the old Plymouth sedan turning into the driveway. Betsy and Terry were home from high school. Car doors slammed, and the two older children appeared looking ashen and shaken. Terry's hair glistened in the sun.

"Mom, Dad, something happened on the way home from school—" Betsy began.

"Betsy hit a pheasant," Terry interrupted. "And it went right through the windshield. I've got glass in my hair, my clothes, and everywhere."

"Honest, Dad, it flew up in front of the car. I never had a chance to stop. It scared us half to death." Betsy was convinced that she was in big trouble. Sandy hovered near her with a hand on her shoulder.

"Are you guys okay?" Butch asked while Mary got up and began carefully brushing glass fragments out of her son's hair.

"We weren't cut, thank goodness. But the windshield is wrecked, Dad. And there's glass everywhere inside on the front seat."

"I'm pretty sure a windshield can be replaced, but you guys can't be. Betsy, why don't you show me. Your mother will work on cleaning up your brother while Judy and Gail get their swim time."

Walking toward the carport, Butch turned to Betsy. "Where was Sandy?"

"Riding with us. It scared him, too. He held up his hand and kept any large pieces of glass from hitting us."

"Well, well, well. I guess we owe Sandy another thank you," Butch said as he examined the car, picking feathers out from under the wipers. "I guess this old gal will be out of commission till we get her fixed. I'll see how soon my guy at the garage can take it. If we're lucky, he'll tell us to bring the car now. Bets, go on upstairs and get changed as soon as you have Mom check you over."

Betsy shook glass bits out of the fabric of her blouse as she returned to her mother on the patio. By this time, her sisters were back in the house getting changed and ready to do their homework.

Upstairs in her bedroom, Betsy studied herself in the mirror. Today's incident impacted her more than her parents knew. Graduation was looming. She hated that her senior year was almost over. It had been so much fun and she had enjoyed her classes, her friends, all the special dances and parties. She was no longer so sure she wanted to be six hours away. Sandy stood behind her.

"Heavy thoughts, Betsy?"

She addressed the angel's reflection. "Yeah, I guess I want to be on my own and in college, but I love my family. I feel homesick already, and I haven't even left."

"You know they'll always be here for you, right?"

"Of course I do. I think what bothers me the most is that the school is so far away I can't come home for a weekend. None of my friends are going this far away." Betsy's eyes welled up.

"There's always Christmas break." Sandy paused. "Betsy, you do realize that I'm coming with you, don't you?"

"Yes, I do." Betsy couldn't bear to tell Sandy that he couldn't replace the relationships with her family and special friends. "Terry and I have really gotten closer since we've been driving to school together. I hate the thought of missing his basketball games and it makes me sad to think that I won't see him dressed up for prom. He talks to me about girls he likes, and he trusts my opinion. Sandy, we had the best time this year when I was teaching him to slow dance. He's a natural, just like Dad. Terry feels the music. Girls love a guy who can dance, and already, he's got them drooling all over him. I'm worried he'll do dumb stuff if I'm not here to talk sense to him or to be a sounding board."

Betsy heard shuffling and giggling coming from her closet. Sandy's eyebrows raised as Betsy put her hand on the doorknob. Yanking the door open, Betsy was greeted with the sight of Judy and Gail sitting on the closet floor, painting each other's toenails. And they were using Betsy's newest favorite polish.

"Hey, you two. Why are you in my closet, and why are you using my stuff without asking?"

Twelve-year-old Judy attempted to stand, knocking over the bottle. Hot-pink nail polish flowed onto the hardwood floor.

Betsy shrieked, "Pick it up; pick it up."

Gail crab-walked backward into the bedroom. Judy tried to grab the rolling bottle, putting her hand in the pink puddle.

Betsy hollered, "Gail, go get the polish remover and some cotton balls." She turned back to Judy. "You're only twelve and Gail is ten. You're not even allowed to wear polish unless you ask Mom."

Sandy held his hand to his head and reclined on the bed to watch the show, shaking with laughter. The angel understood what Betsy was talking about in her reluctance to be so far away. It was hard to leave a comfortable loving nest and step into adulthood.

Forty-Two

January 1976

Archangel Michael requested a meeting with Sandalphon and the other Emig guardian angels. After the initial greetings, Michael said, "It's been a busy few years for the Emigs. Let's have a summary of the last fifteen years before we assess where we are now. Tell me, Sandalphon, how is Betsy doing?"

"Here, let me show you, Michael." Sandalphon swept his right arm in a wide arc. Images appeared on the white background of a fluffy cloud. Betsy appeared in a cap and gown. "This is the child to whom I was assigned. She graduated from high school and went on to the State University of New York for one year. That didn't last long because she was terribly homesick. She came home, found a job as a secretary, and met her future husband." Sandalphon waved his arm again, and the picture changed. Betsy appeared as a bride with a young man at her side. The next image showed Betsy and her husband with two small children. "Betsy and her family relocated to Lock Haven, Pennsylvania, when her husband took a new job. It was wrenching for Betsy to leave her extended family, but she's only a few hours away. She'll be thirty-three years old this

September, so this will be a time when she has to stretch her 'wings' so to speak."

Michael smiled as he nodded. "I understand. What about Terry?"

Terry's guardian took over the narrative. "Betsy's brother, Terry, seems to have nine lives. After all the accidents and predicaments when the family lived on the farm, he went to college and enlisted in the military." Terry's angel shared images of Terry in cap and gown, both high school and college graduation. Another scene captured Terry in an Air Force uniform. Still another showed him in a black tuxedo at his wedding. And then there was a touching visual of a tearful parting from his bride when he deployed to Thailand.

"And he came home unharmed?" Michael asked.

"Yes," his guardian replied. "He did and is now a father and a successful businessman, active in his community, and dedicated to his family. He's one of those outgoing, good guys that everyone loves."

"What about the other Emig children?" Michael asked.

Judy, Gail, and Joni's guardians presented images of Judy and Gail in a progression of years through high school, business school, weddings, and motherhood. More images pictured Joni graduating high school and going off to college.

"How are Butch and Mary faring with all these life changes?" asked Michael.

Butch's angel spoke up. "They are extremely proud of each of their children. They love being grandparents, something they learned from Fred and Cora when they all lived together. Butch and Mary are grateful for their years of farm life. But Mary was shocked when her mother Helen was born into eternal life suddenly in 1965. Mary stoically grieved her loss."

"And what about Fred and Cora?" asked Michael. "I hear their daily impassioned prayers for their family."

"Cora is in bad health with congestive heart failure, but she has rallied in Florida's warmer climate. Fred is leading a senior exercise group called Get Out the Lead and Exercise With Fred," said Fred's guardian.

Michael chuckled, as did the other guardian angels.

"They all remain thankful for the many blessings bestowed upon them... but there is one silly thing I must mention," Sandalphon said reluctantly. "I don't know if you are aware of the structural configuration of the railroad bridge that spanned the gorge near the Emig farm where Betsy was born." He brought forth the image of the architectural rendering.

"That looks familiar. I must say that I'm impressed," Michael remarked.

"Fred and Cora passed the drawing down to Butch and Mary. The younger couple was deeply moved by the symbolism in the drawing when Betsy pointed out the resemblance to outstretched angel wings. Butch and Mary look back on their years at Lyon Brook Farm and see the structure as a symbol of divine protection. In 1964, they got word that the bridge was dismantled. Now there is nothing left except the supporting piers. Although they no longer live on the farm, the couple feels the bridge's demolition may be an omen." Sandalphon shook his head from side to side. "I pray that it's not an omen."

Sandalphon and the other Emig guardian angels turned to Michael. Sandalphon said, "We know that I am to stay with Betsy for her entire earthly life, but what about these faithful guardians?" He gestured to the rest of the Emig angels.

Michael bowed his head briefly and replied, "Let me show you some scenes." He turned to Sandalphon and the others, showing them a series of images.

Sandalphon cried out, "Must that be?" Tears coursed down his cheeks. The rest of the angels covered their eyes in shock.

"Everyone needs to stay in place," Michael instructed. "As you can see, you will be needed. John Calvin—the sixteenth century theologian and reformer—once said, 'The angels... regard our safety, undertake our defense, direct our ways, and exercise a constant solicitude that no evil befall us.' How true."

All of the Emig guardians were extra vigilant after viewing the images that Michael showed them. Mary's guardian angel knew that she hadn't been feeling well for some time and was pleased when she finally made an appointment to see a doctor who referred her to a specialist.

The specialist told the Emigs that Mary's shortness of breath was a symptom of a serious heart condition. Diagnostic testing revealed that her heart valves were diseased. She would need valve replacement on one and repair on another. Mary made an appointment to see a heart surgeon.

Shortly after Mary's cardiac evaluation, Fred and Cora came to visit. In Mary's mind, it was appropriate that the family planned to come together at the Briar Patch for the upcoming Fourth of July holiday. She didn't know what her future would bring.

Four generations of Emig families gathered to

celebrate the United States Bicentennial on July 4, 1976. The hot summer day lent itself to hours of pool time, lawn games, and a large family picnic complete with fireworks.

As the family gathered around the table, Terry and his wife Laura shared the contractor's progress on their new home. Having bought land adjacent to Butch and Mary's three acres, the couple had designed a two-story house on top of the hill overlooking the valley. The dwelling was under roof, and windows and doors were being installed that week. Terry was excited that the power company would be coming out in a few weeks to remove some trees and install poles for power lines. He eagerly showed the family pictures of the house in progress.

Because of the visions Michael had shared with them, the angels remained on alert.

Forty-Three

Three weeks later, Betsy, Greg, and the kids pulled into his parent's driveway after attending Mass. They got out of their car and walked toward the house. It was a picture-perfect Sunday in July with low humidity and a cloudless blue sky. They'd be leaving to return to their home in Lock Haven that afternoon. It had been a lovely weekend.

Greg's father emerged from the kitchen door looking distressed as he met Betsy and Greg on the porch.

"Something terrible has happened," he announced.

"Is Mom alright?" Greg asked tentatively.

"She's fine. We had a phone call." He looked at Betsy. "Terry... there was an accident. Terry was killed."

Betsy's knees buckled. Greg grabbed her to break her fall.

"What? No, it can't be. Who said this? There must be a mistake." Betsy began to hyperventilate.

"Come into the house and call your sister back. Judy's at your parents' house," Greg's dad said as he led the way.

Greg's mother sat in the living room with a box of tissues on her lap. She'd been crying.

With trembling hands, Betsy called her parents' home. Someone answered.

"This is Betsy. Who is this?" Betsy didn't recognize the voice.

"It's Judy." Betsy heard her blow her nose and sniffle.

"Is it true?" Betsy asked.

"Yes. Terry was cutting down a tree. It hit him and killed him."

Betsy's voice cracked. "There must be some mistake. This is not happening."

Judy was crying softly. She paused to get her breath and said, "Bets, it's true. A tree hit Terry in the head. He didn't survive. We need you."

Betsy could barely breathe.

Greg gently took the phone from his wife. "Judy, we'll leave right away. Be there in a couple of hours. How are your mom and dad?"

Judy took a second to answer. "They're a mess, Greg. Mom is the one who found him, and Dad tried to revive him. Come as soon as you can. I'm afraid for Mom, with her heart condition."

Greg hung up and turned to his parents. "Can you keep the kids while we're gone?"

"Of course," his mother managed to say before she started crying again.

The younger couple ran upstairs to pack their suitcases. After loading the car, they kissed Greg's parents and their children goodbye, taking the time to give the kids an extra hug and reassuring them that they'd call frequently.

On the drive to the Briar Patch, Betsy prayed that God would sustain and comfort the family. Her prayers were disjointed, but she knew her Heavenly Father would untangle her thoughts and understand what she was saying.

"I don't know how I can possibly get through this, Greg," she told her husband. "Terry and I were so close. Our birthdays are one day apart. We shared every party since the day he was born. We were two peas in a pod. How can I live without him? How dare the sun shine on this horrible day?" Betsy balled her fists, and her cheeks reddened. She clenched her jaw. "How dare the birds sing, knowing my brother died today?"

Sandy held Betsy in his arms as she railed. Her body shook with sobs.

Greg stifled his own grief as he gave his wife the time she needed to vent. He kept his eyes on the road and drove, murmuring reassurances every so often. Sandy prayed for them all.

Betsy was still struggling to sort through her sadness and anger when they finally pulled into her parents' driveway. Greg stopped the car as soon as they drove over the wooden bridge. Betsy flung open her door and ran to her dad, who was walking across the lawn toward her. She threw her arms around her grieving father's neck.

Butch enveloped his daughter with a hug and sobbed. "We lost our boy. We lost our boy."

"I know, Dad." They wept together, rocking back and forth as other family members crossed the lawn to join them.

Terry's wife Laura joined in the tearful embrace.

Betsy's heart broke as she realized that her young sister-in-law was now a widow, left to raise an active three-year-old by herself. It was a multitude of emotions to bear.

Moving as one unit from the lawn to the deck, the knot of people unraveled as they found seats overlooking the pool. Boxes of tissues were strategically placed on the arms of several chairs. Mary disappeared into the house.

Someone asked, "Did anyone call Herb?"

Another answered, "Yes, he's on his way; Corinne is staying home with the kids."

Betsy turned to her dad. "How's mom feeling?"

"She's weak with grief and shock. She went into the living room to lie down."

Betsy rose and went into the house to check on her mother, who sat in a rocking chair, staring out the window. Betsy fell to her knees and put her head in her mother's lap. Mary stroked her daughter's hair as they both wept. Massive angel wings enveloped the two women, temporarily blocking out the rest of the world.

Betsy lifted her head and pulled away from her mother to grab some tissues. After giving a handful to her mother and keeping some for herself, she blew her nose. "Mom, I have to ask Sandy an important question. Is there anything you would like to know?"

"Yes. Why did this happen? How could God allow such an outstanding young man—a loving son, brother, husband, and father—to die in such an unnecessary tragedy? I don't understand. Why didn't God take me instead? He was only thirty-one. He had his whole life ahead of him." Tears spilled out of Mary's eyes. She turned her head from side to side, looking for a sign of Sandy's presence.

Sandy hesitated before answering. "Betsy, please tell your mother that death was not part of God's original plan. In that perfect world in the Garden, humanity wasn't meant to grow old, to get sick, have accidents, or die. When Adam and Eve committed the original sin, it allowed death to affect the entire human race. That, in a nutshell, is why bad things happen to good people."

Betsy conveyed Sandy's information to her mother.

"Did he feel pain?" Mary asked timidly.

"Sandy, you heard Mom's question, and I want to know if his guardian was with him."

"His death was instantaneous. I can assure you he did not suffer," Sandy said. "According to Luke 16:22, when believers die, angels usher their soul to Heaven. Terry didn't even know what happened until his guardian replayed the incident so he could understand."

Mary had stopped crying and was listening intently to Betsy's translation. She emitted a sudden shuddering sigh.

"Mom, are you okay? Do you have any shortness of breath or weakness?" Betsy asked.

"No, I'm not sure I'd notice right now because my heart hurts so much from losing my son. I need to know if he's all right."

"Sandy?" Betsy beseeched her guardian.

"Yes, he's in peace and not in pain. He doesn't want you to worry. He's feeling the joy and love of God and other family members who have crossed over. They surround him. Luke 9:28-36 tells us that you will recognize and communicate with believers who preceded you to Heaven."

Betsy repeated the message for her mother. She nodded as she dabbed at her tears.

At that moment, Betsy's sisters and sister-in-law came into the room. Judy, Gail, Joni, and Laura gathered around Mary to comfort her with love, even though they felt unrelenting sadness.

Betsy opened the front screen door and walked down the concrete steps to her mother's carefully tended rock garden. Sitting on a large flat stone, she covered her face with both hands and allowed herself to think about Sandy's revelations. Trying to grapple with the depth of her feelings, Betsy asked, "How on earth did this happen?"

"Bets, there's no accounting for the free will of a human being."

"What do you mean, saying that to me right now?" Betsy angrily demanded.

"Terry's angel told me that Terry made arrangements with the power company to take those trees down. At the last minute, he decided he wanted to save some money by doing it himself," Sandy said matter-of-factly.

"What? Really?"

Sandy paused a moment to choose his words. "Yes, he made a bad decision. There is a difference between trusting the Lord and testing the Lord. God's people should not take unnecessary risks and expect Him to bail them out. Yes, God will keep us in all of our ways—but our ways should be His ways. Betsy, remember how Eve was tricked by the serpent in the Garden of Eden? The devil kept telling her that nothing would happen if she ate the forbidden fruit. God had given Adam and Eve the run of the Garden. They could go anywhere, do anything, and eat their fill of anything— except the forbidden fruit. The devil wanted the ruination of Adam and Eve's souls. In Terry's case, something convinced Terry that he could cut down that tree when, in fact, it was beyond his capabilities."

Betsy cocked her head. "What did the devil have to gain from Terry exercising his free will as Eve did?"

"Let me just say this. There is a thin veil between this world and the next. When a believer dies, they are accompanied on their journey to Heaven. David wrote in Psalm 23, 'Yea, though I walk through the valley of the shadow of death, I will fear no evil. For thou art with me, thy rod and thy staff they comfort me.' When one makes the journey from this life into the next, this crucial time is fraught with danger. Demons wait in the interim space to snatch up unprotected souls."

Betsy's eyes widened with each word Sandy spoke. "Demons? And you're sure Terry's guardian was with him?"

"Yes, Betsy, I'm sure. Terry was a Christian believer, and I know his guardian sheltered him."

"So Terry was convinced he could do something that he didn't know how to do, and it cost him his earthly life." Betsy wiped at the tears coursing down her cheeks.

"Yes. He even discussed it with your father the day before. Your dad told him outright that it could be a fatal mistake if he didn't know what he was doing. And Terry responded by telling your dad that he'd just cut the thick brush around the trees. Butch honestly thought he talked your brother out of tackling a tree."

Betsy looked up at the blue sky. "Guess he didn't, did he?"

"No, he didn't." A tear slid out of Sandy's left eye as he sat in the rock garden, his arm around Betsy, her head resting against him.

Surrounded by sweetly scented lily of the valley, Betsy lost track of time until a car pulled into the driveway. Herb had arrived from New York. Betsy watched as he got out of his car and embraced Butch. The two men walked the circular driveway. They talked, stopped, embraced, and cried together like the brothers they'd become.

Neighbors arrived to offer condolences and deliver food. The foil-wrapped platters and bowls filled the refrigerator. At some point, the family would have to eat.

Forty-Four

The tall white spire atop the brick steeple pointed into a cloudless blue sky. Betsy stared at it. It seemed to be telling her, "Terry's up there. Terry is in the heavens looking down on you."

Greg parked the car and opened Betsy's car door. "It's time to go in, honey," he said.

Mourners entered the church, passing Terry's flag-draped casket in the vestibule. Friends, co-workers, neighbors, and relatives from up and down the East Coast briefly touched the coffin as they walked somberly into the sanctuary, searching for seating. The grief-stricken family entered the church through the back door. The main level of the church was packed to overflowing. Sunlight streamed through the stained glass windows. The colors created abstract patterns on the carpeting and the dark suits and dresses of friends unaware that they were part of a colorful collage. As the church continued to fill, ushers showed attendees to the balcony stairs. Long before the service started, all the seats were taken. The only space available was standing room along the back and sides of the sanctuary.

It was time for the family to be seated. The procession of Terry's loved ones began. Seeing the raw emotion of Terry's young widow, beloved parents, and devoted siblings brought many in the congregation to tears. Terry's survivors filed into the reserved pews by family groups. Boxes of tissues sat at each end of the padded benches, a testament to the thoughtful funeral director, a family friend.

Betsy held Greg's hand as she listened to a pastor who had known Terry most of his life. This was the church in which Betsy and each of her siblings was confirmed. It was the church where Joni was baptized as an infant. Judy was married in this church, and now, Terry was being mourned in its sanctuary.

The interment followed the service. The family led an orderly procession of mourners out of the building, along a sidewalk, and into the cemetery. Laura had chosen a burial spot near a grove of trees at the top of the hill. The plot overlooked rolling meadows and valleys, and the view was spectacular.

Betsy screamed silently. It wasn't supposed to be this way. Her parents were not supposed to bury one of their children. This was all wrong, and it wasn't fair.

After the ceremony, the family received visitors at the gravesite, staying until they were the only ones left.

Butch turned and said, "We should go home now. There's lots of food for those who are hungry."

As Greg drove out of the parking lot, Betsy looked back at the cemetery. A part of her was missing now. Panic rose in her chest. It seemed wrong to leave Terry behind, in the ground. She felt like she could die. She couldn't begin to fathom what Laura or her parents were suffering. She closed her eyes as fresh tears rolled down her cheeks.

Greg was intuitive enough to know that her tears were cleansing and therapeutic. Instead of offering his wife empty platitudes, he offered her a pack of tissues.

When the family arrived back at the Briar Patch,

Betsy sought solitude in her mother's rock garden once again. Sandy knew that Betsy was being asked to shoulder her burden of grief and to help her family, because of her connection with him. He cleared his throat.

"Betsy, we need to talk about what the next few years will bring. Your parents have suffered a shocking loss and so have you. Right now, despite the pain, you are still frozen and numb."

"I don't feel numb at all," Betsy cried. "I feel horrible. I can't seem to get my breath. It's like an elephant is sitting on my chest. I've cried so much, even my eyebrows hurt. How can you say I'm numb?"

"As bad as it feels right now," Sandy answered, "it will hurt worse in a few months. God created you to be somewhat frozen in shock right now, because no human can comprehend the full scope of loss in just a few days or weeks. If they could, it would kill them. But as the months unfold, you and the rest of the family will be reminded, a little at a time, of all the things Terry meant to you, so that you can process each loss that follows the death of a loved one. You've all been busy with the arrangements for the funeral and the decisions that had to be made immediately. But without those decisions and activities, your days—and everyone else's—will reveal fresh understandings of what Terry meant to each of you. He'll be missing all the 'firsts' that you and other family members experience from now on. And memories of the last times he did things with you will intrude into family traditions and celebrations—and even ordinary activities like collecting eggs or holding hands around the dinner table."

"I don't think I'll be able to bear that," Betsy said.

Sandy folded his wings around the grieving woman. "I'll be here to help you. In a few months, support from friends and neighbors will probably fall off. They won't understand that grief can be a long process, one you cannot hurry or ignore or refuse. If you do ignore it and try to forget the pain—or worse try to cover it up with things that keep you numb like alcohol, medication, or even too much busyness—it will still be there, hidden, waiting to burst out later."

"So you're saying that I can't go over it, around it, or under it? I have to go through it?"

"Yes, and I'll be with you every step of the way. And since you can ask me things and understand what I tell you, we'll need you to be there for the others at times."

"What on earth do you think I could do for them?" Betsy said, standing up abruptly. "The hole in my own heart is big enough to drive a tractor through."

"Precisely. And as awful as it sounds, there's a reason for that, Betsy. God gave all of you the ability to love. And now that the object of your love isn't here to participate in that sharing, there's a void. In the days to come, you might be tempted to think that God should come down and fill that void, erase your pain. But some of that space needs to remain open. Someday, when you and your family join Terry in eternal life, the reserved space will be his to occupy once again. Do you understand this?"

"It does make sense," Betsy said. "But in the meantime, this really hurts."

"Yes, and that brings up another thing. People who see your pain may try to make you feel better so that they're more comfortable around you. They might say dumb things. If you can remember that they are not experiencing the depth of your loss and that there's no way they can understand it, you will someday laugh at the silly things they told you."

"I don't think I'll ever be able to laugh again. It seems impossible."

"I know you can't imagine it right now, but in time you will adjust to the absence of Terry's presence. You will never get over his death, but you will get through this. You won't 'move on' as many well-intentioned friends might advise, but when you are ready, you will move forward."

"What will that look like?" Betsy asked.

"As long as you are willing to walk through this particular valley of the shadow of death and allow yourself to experience all the emotions of the loss—anger, sadness, and all the rest—your grief storms will eventually grow fewer and further between. You will always miss Terry, but his memory won't sting as much as it does now."

"That does give me hope, if I can hold onto it."

"Remember, you can share all this with your family. And you can tell all your feelings to God. He won't be surprised or put off by your questions. And He'll still love you, even on those days you lash out at Him. You'll especially need to remind your father about that. Terry was the only other man in the family. Butch will miss him immeasurably."

"I feel like Dad's and Mom's and Laura's losses are so much worse than mine. I guess that's why I have to be strong." Betsy pulled a tissue from her pocket and blew her nose.

"No! That's not what I'm saying. No one's grief is more deserved than another's is. Each relationship is special. Everyone knew Terry from a different perspective. Siblings share a bond that differs from a parent's love or a spouse's love. Not better or worse or less important. Different. And when you think of it, you and your brother should have shared the longest relationship of your life. From the time you were a toddler, you didn't know a world without Terry in it. And it's natural to assume he would still be here after your parents go to Heaven. You will have to remind your siblings of their special relationship, too. They are younger. The first breath any of them took was in a world that included their big brother. People will even ask you how your mom and dad are doing, without asking how you are. Brothers and sisters are sometimes ignored."

"Well, that's happened already!"

"But you cannot afford to dismiss your own right to grieve, even when others seem to," Sandy said gently. "For now it's important to allow the process of grieving so that you don't harbor regret and bitterness and resentment in the years ahead."

"And what about Mom and Dad and Laura?"

"They will need to walk that path as well. Don't be afraid to talk about Terry, to remember him and say his name out loud when you are together. It will bring fresh tears, but also laughter."

"Won't it seem like I am ripping off the scab of a healing wound if I keep talking about Terry?"

"Not really. Um...let's see. It's more like you would be lancing an abscess, allowing whatever is poisonous to flow out. Only then can the wound be cleansed so that healing can take place."

Forty-Five

Butch, Betsy, her siblings, and Terry's widow Laura sat in a small area designated for family members of patients undergoing open-heart surgery. The room was painted pale yellow with standard waiting room furniture and seating for twelve. There were six Emig family members, along with their bags of magazines, snacks, and games. The surgeon had told them the procedure would take four or five hours, and they came prepared.

Terry had been gone three months. On the one hand, it seemed like only yesterday. On the other, it seemed like they had lived with heart-wrenching pain for an eternity. The pall of grief was temporarily blunted by concern for Mary. Nothing could happen to Mary. It would be unbearable for the family, so soon after Terry's death. Mary's childhood rheumatic fever had ravaged her heart valves. The cardiologist was amazed that she'd remained asymptomatic until the age of forty-nine. When the shortness of breath began, Mary thought it was because she was out of shape and started a light exercise program. Soon, Butch noticed that her lips would periodically turn blue. It was unnerving.

Now in the waiting room, Mary's family kept an eye on the clock while they played Uno. Butch couldn't sit still. He paced into the hall from the waiting room and back.

Once in a while, he paused to gaze through the window at the street below. The girls took turns walking to the cafeteria for coffee. An hour later, the telephone on the wall rang, startling everyone. A voice asked for a member of the Emig family. Butch took the phone and listened to a nurse give him a surgical procedure update and Mary's current condition.

When he hung up he turned to his thirty-three-year-old daughter. "Bets, when they call again, will you talk to them?"

"Sure, Dad." She reached over to grab his hand. "I know how hard this is." She watched as his lower lip trembled, and tears filled his eyes.

"I can't lose her, Bets. I just can't..."

"We're not going to lose her, Dad. We've got a great doctor. Mom's going to recover in no time, you'll see."

On one of her trips to the restroom, Betsy noticed a small chapel. She opened the door and walked in. Lowering herself on the edge of a cushioned chair, she surveyed the room. Votive candles burned in clear glass holders on a small altar. It was serene and quiet. Betsy slid back in the chair to pray.

"Heavenly Father, I beg you to hold my mother in your arms during this surgery. Guide the hands of the doctors and nurses and utilize their skills to fix her diseased valves. Merciful Lord, restore Mom to good health. You know our recent loss. You know how hard it is for us to bear. Lift our hearts and spirits, Heavenly Father. We pray that you bless us with Mom's speedy recovery. Amen."

Betsy turned to her guardian Sandy, "You've been unusually quiet in all this. Do you have any insight for me?"

Sandy replied, "Your prayer was well said."

Betsy turned to face Sandy. "You know how this is going to turn out, don't you?"

"Yes, I do," Sandy replied.

"Well?" Betsy stood up with her hands on her hips. "Are you going to tell me?"

"You haven't asked."

"I'm asking now."

"In ten days, you'll be taking your mother home, and she'll make a full recovery."

"That's great news." Betsy threw her arms around Sandy's neck.

"There's more," Sandy began.

"More what?"

"She'll need more surgery in the future," Sandy lowered his head. "It'll be hard, but she'll recover."

Betsy soberly nodded her head. "I can't say anything, can I?"

"No, you can't. But you'll be the support person because your dad will not be able to."

"What does that mean?"

"He's hanging on by his fingertips. He puts on a brave front for you girls. That's all I see right now, Betsy. Trust in the wisdom and mercy of the Lord. I can't emphasize that enough. God will be with you always. He will never let you down."

"And you, Sandy?"

"The Lord is the One who sent me."

Three months later, Mary was back in the hospital for surgery. It wasn't a good start for 1977.

After Mary's recovery, Butch suggested they make plans for a vacation. A week at Pine Bay Farm, their favorite spot on the St. Lawrence River, might be just what the doctor ordered. Located deep in the Thousand Islands, New York, the secluded cottages provided a peaceful, laid-back spot to soothe their souls. They picked a week in August and made a reservation.

Butch and Mary sat on the porch of Cottage Twelve to watch the summer sun slide over the western horizon, its kaleidoscope of colors reflecting across the majestic St. Lawrence River. Their boat was docked nearby.

The couple enjoyed daily exploring as they drifted in the boat with their fishing lines trailing in the water. One day their boat was pulled by the current into a peaceful bay. Butch spotted a yellow cottage on a flat lot with several matching outbuildings and a good-sized boathouse. He had a flashback to Lyon Brook Farm, and it gave him goosebumps.

"Mary, look."

Mary was tightening the handle on her fishing reel. She looked up. "Oh, my goodness." She put her pole down. "Wow, it looks like they used a lot of river rock to build that retaining wall along the shoreline."

"I see some good-sized boulders in there. Now, that's impressive," Butch observed. "Hey, look. What's that?" He pointed to a sign on the front lawn that neither of them could read. "Let's get a little closer."

Butch started up the inboard engine and pushed the throttle forward. Steering the craft closer to the property, he came parallel to the wall. Butch shifted into neutral.

Mary gasped. "Honey, it says For Sale."

"Can you see a phone number?" Butch squinted.

"Yup, give me a minute and I'll write it down." Mary opened the tackle box to retrieve a small pencil and note pad. Butch maneuvered the boat.

She looked up, ready to write down the information.

Butch heard a sharp intake of breath.

"Mary, what's wrong?"

"Nothing, honey. There's a cardinal on the For Sale sign."

"So?"

"Some people believe it's a visit or a sign from a loved one who has passed on. You've never heard of that?"

"Uh, no."

"Well, here we are, looking at this sweet river house that reminds us of our farm. I'm writing down a phone number to inquire about the purchase, and a cardinal appears on the sign. He's staring at us and hasn't moved the entire time."

"Mary, what are you thinking?"

"I think it's a sign from Terry."

Butch studied the bird. "You know how many times Terry and I talked about finding a place up here? Dozens. He even offered financial help if we found the right one." He pulled a handkerchief out of his back pocket to blow his nose.

"Having our own river house is at the top of our bucket list," Mary added as she watched the cardinal fly into a nearby maple tree.

Butch continued to think out loud. "Terry would sure love this place. It's got an amazing location and a spectacular view of the shipping channel. Now I'm even more curious about it. It doesn't appear that anyone lives here. I wonder when it was built and how big the lot is."

"Let's call and find out. Maybe we'll get a chance to look at it while we're here this week."

"I think I'm done fishing now," Butch said. He reeled in his line, secured his fishing pole, and adjusted the throttle to head out of the small bay.

"Me, too," Mary agreed as she reeled, clipped the hook in place, and closed the tackle box. "I think we need to get to a phone."

Butch turned to Mary. "You know, Terry died thirteen months ago today. Do you think he could have anything to do with this?"

Mary teared up. "I wouldn't be surprised, honey. The Lord works in mysterious ways."

"I didn't say the Lord; I said Terry," Butch growled. "The Lord took our son away. That's a hard pill to swallow."

"I can't let you get away with that, Butch."

"Get away with what?"

"Putting the blame on the Lord. I know you feel some guilt and responsibility for Terry's death. But this anger at God—it's misplaced." Mary looked at the sun's reflection, skipping across the water in the wake of another boat.

"How so?" Butch seemed sullen, but he was listening.

"I've had a lot of conversations with Betsy about this. Maybe if you didn't storm out of the room every time his name is mentioned, you would have heard us. But now you're trapped in this boat with me, and this is my chance. Please hear this. Terry was a grown man when he made the decision to cut down that tree. He had no experience. But he went ahead with it anyway, even after you told him not to, and it was the death of him. It wasn't your fault and it's not God's fault." Mary brusquely brushed away tears that had involuntarily started streaming down her face. "In fact, it was God's blessing that he didn't suffer."

Butch refrained from commenting. He couldn't have gotten one word past the lump in his throat.

The guardian angels could see that it was a turning point for Butch. Mary had hit a nerve. No one had called him out quite so succinctly. It took his wife, watching him suffer for a year, to reflect back to him. It worked. It made sense. The angels applauded.

After docking the boat, the couple walked the path to their cottage and put the beverage cooler on the porch. Although it was 1977 and the cottages had other modern conveniences, there was no phone. Driving a short distance to the main office, Butch called the number Mary had written on the piece of paper.

Someone answered the phone and Butch expressed his interest in the riverside property. Seemingly, he had contacted the executor of the estate, attorney Stefan Thomas. The two men arranged to meet at the lawyer's home in Alexandria Bay.

"Let's go, Mary. He can see us now."

"Wow, that's nothing short of amazing."

A half-hour later, they were sitting across the table from a friendly white-haired man. Butch and Mary connected with him as if he were an old friend. The couple found themselves sharing their family story, including the fact that they'd been vacationing in the area for years

Soon, Mr. Thomas got down to business. "Butch, Mary, I like you folks a lot. To be honest, I'd like to see you get this place."

Butch's eyebrows lifted.

Mr. Thomas continued. "This is what I can tell you. The deceased owner had no heirs. He left the property to a local church. The church's board has unanimously decided to liquidate the property as soon as possible to avoid paying taxes on it. This might bode well for you folks."

"Mr. Thomas, we're interested in looking at all the buildings since we've seen the place from the water. Can that be arranged?"

"Absolutely. You can look this afternoon if you like."

He reached over to the nearby buffet and grabbed a ring of keys. "Here. They're all labeled. You go look at the property. In the meantime, I'll try to reach someone at the church."

"Thanks, Mr. Thomas. We'll head there now." Butch handed the keys to Mary. She slipped them into her purse.

The lawyer stood up. "I think I can get this property for you at an affordable price. I'll get back to you on the exact amount after talking to the folks at the church. Maybe I'll have some news by the time you return the keys."

The couple shook hands with the attorney and walked the uneven slate sidewalk to their car.

"Butch, I feel like I've entered the Twilight Zone."

"I do, too, honey. I can't quite put my finger on it."

They drove directly to the yellow cottage on Indian Point Road. After looking at the house and each building, Butch and Mary sat on the warm cement patio, looking out over the water. "I love the view, Butch."

"Me, too." He reached for her hand. "It's almost like Terry is giving us permission to enjoy life again..."

"The place needs a lot of work. Are you up for it?"

"I think so," Butch replied. "I already know we can divide the big bedroom and add another bathroom." He looked from left to right. "Mary, just look at this view."

"I know. Heavenly." She leaned her head on his shoulder.

After making sure everything was locked up, they drove back into Alexandria Bay.

Mr. Thomas greeted them on the porch of his neat craftsman-style home. "I've got news from the church." He quoted them a price for the river property.

Butch's eyes widened. "Say that again."

Mr. Thomas repeated the price.

Mary's index finger touched her parted lips.

Butch said, "You've got a deal."

The couple went inside to sign a purchase agreement.

When the closing date arrived, the couple went to the bank in Alexandria Bay, expecting to see Mr. Thomas. Instead, they were greeted by a tall thin bespectacled man who introduced himself as Mr. Hart.

"Where's Mr. Thomas? Butch asked.

"You mean, Stefan Thomas?"

"Yes, he's the gentleman we met with a few weeks ago. We signed the purchase agreement in his house," Butch shuffled his feet. *Please, Lord, don't let this deal go wrong.*

"Ummm I don't know how to tell you this, but Stefan Thomas has been dead for over a year. You must be mistaken about who you met. However, the papers are all in order and were signed and notarized by his former clerk."

The color drained from Butch's face.

"May we sit down?" Mary asked. Her hands were shaking.

"Please do." Mr. Hart ushered them into an area with upholstered chairs and a table. "Are you all right? Can I get you some water?" Without waiting for a response, he poured two glasses.

They drank. "Thank you." Butch said, "We're having a hard time grasping the news about Mr. Thomas. I'm afraid you wouldn't believe our story, Mr. Hart. So if the papers are all in order, can we go over the agreement to make sure we understand everything?"

"Of course, Mr. Emig." After Mr. Hart's explanations, Butch and Mary signed on the dotted line. The small fishing camp with two hundred forty feet of waterfront became theirs.

The couple's guardian angels stood outside, arms

crossed over their massive chests. Mary's angel said, "A job well done, my man. Or should I call you Stefan?"

The second angel took a deep exaggerated bow. "Thank you for your help. We followed our instructions and made it happen. Butch, Mary, and the family will enjoy much happiness in that little yellow river house."

Forty-Six

On the one hand, no one loved surprises and secrets more than Butch and Mary. On the other hand, no one was more excited than Butch to share the news.

Two days later, after taking inventory in the cottage, Butch and Mary loaded up the car and drove back to Pennsylvania. They now had an idea of what household goods were needed and what work had to be done. Neither one felt they could contain their excitement about being bona fide property owners on Indian Point Road.

After telling the girls about the river house, including the strange account of their initial discovery and subsequent offer to purchase, the couple brought out a wide-brimmed straw hat and put it upside down on the table. They asked the girls to gather around.

"We're going to name the river house. There's no limit on the number of suggestions you can make. Just put them in the hat, and we'll draw them out and vote on the ones we like." Everyone was soon laughing as they pondered catchy names and wrote their entries on small pieces of paper.

Mary said, "We're going to show you pictures of the four outbuildings that also need names. Hopefully, seeing the structure will stimulate your creativity."

With all the suggestions submitted, Mary shared

each entry as she pulled it from the hat. As soon as she said "Briar Bay," everyone cheered.

"That's it," squealed Judy. "It makes perfect sense. With the Pennsylvania house called the Briar Patch, it's only right that we should name the river house Briar Bay."

The sentiment was unanimous. The name was perfect.

One after the other, they chose names for the outbuildings: The Lodge, The Shed, The Oar House, and The River Rat Boathouse.

Sandy hovered next to Betsy and leaned in to whisper in her ear, "Your mother was correct about the angelic intercession. Terry beseeched our Heavenly Father for a big favor. We angels know that a prayer was heard and answered. Heavenly strings were pulled for Butch and Mary to realize their dream of having a summer house on the St. Lawrence River. They were supposed to have this property."

Betsy's eyes filled with tears as she joined in the celebration with her family.

Despite the long-awaited purchase of a river house for the family, Butch and Mary's family carried a burden of overwhelming sadness from Terry's loss. The grieving process, while normal, seemed endless. Sandalphon knew it was time to call for assistance once again.

The Archangel Michael approached Sandalphon, extending both hands. "Peace be with you, my brother."

Sandalphon similarly greeted his superior.

"I understand there's continuing anguish in the Emig family. We have enjoyed welcoming Terry, but certainly understand the depth of their loss. "

"Yes, Michael." Sandalphon saw no benefit in mincing

words. "It's hard to watch and not know how to help. Can give us some guidance?"

"Certainly," Michael said. "When we met before, you were able to show me how this family had fared through the years. It was impressive to see them thrive. Unfortunately, I had to show you the coming tragedy and caution you to stay on guard. With this meeting today, you ask for suggestions on helping the family move forward, correct?"

"Yes, that is correct."

"Let me illustrate where you can focus your energies right now. Butch has made some plans for renovation of the cottage. See if you can urge the family to pull together and do the construction together in Terry's honor. Betsy can be a big help there. I'm sure that if she asks, the young in-law men will jump at the chance to learn from Butch. And their time together will remind Butch that even though he no longer has Terry on earth, he still has loving sons."

"That's a great help," said Sandalphon.

"There are still many trials and many joys to come for the Emigs. The next years will bring the deaths of Cora and Fred, even as the family continues to grieve the loss of Terry. Grief never ends, but it does change and get a little easier as they adjust to the absence of the loved one. Remind your charges that grief is the price they pay for having loved."

Sandy nodded in understanding.

Michael paused. "Life goes on, and new souls will enter the family, too."

Sandy straightened his back and fluffed his wings.

"This is just what we needed," Sandy said. "We now know how to best serve our charges. Thank you, Michael, we appreciate your wisdom."

Michael turned to leave. "Anytime, Sandalphon. You know where and how to reach me."

Forty-Seven

Spring 2000

The next twenty years seemed to speed by as the Emig family moved from grieving to surviving to thriving. Terry's death spurred Betsy to act on her childhood dream to become a nurse, completing her studies at the age of thirty-nine. Joni married, and Butch and Mary danced at the wedding. Fred and Cora's move to Florida added years to Cora's life, allowing her to remain on earth until she was eighty-five years old. Fred died a few years later. Together, they left behind a legacy of love, shared Sunday dinners, and wonderful memories of unconditional love to sustain their surviving family.

Grief was a recognized, if unwelcome, visitor by then and the family drew together. They had learned much since Terry's passing. While sad, they knew that Fred and Cora had lived a full life. The sadness was mixed with joy, knowing that Fred and Cora were greeted by Terry when they were received into eternal life.

In late 1999, it had become apparent that Mary needed yet another heart surgery. As a high-risk seventy-four-year-old, Mary was not the kind of patient most cardiac surgeons wanted to tackle. Finally, in mid-spring of 2000, a top-notch cardiac surgeon agreed to examine Mary. After the exam, the doctor scheduled a heart catheterization. Mary was recovering from the catheterization when she suffered a complication. Panicked, Mary called the family nurse—her daughter, Betsy.

"Please come. I'm scared." Mary sniffed back the tears.

"Mom, what happened?" Betsy's heart skipped a beat.

"They've got to do emergency surgery on the artery they used for the catheterization. I'm scared, I need you, please come."

Betsy was at work, but after securing coverage for her position, she left immediately. She drove home to throw some clothes into a suitcase and left a note on the counter for Greg.

Betsy hopped on Pennsylvania Interstate 80 for the first leg of the three-hour trip to Lehigh Valley Hospital. The mountains, covered with lush greenery, loomed above both sides of the highway. Every few miles, she passed a farm nestled in the rolling hills. It was a beautiful day with light traffic. But Betsy couldn't enjoy the scenery or the weather. All she could think about was her mom.

Ahead, Betsy saw a large tractor-trailer laden with building lumber. The load was secured on the truck bed with multiple webbed straps, but the sight of it made Betsy feel uneasy.

Sandy spoke clearly and calmly to Betsy. "Those straps are going to break."

"What?" Betsy asked incredulously.

Her guardian angel elaborated. "The straps are going to break, and that lumber is going to spill onto the road."

"Holy Mother of God!" Betsy began to sweat; her heart was pounding. She was a few car lengths behind the truck. Both vehicles were traveling at seventy miles per hour.

Sandy urged, "Pass him, Betsy. Get away from him. Do it now!"

Betsy obeyed, but when she pulled into the passing lane, the truck accelerated. "Good grief, what is he doing?" she asked. Accelerating so she could overtake the truck, Betsy kept an eye on the load of lumber.

She watched in horror as the straps holding the stacks of wood in place started snapping. The broken belts twirled uselessly in the air. Everything seemed to move in slow motion. When the third strap snapped, the lumber shifted.

Sandy gave a sharp command. "Pedal to the metal, Betsy. Get away from him as fast as you can."

Betsy pressed the gas pedal to the floor. She watched the speedometer register seventy-five, eighty, eighty-five miles per hour.

As her small four-door sedan pulled away from the big rig, Betsy watched the scene unfold in her rearview mirror. The stacks of wood rotated sideways, cascading onto the road. The first pieces missed the back of her car by a few feet. She was just one car length ahead of the blockage that would stop all eastbound traffic on Route 80.

The young woman safely pulled away and eased off on the gas pedal, allowing her speed to return to normal. Coming to a rest area, Betsy took the exit and let her sedan idle as she sagged against the steering wheel. "Sandy, that was a close one. Thanks for talking me through that. I'm so grateful."

Sandy replied, "You are quite welcome. You know I'm always going to be here for you. We're a good team. You need to get a drink of water and stop shaking before you continue on your journey. Your mom needs you in one piece."

Betsy arrived at the hospital and found her way to

Mary's room. She was sitting in a chair by the window when her groggy mother was wheeled in from recovery.

Mary felt someone holding her hand and looked over to see her eldest daughter. "Hi, honey, you got here fast."

"It seems like that to you because you had an anesthesia nap. It took me three hours to get here. Boy, do I have a story to tell you. Where's Dad?"

"Oh, he went for lunch while I had the procedure. I think he said something about making some business calls. He should be back soon."

Mary looked at the doorway as a tall gray-haired man in a white lab coat entered the room.

"How'd it go, Doc?" Mary asked as she shifted the pillow under her affected arm.

"Great! I'm sorry for all the excitement, though. We got it all sutured, nice and secure." The doctor pulled up a chair.

"This is my daughter, Betsy. She's a nurse," Mary proudly proclaimed.

Just then, Butch walked into the room.

"Good, I'm glad you're both here," the surgeon said. "I think it's nice to have more ears when information is given. Mary, you'll need a valve replacement and I've decided that I can do it with a pig valve. I'm confident that you'll feel much better after the surgery."

"That's good news." Mary smiled from ear to ear. "Will I snort when I eat?"

She and Betsy burst out laughing. Butch rolled his eyes.

"I'm sorry," Mary said, "I just couldn't resist."

"Believe it or not, you're not the first to say that. But I love it when my patients have a good sense of humor." The doctor continued to give them more specifics about the procedure. "I'll let you know a date as soon as I check with scheduling. My office will call you with details." Turning to Betsy and Butch, he said, "It was nice meeting you. I'm sure we'll see each other again. You'll probably be able to take her home tomorrow. I make rounds fairly early, so as soon as I check that surgical site, she'll be discharged."

Two weeks later, Butch, Betsy, Judy, Gail, Joni, and Laura waited for news from the operating room. Butch sat forward with his elbows on his knees. He clasped his hands together and looked around at each of the girls. "This recovery is going to be tougher than before. She's older now. We have to give her something to look forward to."

"Like what, Dad?" Gail asked as she flipped the pages of a magazine.

"Maybe a special spa day outing?" Joni suggested.

"How about a trip?" Judy tossed her bid into the ring.

Butch responded thoughtfully. "Your mother's been wanting to go back to our stomping grounds in New York."

"What a great idea, Dad. A 'sentimental journey.'" Betsy looked at her sisters with a gleam in her eyes.

"Isn't 'Sentimental Journey' a Glenn Miller song? You and Mom danced to that tune a lot," Judy mused.

"Yes, it's one of our favorites to this day." His eyes glistened.

Gail pulled a tablet and pen out of her backpack. "Let's make a list of all the places you'd like to visit, Dad. You tell me, I'll write, and then we'll figure out an itinerary. Okay, go! What do you want to see?"

"Let's see... New Berlin, the house where she grew up, the school where we met at a dance, and St. Andrew's where we got married. Then I'd like to see the one-room schoolhouse where I went before going to Oxford Academy." Butch sat up straight in the chair, his face animated. "I almost forgot. We have to stop at the swimming hole under the railroad bridge—or where the bridge used to be. And we have to see Lyon Brook Farm to see what changes Herb and Corinne have made to the farmhouse and the apartment."

The girls could see the excitement in Butch's face as he talked about the trip. Gail wrote Mom & Dad's Sentimental Journey on the top of the lined tablet in all capital letters.

As Mary recovered from her surgery, Butch visited her every day, and the couple talked about the trip. His excitement was contagious. Butch made a countdown calendar for Mary with a mid-summer target date. According to Butch's schedule, Mary had eight-weeks to recover.

Forty-Eight

On the day of departure, the five daughters, with all their luggage, piled into Butch and Mary's van. Within fifteen minutes, the van was cruising on a four-lane divided highway.

Butch said, "Wish we'd had this four-lane when we drove back and forth from Oxford, house hunting. Would've saved us a lot of time."

"It sure would've," Mary commented.

"I'm glad for this kind of progress. I can't wait to show you the dirt roads where I rode my pony to Public School Thirteen."

"Is that the one-room schoolhouse, Dad?" Judy asked.

"Yup, I went there until the end of the third grade before my parents pulled me out and sent me to Oxford Academy."

"Why did they pull you out?" Gail inquired.

"My grades were terrible. They went to visit the teacher. As soon as they saw her, they knew she was out of her league, teaching eight grades simultaneously. She admitted having some of the older kids teach the younger ones. My father was a teacher before he bought Lyon Brook Farm, and he knew that wasn't working because I couldn't add, subtract, multiply, or divide. When I got to Oxford

Academy, I had to spend all my recesses and time after school getting tutored."

During the drive, the girls questioned Butch and Mary, gently probing for memories of all the places they'd be visiting. It was an enjoyable stroll into the couple's history and always included their love of music and dancing.

Arriving at the hotel late in the afternoon, the family unloaded the van and settled in their rooms. They walked across the parking lot to Fred's Inn, where Butch assured them they would have the best steaks they'd ever eaten.

"When did you eat here last, Dad?" Gail asked skeptically.

"Well, now that you mention it, back in the... oh my goodness, it was almost forty years ago."

The girls laughed and Gail said, "Let's hope the steak is still good."

Arriving in New Berlin the next day, the first stop was St. Andrew's Episcopal Church. Everyone piled out of the van and stood on the sidewalk to admire the old stone structure.

"Your mother and I were married here on June twenty-seventh. It was during the war, 1942. She was seventeen; I was twenty. Good Lord, we were young!"

Mary chimed in. "I remember the big hats all the women wore back then. Aunt Gertrude designed and made my wedding dress with a beautiful train. I believe she bought my headpiece in New York City. She couldn't get anything like it around here. It was made of glass orange blossoms."

Butch turned to face his wife of fifty-nine years. "You were the most beautiful vision I'd ever seen." He turned to his girls. "Seeing your mother walk down the aisle on her father's arm, I felt like the luckiest guy in the world."

The girls were all fumbling for tissues as they watched Butch reach out for Mary's hand.

Betsy leaned over to Judy and whispered, "The trip was worth it for this moment right now."

Judy nodded imperceptibly.

The massive red wooden doors to the church were locked. The family was disappointed at not seeing the inside of the church but settled for taking pictures of the "bride and groom" on the steps in front of the locked doors.

"What did you do after the wedding, Mom?"

"We went back to my house for the reception. We played Big Band music on the Victrola and danced on the patio. It was such a nice day. Everyone was outside most of the time. Remember, this was wartime, and we had a small wedding. A photographer who worked for my dad's newspaper took pictures of the wedding party on the lawn. After we ate, we left on our honeymoon."

"Where did you go?" Joni asked.

"You gals will think this is funny, but because of the war and gas rationing, our going away required some ingenuity."

"What does that mean?" Gail asked.

"Uncle Chet was on two weeks' leave from the Army before he went overseas. Chet and your father pooled their gas coupons and we rode in Chet's car with him and Aunt Lorene—and your cousin Linda, who was just over a year old. We shared a cottage on Silver Lake, near Batavia. They needed a vacation, and we needed..."

"And you needed a honeymoon," Betsy finished her mother's sentence.

"Yup, that's about right." Mary giggled.

The family walked down Main Street, stopping in front of an imposing brick high school set back from the street. The massive grounds were spectacularly manicured and landscaped.

"That, girls, is where I met your mother." Butch gestured to the building.

"My best friend Roberta asked him to be her date at a school dance," Mary said. "He flirted with me, even though he was her date, asking me to dance and then asking where I lived. I tried to resist him; after all, he was Roberta's date." By that time, both Butch and Mary were grinning.

"What happened then, Mom?" Joni stood with her hands on her hips. "Dad?"

"I ended up writing my phone number on a piece of paper and giving it to him. And that was that," Mary said as she brushed off one shoulder then the other in self-satisfaction. "We danced off into the sunset."

Further down the block, Mary's angel stood back to back with Butch's guardian. "We made that happen, didn't we?" one asked the other smugly.

"They were meant to be together," the other said. "Roberta was a momentary distraction. We did a good thing." The angels turned to high-five each other.

Betsy was taken aback, watching her parents' guardian angels interact. Quickly regaining her composure, she said, "You know, Mom and Dad, there's one thing I vividly remember as a kid."

"What's that?" Butch asked.

"Rolling up the living room rug, the sound of music playing, and you and Mom commandeering the dance floor with such style and grace. We kids sat cross-legged on the couch, mesmerized by you two gliding across the floor. We all love hearing any Glenn Miller or Tommy Dorsey Big Band tunes, don't we?"

Judy, Gail, and Joni nodded.

Laura joined in. "Whatever they say, I agree."

"I think it's time we move on down the road to visit the farm. Load up," Butch ordered.

Mary looked at each of her daughters and Terry's widow as they moved toward the van. "I feel so incredibly blessed to have this special weekend with you gals."

"I second that emotion," Butch announced as he got behind the wheel.

Driving from New Berlin to Lyon Brook Farm, the family enjoyed a scenic ride along the Chenango River. They turned off Route 12 to continue on the back road toward Oxford. The van approached a ramshackle wooden building, complete with a short squat bell tower.

Butch announced with surprise, "There it is!"

"What?" the chorus from behind the front seat called out.

"Public School Thirteen, the one-room school I went to."

The windows were boarded up. Weeds around the building reached up to the bottom of the rotting wood around the window frames.

Mary said, "I wonder why a historical society hasn't stepped up to preserve this old schoolhouse?"

Butch answered, "Money."

"I suppose it's that simple," Mary returned, "but you'd think..."

"We all love antiques and shabby-chic decor now, Mom," Joni said. "But this is a small farming community with equally small budgets. There's probably not a huge outcry to spend money preserving this schoolhouse."

The van slowed as Butch pulled in front of PS13. "Oh my gosh, there's the hitching post for the kids who rode horses to school. I'm surprised it's still standing."

A flashy red Corvette sped past, barely making the left turn onto Lyon Brook Road. The rear end of the sports car fishtailed as the driver accelerated, kicking up loose gravel.

"Good grief," Mary shook her head. "Look at that, Butch. Even in the country, these kids drive as if they have no common sense."

"I wonder if the driver knows the road. If not, he's in for a surprise." Butch put the van in gear, and they, too, made the left turn, following the swirling dust trail of the sports car.

A quarter-mile up Lyon Brook Road, Butch pulled into Herb's driveway. They were greeted by a fancy sign announcing Lyon Brook Enterprises, Herb Brunner, Proprietor. Butch and Mary sat in silence, taking in the changes they saw before them. It was shocking to see that the entire front porch had been removed from the house. All the windows in both the main section of the house and the attached apartment had been replaced. A new roof covered the entire structure. The barn and outbuildings had been freshly painted. Herb still used the same shade of yellow that had set the farm apart from its neighbors for decades. It looked sharp.

Butch beeped the horn several times. "Come on, everybody, pile out. Let's say hello."

Mary and Butch walked onto the side porch. Butch was lifting his hand to knock on the door when it flew open.

Herb Brunner, who sported a full head of thick white hair, greeted them. "Come in, come in. Get the girls in here. We've got refreshments ready. Corinne has been baking all morning."

Everyone sat around a large harvest table in the kitchen, overlooking the back yard and distant chicken houses. It brought a lot of memories back for Butch and Mary.

"I like what you've done. What's happening with the front porch?" Butch asked. He remembered how his parents had rocking chairs lined up next to the railing.

Herb laughed and slapped his leg. "I knew you'd ask about that. Yeah, we're replacing it. There was a lot of rot, and we've had to fix some of the siding on the house. So Fred and Cora's new and improved porch is going up in the next few weeks."

Butch leaned toward his friend. "Do you really call it Fred and Cora's porch?"

Corinne spoke up. "Sure as shooting, we do. He told me right off the bat that Fred and Cora spent a lot of time out there, and that's what it was going to be called. He loved them like parents." Corinne pulled a cloth hankie from her blouse—just in case.

"Corinne, they loved Herb like a son. It was mutual." Butch reached out to pat Corinne's hand.

"Say, what's next on your agenda, Butch?" Herb asked.

"We want to take the girls up to the swimming hole by the bridge abutments. It sure is strange not seeing that railroad trestle overlooking the farm."

"Well, why don't you do that, and then come back down for dinner. I'd like to spend more time with you before you go."

"Okay, we'll do that. Saddle up, girls."

They pulled out of the driveway and drove up the dirt road at a leisurely pace. Butch pointed out the first visible bridge abutment.

"See that big stone stack? The steel structure of the

bridge was anchored into dozens of them all along—" He slammed on the brakes. "What the heck?"

They could see brush and trees ripped in half or flattened behind a partially crushed guard rail. Butch found a safe place to pull off to the side, and everyone got out of the van. Peering over the edge of the road, Butch saw it first.

"Holy mackerel, it's that fancy red sports car. It never made the curve in the road. Must have jumped the guard rail and flew nose-first down the hill. I'm going down to see if the driver is still in the car."

Butch made his way down the steep path, careful not to slip on loose stones.

"Oh, Lord! Driver's slumped over the steering wheel," he called up to the women peering down at him. "The only thing keeping this car from sliding off into the water is a small clump of bushes. The front bumper and headlights are underwater." Butch continued to assess the situation. "If we try to get him out of the car, just opening the door could cause enough movement that the car will finish its swan dive into the water."

"What should we do?" Mary asked.

"Drive the van down to the farm to get Herb. We have to get this car stabilized. Before you go, send Betsy down to take a look at this fella."

Mary glanced at her eldest daughter.

"I'm on my way," Betsy said. She picked her way down the steep path her father had taken. Mary and the girls left to get Herb.

"How's this guy doing, Bets?"

"If I could get closer to the car, I could see better. Looks like he's in and out of consciousness and breathing on his own. But I'm worried."

"Why, honey?"

"Well, he's not a kid, like we thought. He's much older. This kind of trauma may affect him more than a younger person. He may have some internal injuries. It's hard to say."

Butch and Betsy heard Herb arrive before they could see him.

"Sounds like he's driving a tank, doesn't it?"

"Sure does, Dad."

Herb appeared at the top of the creek bank. "Butch, I'm gonna feed you a hook to put on his undercarriage. Do you think you can get to it?"

"Yeah, if you give me a minute. I'm not a spring chicken, you know."

Butch could hear Herb laughing.

"What tractor did you bring?" Butch asked.

"I don't fool around, Butch. I didn't bring a tractor."

"It sounds like a tank."

"Well, just about. I bought a tow truck a couple of years ago. They're good for pulling tractors out of the muck. Let me know when you have the hook in place, and I'll start the winch."

Butch grabbed the hook and tried to make his way through the thick brush to the rear of the car.

Betsy could hear his labored breathing. "Dad, hand me that thing. I'm closer to the car. What am I looking for? Where does this hook go?"

"Well, not the bumper; that would pull right off. You have to get it on the undercarriage."

Betsy squatted and leaned forward onto her hands to look under the Corvette.

The last thing she expected to see was someone looking back.

Forty-Nine

"Well, now. Who are you?" Betsy said quietly.

"Raphael. You can see me?"

"Yup, I can."

"How is that possible?"

"Let's just say I'm special. Whose guardian are you?"

"The driver's; his name is Bradley Sawyer."

Betsy pointed at Sandy. "You two know each other?"

"Yeah, we go way back." Sandy compacted himself and beckoned to Betsy. "Hand me the hook, Bets. Raphael is keeping the car from sliding into the drink, right?"

"That's right. You can call me Ralph. I'm glad you came along. Bradley took a blow to his head."

"I'm Betsy, by the way."

"I heard."

"Bets, who are you talking to? Is Sandy helping?" Butch hissed. He could only see the back of her shirt through the bushes.

"Yeah, Dad, Sandy's got the hook. He's attaching it to the undercarriage. We've got another angel here who's holding the car steady."

"The hook is secure, Bets. Let me help you get clear of the car and out of these bushes." Sandy stood his full height and gently transported her next to Butch. Butch's jaw dropped.

"Dad, close your mouth. You'll give me away. Tell Herb to start the winch. You don't need to tell him we've got two helpers."

"He'd think I was nuts," Butch said with a chuckle. "Tell Sandy I said thanks."

The winch whined with the weight of the Corvette. The flashy red sports car lifted totally clear of the brush and small trees with Ralph guiding it over the buckled metal guard rails. As soon as the car was lowered to the ground, Butch and Betsy rushed to the driver's side door. It opened easily.

The stranger's eyes fluttered open. "What happened?"

"Your car left the road and went over the embankment and into Lyon Brook," Butch answered.

"Oh, no! Is the car ruined? It can't be ruined; it's a gift," the man moaned.

"A gift? This expensive car is a gift?" Betsy asked in astonishment.

"I promised myself that if I ever had the money, I'd buy the red sports car that Paul always talked about and give it to his brothers."

Butch had a flashback. "Paul? What's Paul's last name?"

"Fisher, Paul Fisher. Did you know him?" the driver asked as his eyes closed for a moment.

"I had a Paul Fisher working for me for a while, but that was fifty-some years ago. He used to talk about saving up to buy a red sports car."

"That's him. That's Paul."

"So the car is for his brothers, Randy and Jim Fisher?"

"That's right."

Bradley's guardian angel took Sandy aside. "I don't know if he'll be able to tell the whole story because of this head injury making him sleepy right now. But Bradley spent time in jail for attempted bank robbery. It was decades ago. You remember, around the time the hayloft in the barn collapsed."

"I remember; keep going," Sandy said.

"Well, when Bradley got out of prison, he found the Lord. He's been living his life on the straight and narrow ever since. But back then he was the leader of the gang that pulled Paul in—he used to go by the name of Buzz. He had no idea Paul was mentally unstable, and he felt responsible for Paul's death. His brother died in the barn that night, too. Anyway, Bradley won money on a scratch-off lottery ticket and decided he was going to buy the sports car Paul always talked about. So he's here to deliver it to Paul's brothers, if they're still around. He didn't count on having to know how to drive something that powerful up a winding narrow dirt road."

Betsy overheard Ralph and asked Butch, "Do you know who Bradley Sawyer is, Dad?"

"Now that I'm thinking about Paul Fisher, the name rings a bell. I think he was one of those gang members out of Norwich that Paul hung out with. He went to prison for bank robbery. Why? Is there more I should know?"

"Yes," Betsy said. "According to the man's guardian, this man is Bradley Sawyer, who used to be known as Buzz. He's the brother of the guy who died in our barn the night the hayloft collapsed. When he got out of prison, he found the Lord. And now he's trying to do something nice for the Fishers. You should tell Herb 'your theory' about who he is." Betsy made air quotes with her fingers.

Butch did just that and the two developed a plan.

Herb glanced at the vehicle. "Hmmm, some bodywork, buffing out the scratches, fixing a few dents. We'll check to see if the headlights are working since they were underwater, and look at the undercarriage for any damage. I think I know someone who can do the job."

"Good," Butch said.

The ambulance arrived, and the EMTs put Bradley on the stretcher. Herb held up his hand as he and Butch approached.

Butch knelt close to the pale man on the litter. "I know you're Bradley Sawyer, and I just want you to know this red Corvette can be fixed. Herb can make sure it's as good as when you drove it out of the showroom. He'll see that the Fisher brothers get the car and tell them who it came from. You need time to heal without worrying about a thing."

"That'd be great. I'd really appreciate it. Tell the Fishers I'd like to stop by someday after I'm back on my feet."

"We'll make sure they get the message

The EMTs lifted the litter into the ambulance. They drove up the road to find a turnaround and came back down with the lights flashing.

Herb threw his arm around Butch's shoulders and said to the ladies, "Now that you've seen the swimming hole, are you ready for dinner?"

"Yes," all the Emigs replied in unison.

"Follow me." Herb climbed back into the massive tow truck and led the way back to Lyon Brook Farm.

Fifty

Sandalphon and Michael met mid-morning to discuss the Emig family's past and future.

Feeling playful, Michael joked, "I should have brought some angel food cake for a snack."

Sandalphon laughed, and his big wings bounced up and down. "Well, it's been a few years, so I hope it's fresh. I haven't really seen you since shortly after the trip the family took back in 2001."

"Yes, I was delighted that Butch and his daughters planned that wonderful trip to New York. It made the couple so happy to visit their childhood homes, schools, where they met, and best of all where they married." Michael straightened his robe.

"Indeed, there were some interesting developments on that trip that allowed Butch and Herb an opportunity to do something special for Bradley Sawyer," Sandy noted. "Raphael told me that Bradley made a full recovery and paid a visit to the Fisher brothers. They could see how genuinely repentant he felt about his part in Paul's downfall. So they worked together to establish a center to help those with mental illness in the Chenango County area and kicked off the campaign by auctioning off the Corvette."

Michael nodded. "Excellent."

"Sadly, that trip was the last time Herb and Butch saw each other. Herb died from a stroke in his sleep a few weeks later. Betsy and I attended the funeral. Herb was a big part of her growing up too. Corinne told Butch and Mary at the funeral how much their visit meant to both of them."

"Sandy, how are Butch and Mary doing in their advanced age? And their daughters—now that they're in their fifties and sixties?"

"Their angels tell me the extended family keeps growing. Twelve great-grandchildren have arrived—including a set of twins. Two more grandchildren married. I saw Butch and Mary at their weddings. And while they may no longer jump and jive as they once did, they still seem to enjoy holding each other and swaying to the music." Sandy couldn't contain his smile at the vision.

"An interesting thing happened as a result of Butch and Mary's visit back home," Sandy continued. "Betsy and the girls enjoyed being together so much that every year around Labor Day, they gather for 'Sisters Weekend.' Whoever has a milestone birthday, a retirement, or other special event is celebrated. And they sometimes gather at Briar Bay to include Mary and Butch."

Michael nodded, "Go on; I know you have more."

"I do. Sadly, Judy's husband had a massive stroke and died in 2008. It was heart-wrenching. Judy and Bill had been planning a get-away-weekend to Nashville the following spring. Betsy and the other siblings thought it would be a perfect time to have Sisters Weekend. The girls made reservations for two big suites. They held Judy together with love and laughter on that memory-making trip."

Sandy fluffed his wings and smoothed his robe.

"The ingenuity of this family and the love they have for each other never ceases to amaze me," Michael reflected.

"We pray for them daily. As Butch and Mary age and the end is near, it will be a test of faith and courage for their daughters. Butch and Mary have been the example to follow, just as Fred and Cora were before them—the glue that binds those ties and traditions. As the eldest, that role will fall to Betsy soon."

Sandy said, "We've seen half the family move to other states, including Betsy and Judy, who live in North Carolina. That, in and of itself, makes reunions more difficult to manage."

"Indeed," Michael said, "Changes are coming; we must do what we can to help. Thank you for calling upon me once again, Sandalphon."

"As always, thank you, Michael, for listening and supporting us." Sandy watched as Michael spread his wings and departed into the clouds.

Fifty-One

Betsy held a hot mug of spiced chai tea in both her hands as she sat on the back porch of her home, looking out into the woods. More than a decade had passed since the family's sentimental journey to New York. A single tear made its way out of Betsy's right eye and down her cheek.

Sandy was nearby, waiting for her to speak.

"I never expected things to go this way, Sandy. The past few months have just taken my breath away."

"I know your heart is heavy. Sometimes it helps to talk it out. I'm here." Sandy moved to sit opposite her.

"I'm a nurse. I should have seen this coming, but we were all so focused on Dad, even though he was always the hardy one. When he started getting so short of breath, we all thought it was COPD. Instead, it was aortic stenosis. Even at the age of ninety, he came through the surgery with flying colors."

"It was a blessing, that's for sure," Sandy confirmed.

"But how did I not see the effect his illness and surgery was having on Mom? I could see how tired and pale she looked. We tried to get her back to the house for an afternoon nap every day, but hours of sitting in the cardiac intensive care unit sure took its toll."

"I think you're being too hard on yourself. You and Judy were juggling a lot."

"But this kind of thing was exactly why Mom and Dad moved to North Carolina in the first place to live with Judy. I was her back up when she had to travel for business. And I feel like I failed."

"You didn't. You both set aside your own lives, fears, and emotions after your dad's surgery. And you watched out for your mom's well being, getting her back and forth to the hospital. That is a full plate for anyone," Sandy pointed out.

"When Mom came to me at eleven o'clock on the night of Dad's third post-op day to tell me she needed to see a doctor, I knew it was bad. I took her to the nearest emergency room and she was admitted with internal bleeding. I thought she was just exhausted."

"You can't know the future, Betsy. You can only deal with what you see. And even then, despite the seriousness of their respective conditions, the Lord was not finished with them. It touched my heart when, every day, you dialed the phone so your mom and dad could talk to each other," Sandy observed.

"Judy and I hoped they would have more time together once they were discharged and back home. After four days of transfusions, I was able to take Mom back to Judy's. I got Mom into the house and settled in bed. Then Judy arrived with Dad. When he saw Mom asleep, he kissed her and said, 'Is it really you, princess?' Mom opened her eyes and said, 'Yes, it's me. Are you really here?' Judy and I lost it. We cried buckets."

"I certainly can see why. Their love and devotion showed the meaning of the words, 'for better, for worse, in sickness and in health.'"

"Judy and I left the room to find a box of tissues. We

made a promise to each other that day that we'd do our best to keep them together. But it was only six weeks later that Mom died. She might have lived longer if I..." Betsy's tears were flowing freely.

Sandy reached out to take Betsy's hand. "You have to remember that Mary was a believer. She trusted in God for every day. And she knew that Psalm 31 says, 'My times are in Your hands.' What a wonderful legacy of love she left. You'll always miss your mother, there's no doubt about that. I encourage you to fall back on the memories you have of her. In time, memories will bring smiles instead of tears."

"Sandy, how do you always know the right thing to say?"

"Because, I'm an angel of God."

Butch healed from his cardiac surgery but not from the loss of his beloved Mary. One year later he developed severe abdominal pain and Betsy took him to the emergency room. He was admitted and had surgery. After a week's stay in the hospital, he was transferred to a rehab center, where he struggled to recover. Working with a physical therapist, Butch had goals set for him. He could be discharged to Judy's home as soon as he was able to acclimate to using a walker and could dress himself without help.

For the first two weeks, Butch's progress was encouraging. One day when Betsy went to visit, Butch was in bed. Judy sat next to him.

"Bets, I just don't have the strength in my legs to lift them. PT says they can't do any more for me."

"Dad, it's okay."

"There's more." He grimaced.

"Dad?" Judy questioned.

"I thought I had more time."

At the age of ninety, Butch had fought the good fight but no longer had the will for the daily battle. He wanted to be with Mary.

There was silence in the room as the women digested what their father told them.

"What day is it?" he asked.

"It's June tenth," Judy said.

"I'm going to be with your mother for our anniversary on June 27. We'll be going on a cruise, and we'll be dancing to Big Band music."

Judy and Betsy smiled and agreed that his anniversary vision sounded lovely. Blinking back their tears, the girls knew that they'd treasure every moment with their dad for as long as they had him.

In succeeding days, as Butch got weaker, he requested prayers and Bible readings. His favorite was Psalm 23.

Two weeks later, Betsy entered his room, noticing that her father was pale and still. She leaned close to whisper in his ear. "Hi, Dad, it's Betsy; I'm here." There was no response. Laying her head on the pillow next to his, she began to recite the Lord's Prayer. "Our Father who art in Heaven..."

Butch began making sounds in the exact cadence as Betsy's words. He was praying with her! Their guardian angels rejoiced.

Betsy realized she'd been given a gift. She prayed, "Please, Lord, when Dad dies, give me a sign that he made it to Mom's side."

She drew a chair next to his bed and sat quietly, holding Butch's hand until Judy arrived. Staying later than usual that day, Betsy was reluctant to go home. She was sure she would get a call in the middle of the night to say her father had died. But the phone didn't ring. Betsy slept until the alarm went off at seven.

As she dressed to leave her house for the rehab center that morning, Betsy looked out her bedroom window. The storm clouds were building in dark layered formations across the sky.

Sandy stood behind his charge. The overcast sky and generally gloomy day reflected how he knew she was feeling. He knew her heart was heavy with anticipatory grief.

Arriving at the center around nine, Betsy walked the familiar long hallway to her dad's room. She paused in the doorway. Judy was already sitting next to the bed, holding her father's hand. The light from the only window in the room diminished as dark storm clouds enveloped the building.

The two sisters hugged, knowing that their time with their father was coming to an end.

The sky took on a deep purple hue, the prelude to a frightening, but spectacular show. In minutes, an intense wind began to howl. Driving rain pelted the window. Lightning flashed repeatedly.

Butch's breathing slowed. The women counted the seconds between breaths as a sense of peacefulness enveloped each of them. When Betsy recited Psalm 23, Butch's facial features relaxed.

There was a startling crack of thunder, accompanied by a flash of lightning. The women flinched. Butch remained still.

Suddenly, his eyebrows lifted, as if he saw something pleasing.

"Do you think he sees Mom?" Judy asked.

"I wouldn't be a bit surprised," Betsy said.

A low, deep rumble of thunder shook the windows.

The floor of the darkened room vibrated and the lights flickered.

One corner of Butch's mouth curled upwards.

As Betsy said the words, "Yea, though I walk through the valley of the shadow of death, I will fear no evil," Butch exhaled for the final time. It was June 26, the day before Butch and Mary's seventy-first anniversary.

Betsy and Sandalphon moved to the window and watched as Butch's soul left his body, traveling toward the light. He was hand in hand with his guardian. Sandalphon wished that others could have seen what Betsy saw. The wonder on Betsy's face said it all.

The storm outside subsided. Beams of late afternoon sun sliced through a section of the dark clouds, paring away an opening for brilliant rays of light to touch the ground outside Butch's window.

"Sandy, look. Do you think that's a sign? Did God give me a miracle? Did Dad make it to Mom's side?"

"I'd say it's definitely an answer to your prayer. You asked. God delivered."

Fifty-Two

Butch and Mary's final wishes were that their ashes be combined. Some were to be spread on Terry's grave, and the remainder committed to the water in front of the family's summer home. The occasion called for an extraordinarily special Sisters Weekend.

The entire family gathered at Briar Bay over Labor Day weekend. Inviting neighbors, the girls hosted a celebration honoring their parents' lives. Toasts were made, and funny stories were told.

Betsy turned to Sandy and whispered, "Mom and Dad would have loved this!"

"Correction, my dear. They are loving this."

"They're here?" Betsy asked in a high-pitched voice.

"Who's here?" Judy asked.

"Ummm... well look who just came around the corner." Betsy covered for herself as she pointed to the next-door neighbors.

"Sandy, that was a close one," she whispered. "Mom and Dad are here?"

"Uh-huh. See the two cardinals sitting on the railing by the hot tub?"

Betsy couldn't hide her joy. "I'm so happy they can see how much they're loved. Please tell them how much we miss them."

"Tell them yourself; they can hear you."

Betsy moved through the party guests to stand adjacent to the hot tub.

Just as she got there, the colorful, red bird offered the more muted female bird a seed from his beak. She gently took it from him.

Sandy said, "That's called the courtship kiss in cardinal behavior. He's wooing her."

"Dad wooed Mom for seventy years, Sandy." Betsy chuckled as she leaned toward the two birds.

The male cardinal dipped his head, and one of his feathers dropped onto the hot tub cover. Betsy's eyes glistened as she picked it up. The birds took flight into a nearby tree. Betsy walked through a gathering of guests sharing greetings and approached Joni. They stood arm in arm, listening as neighbors related funny stories from years ago. The red feather was in her pocket, and Betsy's heart was full.

After the guests left, it was a joint effort to clean up and prepare for the evening events.

The men set up chairs around the fire pit. As the sun slipped behind the trees on the western shore of the St. Lawrence River, the sky darkened. Each family member ignited a wick inside a white paper lantern, sending it into the inky-blue starlit night. They watched from the front lawn as the lights became pinpoints in the distance. The rest of the evening was spent telling stories around the fire. Peals of laughter echoed across the bay.

The following day revealed smooth water and a cloudless sky. The slight breeze was perfect for the private ceremony the sisters had planned.

Gail and Betsy combined their parents' cremated remains and placed them in a heart-shaped biodegradable box, sealing the box with superglue, as directed for a water burial.

The family left the dock in a fishing boat and two kayaks. As they moved into the deeper water of the bay, Glenn Miller music played through the boat's speaker system.

Butch and Mary's daughters each placed a hand on the heart-shaped box. Family members bowed their heads. After a few moments of silent prayer, the girls prepared to commit their parents' mortal remains to the body of water they loved so dearly.

Joni, sitting low in her kayak, adjacent to the boat, received the heart-shaped box and reverently placed it in the water. The family watched until it sank out of sight. The chorus of "Sentimental Journey" sounded from the speakers.

Suddenly, two identical whirlpools rose to the surface. Side by side, they moved in perfect syncopation across the surface of the water toward the house. Everyone watched in stunned silence, then looked at one another as if to say, *Did you see that?*

Nine guardian angels formed a semi-circle atop the calm water of the bay. The divine visitors sang praises to God on high from Psalm 68. "Sing to God, sing praises to his name; lift up a song to him who rides upon the clouds—his name is the Lord—be exultant before him."

Betsy sat down in the stern of the boat. She faced her sisters as she recalled, "Before he died, Dad told me and Judy that he and Mom would be going on a cruise and dancing to Big Band music, and here we are. He was absolutely right."

At that moment, each of the girls knew it was a sign from their parents—a joyous symbol of a couple in love gliding across the surface of a new dance floor in their last dance.

Acknowledgments

When I began writing my first book, I thought it would be a solo effort. Boy, was I wrong. Without the guidance and input of dozens of people, my work would be flat, dull, and uninspiring. Consequently, with *Sheltering Angels*, I knew that I needed my supportive network from the beginning.

To all my faithful friends in the Cary Senior Writers' Group, thank you. You listened each week as I read sections of *Sheltering Angels*. You gave me valued critique and excellent suggestions to add depth to my characters and the story. To each of these dear friends who have encouraged me and prayed for the book's success every step of the way—Ellen K., Terry, Laurie, Jim, Dea, Emily, JoAnn, Linda, Janet, Barbara B., Kate, Willa, Louise, Cynthia, Karen P., Karyn M., Pat, and Barbara P.— I can't thank you enough. I could not have done this without you.

A special thanks to my friend Retired Detective James Lewis. Searching on the internet for instructions to blow up a bridge would have brought the FBI to my door, so I called Jim. He's able to think like a criminal because he's dealt with all kinds. My research on police investigative technology and equipment to solve crimes in the 1940s was woefully inadequate. Again, I called Jim Lewis, of course, he knew. Thank you, sir.

When I got stuck trying to cover several decades with the Emig family in one chapter, my dear friend Ellen Kennedy brainstormed with me to come up with the archangel/guardian angel periodic confabs. It worked. It was brilliant. Thank you, Ellen.

Many thanks to my fantastic Beta readers who promised to give me the unvarnished truth. These precious friends invested so much energy in the manuscript as it became fleshed out. To Yvonne Lewis, Lynn Stoeckel, and Laurie Winslow Sargent, thank you seems so inadequate for everything you did for *Sheltering Angels*. Helping to tie up loose ends, dealing with a problematic timeline in the family's history while developing as much passion for the story as I had was amazing to witness. These talented ladies did a phenomenal job in the initial editing process and gave me feedback, even when it was uncomfortable.

The greatest gift someone can give me is to read what I've created. Thank you to my friend, Terry Hans, for reading the nearly finished product, explicitly looking for errors or discrepancies. An author is so immersed in the work that it's sometimes impossible to see glaring errors.

A big thank you to my patient husband, George, who listened to me read every single chapter in the book. Although not a writer, he told me when something didn't sound right, and he was correct—every single time. I love you, George.

I give honor, praise, and glory to our Almighty Father for giving me the desire and talent to tell stories. My hope is that someone may benefit, be lifted up, or be inspired by *Sheltering Angels*.

One would think that a fictional work would not need research; however, one would be mistaken. What I wrote about angels had to be Biblically correct. I needed to find out what angels are and what they are not. I had to confirm what they can and can not do. The research was fascinating, and every bit of it is backed up by scripture. These are the sources on Angels:

> *Angels: Ringing Assurance that We Are Not Alone* by Billy Graham
> *Angels Among Us* by Ron Rhodes
> *Angels The Host of Heaven* by Dr. David Jeremiah
> *Angels on Assignment* by Charles and Frances Hunter as told by Roland Buck

Elisabeth Beard, aka Betsy, a consummate professional editor, became my friend. Betsy kept me focused on the trajectory of the story, which parallels events in my own life. Sometimes it was a complicated and challenging subject matter. With her guidance, I was able to dig deeply into the process of love, loss, and grieving. Hopefully, these insights will help someone else in their journey.

Thank you, Deborah Bradseth of Tugboat Design, for another beautiful cover. I appreciate your professional touches to make my vision a reality.

Last but certainly not least, I want to thank Wally and Betty Turnbull of Torchflame Books. I appreciate your unwavering support. I feel wrapped up and secure in your professional expertise. It's been a pleasure to work with both of you on *Sheltering Angels*.

About the Author

Nancy Panko is a retired pediatric RN who loves to write. *Sheltering Angels* is her second novel. Author of award-winning *Guiding Missal*, Panko is also a frequent contributor to *Chicken Soup for the Soul* books. She has been published in *Guideposts*, *Women's World*, and *Cary Living* magazines. Nancy is a member of the Cary Senior Writing Circle, The Light of Carolina Christian Writers, and The Military Writers Society of America.

Nancy and her husband moved from Lock Haven, Pennsylvania, to North Carolina in 2009 to live near their two children. They have four grandchildren and three granddogs. When she isn't writing, you can find her reading a good book while pontoon boating on Lake Gaston.

Connect with Nancy:
www.NancyPanko.com
Facebook: Nancy Emmick Panko
twitter: @nancypanko

CPSIA information can be obtained
at www.ICGtesting.com
Printed in the USA
FSHW012225051020
74489FS